What's
Not Said

What's Not Said

Not Said

A Novel

Valerie Taylor

SHE WRITES PRESS

Published September 2020
Printed in the United States of America
Print ISBN: 978-1-63152-745-6
E-ISBN: 978-1-63152-746-3
Library of Congress Control Number: 2020906822

For information, address:
She Writes Press
1569 Solano Ave #546
Berkeley, CA 94707

She Writes Press is a division of SparkPoint Studio, LLC.

This is dedicated to the ones I love:
My family—Lindsay, William, Jeanne, and Cecilia

The cruelest lies are often told in silence.
— Robert Louis Stevenson

1

To Om or Not to Om

K assie prided herself on being a control freak—not the *my-way-or-the-highway* kind of bitch, rather the *do-the-right-things-right* stickler for details. After all, being a perfectionist flowed through her DNA.

Indeed, Kassie didn't alphabetize her spice rack as her mother did. But once upon a time as she prepared to leave for her freshman year in college, she counted the number of cotton balls she used in a week and then calculated a semester's worth. When she ran out two weeks before finals, she'd discovered her plan had one flaw—her roommate. Lesson learned. She hot-footed it to the nearest drug store and gifted her roomie a package to call her own.

Kassie would freely admit she also had a well-developed time management gene. The best part of her day was when she planned the next. When the Franklin Covey store closed in Boston, she took it personally, swearing she'd never shop at that damn mall again. Oh sure, she could order her supplies online, but the thrill of touching the freshly printed planners and sniffing the plush leather binders was stolen from her. How would she ever survive? A quick visit to the Kate Spade store took care of that near disaster.

So imagine what was going on inside her highly compartmentalized mind when the day hadn't started quite the way she'd intended. She rationalized time was on her side. The hands on the oversized, round clock hanging prominently on the hospital's waiting room wall read four-seventeen. Was it early morning? Middle of the night? Didn't matter.

Either way, like her cotton ball miscalculation, this trip to the ER was a minor speed bump. Her plan had arms and legs. The day's agenda was as simple as one, two, three—get to the Red Sox game at Fenway, celebrate afterward, tell her husband she'd filed for divorce. Piece of cake. All she needed to do was get Mike out of the hospital and back home so she could jumpstart the rest of her life.

Leaving nothing to chance, four years ago with the help of her lawyer, Kassie drafted longhand on a single sheet of yellow, lined paper what she'd say to Mike and hid it in her black Kate Spade wallet along with a list of baby names on frayed blue and pink Post-it notes. She practiced a million times—role-played with her best friend Annie, recorded it on her iPhone, and recited it solo in front of her bathroom mirror. By now, she knew the simple words by heart. She was ready. Now it was up to him.

Granted, the calendar on the wall behind the nurses' station in the ER lobby said it was Good Friday. *Screw that.* Come hell or high water, it would be Kassandra O'Callaghan's Independence Day. It just had to be. She'd put it off long enough. Maybe there'd be no parades, no fireworks on the river, no Boston Pops at the Hatch Shell, but there'd be a declaration of freedom . . . her freedom.

For more years than she was willing to admit, Kassie tried to convince herself that telling her husband she wanted a divorce shouldn't be so distressing. After all, she was a mature woman, a successful marketing executive in her own right. Throughout her career, she'd handled many thorny interactions—money-grubbing ad agencies, arrogant creative directors, egotistical copywriters. To her credit, she'd confronted every business challenge thrown at her and triumphed, most of the time anyway.

Kassie's professional, confident persona was merely that—a mask she'd perfected throughout three decades of climbing the corporate ladder with its discrimination and bosses who relished the bar, both drinking at it and moving it. This was contrary to her personal life where she avoided conflict, especially when it came to Michael Ricci. Ever since he was her Italian professor in college, she approached him with deference, expecting him to grade her every performance. And grade her he did, as a student, a lover, a wife.

"Sometimes I think you leave your brain at the office," was a Mike-ism Kassie heard way too often.

Would that be his reaction to her news? Would he take her seriously? Did couples who were married three decades, *a.k.a. forever,* get divorced or did they just suck it up and choose to live together separately?

Had he been unfaithful? Sometimes she'd wished he had been. At least that would mean Mike was passionate about something, if not her.

Would he be surprised? Or maybe he'd be relieved. It was no secret their relationship began deteriorating a few years after they married, after the miscarriage. Kassie spent much of the first half of their marriage trying to save it, and most of the second half trying to escape it.

Several years ago, well at least over the last four to be sure, she'd start each year with one goal: get the hell out. And then something unpredictable, either work or family related, derailed her, making her put off what she knew deep in her heart and soul she had to do.

"Coward," Annie had said over and over and over.

"No, just waiting for the opportunity. When it knocks, I'll be ready. You'll see," Kassie would say, wagging her finger.

To stay motivated, she established annual mini bargains. If she filed for divorce, she'd buy a new car, or a diamond ring, or take a cruise around the world. Yet, even her mind games hadn't worked.

Motivation wasn't the issue. There were other barriers to exit. She and Mike weren't getting any younger. Both were middle aged, though he had ten years on her. They'd spent more than half of their lives putting up with each other's quirks. Change wasn't in their vocabulary.

Yet Kassie believed Mike deserved to find someone he'd smile at when he woke up in the morning, as she had. And, frankly, she'd grown tired of being scolded by Annie and of delaying the inevitable.

So, when the new year began with Annie chastising her again, Kassie posted a "Just do it" note on her computer monitor at work. And she made a list of what it would take. At the top: courage and a long holiday weekend. Courage, because if she trusted anyone's opinion of her, it was Annie's. And a long weekend, like Easter, because she reasoned if she announced the divorce on a Friday, Mike would have the weekend to process and cool down before the next workweek began. And she'd have the weekend to celebrate—step two on her agenda. Ooh la la.

Earlier that week with D-Day approaching, an endless *you-can-do-this* message looped through her mind. Kassie felt as if her blood cells could break through her skin and explode like Mentos in a bottle of Coke. The person she was about to confront wasn't some impersonal business associate. This was Mike, someone she once loved. Someone she'd expected would be the father of her children. She had to do something to keep her emotions in check the night before the big reveal or she might chicken out *again*.

Annie suggested a distraction might do the trick. "Take Mike out to dinner or a movie. Keep busy. The night will fly by. You'll see," Annie said.

Though a good idea, Kassie was skeptical. There was one problem. Thursday night had always been "Must-See TV" in the Ricci-O'Callaghan household. It was the night when America's sitcoms and dramas soared—the likes of *Cheers, Friends, Seinfeld, Grey's Anatomy*. Mike never did much else on Thursday nights other than watch TV, no matter the current lineup.

"Shoot me. I'm a homebody," he'd grumble.

Mike had his rituals, as most people do. Kassie accommodated his more often than not. On her way home from the office on Thursday nights, she would buck traffic, struggle to find a parking space, and pick up a pizza for Mike from Boston's North End.

"If you can't get good pizza there, you can't get it anywhere," he'd say. Another Mike-ism.

It didn't matter Kassie had to go out of her way to get his favorite pie or that she rarely ate pizza. Early on in their relationship, Kassie slipped into the habit of putting Mike's needs first. She wasn't proud of subordinating hers. In her way of thinking, habits created within a marriage—whether good or bad—became normalized and accepted. Over time, rationalizing her subservience toward Mike became Kassie's survival mechanism, as did her having a life outside her home.

Take Mike's pizza routine. Though Kassie would remind him his doctor had cautioned him not to eat pizza, Mike would eat it anyway. He always had it with pepperoni and mushrooms, just as he always ate Cheerios for breakfast. He'd wash down his pizza—not the Cheerios—with a beer or two, plunk his dishes in the sink for Kassie to wash, and then head for his favorite Barcalounger in the family room for an evening of comedy and drama. If this kept Mike happy and allowed Kassie some pseudo-freedom, that was fine with her.

So imagine her surprise when Mike said, "Let's do it," when she suggested they go out for dinner on a Thursday of all days. When he added, "Oh, date night. We haven't done that in a while," she had to admit his reaction was not what she expected. It'd been eons since they'd been there, done that. Nevertheless, she was delighted to check "plan Thursday night" off her list.

Other than feasting on lobster, dinner that evening at *Naked Fish* proved uneventful. Not much meaningful dialogue transpired between them anymore. Their conversations these days were often one-sided. Life with Mike was all about Mike, every day, all day—unlike the early years when Mike started his marketing consulting business, and Kassie's own marketing career looked promising. They had so much in common then, it seemed. Within a few short years, they'd become a power couple in Boston's advertising and marketing world.

Life was one big turn-on. Their dinner table repartee then was full of excitement, problem-solving, and luscious gossip about who was screwing who at the office, figuratively and literally. Sex often was their dessert served at the table, on the floor, against a door. Ah, those were the days.

Nowadays, Kassie would start, "How was your day?"

"Okay, how was yours?"

Then she might say something like, "We met with Sam today. You remember the asshole who—"

Only to have Mike interrupt with something like, "We just signed Eagle Bank today. They wanted to do TV ads, but we recommended they start with radio. Walk before flying . . ." He'd pause, expecting her to laugh.

She didn't. She'd let him ramble, inserting her travel plans into the conversation whenever he shut up and took a mouthful. He'd never remember she told him when and where she was going, but she knew she had. Her conscience was clear, at least somewhat.

A similar scenario repeated itself that night at dinner, without the sex. She reminded him she would be flying to Washington, D.C., over the weekend to pitch a new assignment to Georgetown University on Monday. When they returned home after dinner, Mike retired to his chair and the TV, and Kassie bolted to their bedroom, which they still shared . . . *imagine that* . . . presumably to pack.

Kassie had her rituals, too, most aimed at slowing the inescapable aging process. Despite the butterflies flittering from her stomach to her chest, or because of them, she stuck to her nighttime routine, detailed on green Post-it notes with red tulips on her side of the double-wide bathroom mirror.

"You're not in college anymore. Take those notes down before I do," Mike said on more than one occasion. She loved them. Maybe because he hated them.

Although she knew the list by heart, she read it aloud. "Brush teeth, floss, remove make-up, moisturize all over, stretch, meditate."

She tried to relax on her mauve meditation pillow and changed up her usual practice, chanting instead the short and sweet words she and her lawyer drafted. With deep cleansing breaths, she began.

"Om. Mike, there's something we need to talk about."

"Om. We've been working on us for a very long time." *Not true, I've been working, he's been skating.*

"Om. I don't mean to hurt you, Mike, but I've filed for divorce."

"Om. It's not you, it's me." *Am I really going to say that?*

"Om. You'll be served papers next Tuesday. Where do you want to receive them?

"Om. Better here than at the office, eh?"

She bowed her head and raised a prayer to sweet Jesus and her mother to give her the courage and strength to survive the next twenty-four hours.

With that, Kassie popped a Tylenol PM for good measure, climbed into the California king waterbed she wished they'd replaced years ago, and with steamy visions of where she'd be sleeping the next night, sunk into a toasty, soothing sleep. For a while, anyway.

In a drug-induced fog, Kassie opened one eye. The bedroom was dark, except for a smidgen of light outlining the bathroom door at the opposite end of the bedroom. That was odd. She rolled over and searched for Baby Ben. She knocked over a soy candle and the familiar aroma of green apples floated in the air. Thankfully it wasn't lit.

Fumbling around, she found the clock. Without her glasses, Kassie pulled the clock right up to her face. Ten after two give or take. She never could remember if the clock was ten or twenty minutes fast. Kassie started setting her clock ahead five years ago as a New Year's resolution. She always tried to tackle one more thing before leaving the house, so she figured finagling with the clock would break a bad habit. Not so much. Instead, her brain recalculated the time, and she'd end up either late or right on schedule. It wasn't the problem solver she'd hoped it would be, but it entertained her. It may have even replaced a few of the brain cells the wine she drank had killed.

A quick swing of her arm and sweep of her leg across the bed confirmed Mike was elsewhere. With a grunt, Kassie threw back the heirloom quilt that once belonged to her mother and lifted herself out of the waterbed. She flipped on the lamp she and Mike had made from seashells they'd collected on the beaches of Cape Cod, sat on the wooden bed frame, and tried to figure out what was happening. In her mind's ear, she could hear Mike scold her for sitting on the edge of the bed.

What are you trying to do? Break the bed? Flood the whole house?

But then she heard moaning and got a whiff of an unmistakable odor wafting from the bathroom. A line etched between her brow. No doubt about it. Mike was puking.

The lobster?

She ambled toward the bathroom, giving her arms a good wake-up shake. "Gee whiz, Mike, you must've pulled the short straw tonight. My lobster was de-licious!"

Kassie opened the bathroom door. She stood speechless.

2

KassieCare

You've got to be kidding. Not again. Kassie's hands covered her ears.

Sitting in the emergency room lobby at Boston Clinic in the middle of the night, she heard the sirens first in the distance, and then right on top of her as ambulances arrived. She never got used to their shrillness or their meaning. Somebody was in deep trouble.

It was déjà vu all over again. Her memories of Boston Clinic were vivid and heavy-hearted. She'd never forget the day she was there long ago when she'd miscarried, and the many nights and days more recently as Patricia O'Callaghan, her mother, had fought and succumbed to lung cancer. Her death a year ago left Kassie parentless. *Adults need parents, too, don't they?*

Kassie guessed her mom wouldn't be happy she'd decided to go ahead with the divorce. She'd stayed with Mike mostly to appease her mom, who almost always defended him when Kassie broached the subject of divorce with her.

"It's up to you, KO, to do everything you can to save your marriage," her mother would say.

"I've tried. But you can be lonely even if you live with someone. Believe me, I know."

"But he's not an alcoholic. Doesn't beat you. Doesn't fool around. He puts a roof over your head and food on the table. And he *let* you have your own career. What else is there?"

"More. I want more. Someday I'll show you what more means."

Her mother didn't live to see what *more* meant to Kassie, but someday had arrived. Despite her well-thought-out game plan, she anticipated telling Mike she'd filed for divorce much the same way she approached going to the dentist—dreading it ahead of time, but breathing a sigh of relief when it was over.

Little did Kassie know going to the dentist would be like a walk in the park when that Good Friday was history. Things started to spiral from bad to are-you-kidding-me bad when Mike insisted she take him to the hospital. Collapsed on the bathroom floor, he looked pitiful. The color drained from his face. Crying. In all the years she'd known him, she'd never seen him tear up. Not for funerals, weddings, movies, nothin', never. There were times she doubted he even had tear ducts.

"I tried to pee," he'd said. "But the room swirled. I lost everything. I found the john, right?"

"Not to worry. I'll take care of it."

Kassie grabbed an oversized towel and draped it around his shoulders, making him look like a heavyweight boxer between rounds. She mopped up the curdled stinking mess, succeeded in not gagging, and sat on the cold white tile beside him.

"I need to go to the hospital." Mike rested his head on her shoulder.

"Now?"

"Yes, now."

She rubbed the back of his shirt which he'd soaked through and suggested if he tried to sleep, he could go to the doctor in the morning. Who wants to go to the ER in the middle of the night?

"Kassie, get me to the hospital. Now."

Something was terribly wrong, something beyond bad shellfish.

"You look like hell. Can you make it to the car, or should I call an ambulance?" Kassie was relieved when he chose to drive. No reason to wake the neighborhood.

Though almost a foot shorter than Mike, Kassie had muscles enough to hike him to his feet. At just over six feet and two-hundred pounds, Mike loomed larger than he was, especially when Kassie stood by his side. They would never pass as the perfect Hollywood-looking couple, though their romance was as volatile. But it didn't matter to them. The difference in their size, they'd agreed, was one of the things that attracted each to the other in the first place.

She curled her arm under his armpit. "Heave ho. Let's get you up."

As he stood, she saw the tears up close streaming down Mike's unshaven, handsome face. Her heart throbbed over what could have been. Her eyes blinked, stifling her own waterworks.

Mike shuffled into the bedroom, still with the towel around his slumped shoulders, and perched himself onto the wooden bed frame and scowled. "Don't say a word."

She swallowed so hard her left ear popped.

"Let's get you dressed." Kassie wiped his face with a warm wet washcloth. "Better?"

"I'll need your help. Get me clean underwear."

What? Kassie had never been in his bureau. Mike had proclaimed it off limits to her. When they were first dating—not quite cohabiting—in Columbia, Missouri, he taught her to fold his clothes to his specifications, and then he'd put them away. She respected his privacy then. He was her college professor, and she'd do just about anything for him, especially when it involved his boxer shorts. Once they married, the laundry routine continued. She never gave it much thought as it was one less chore she'd have to do around the house.

"Second drawer."

"Good thing we dumped all those old, decrepit undershirts and shorts!" Kassie tried to lighten the mood. Mike didn't laugh, or maybe he wasn't listening, which was more likely the case.

Mike dressed with a little grunt here, and a big grunt there. Or maybe it was a little fart here, a big fart there. You never could tell with Mike. Whatever noises Mike emitted woke Topher, Kassie's yellow tabby, who had curled up on her side of the bed. Topher yawned, stretched, and swiped his white paw over his sleepy eyes as cats do. *What are those humans doing at this strange hour?*

"I think I'll try to pee again." Mike headed back to the bathroom.

Kassie fussed around the room, mumbling to Topher about neither of them having a good night's sleep. Not the best day to be sleep deprived. After a few minutes, she checked on Mike. He stood there with a pained grimace on his face.

"No luck?"

"No luck."

"Mike, your feet! They're swollen big time. Oh my God! Can you wiggle your toes?"

Mike looked down and tried. "No, not really. Salt from dinner, ya think?"

"You'll need to wear your flip-flops. I'll go find them. Don't go anywhere." Kassie threw her hands in the air.

She left him to finish dressing and ran downstairs. She dug through the hall coat closet and found an old pair of cheap black flip-flops from last summer. A stack of five Red Sox hats caught her eye. Sorting through them, she grabbed her favorite red one. A gift from a friend. She closed her eyes, breathed in its lingering scent, and smiled. *It won't be long.*

She ran upstairs, tossed the hat on the bed, missing Topher's head by a hair. "How you doin'? You ready?"

"I am, but you may want to wear something else."

Kassie glanced down at her short black silk nightgown. *Oh crap, can't go like this.*

Topher had moved from the bed to the honey-colored chaise lounge, resting his head on the lap of the dark-tan teddy bear with a pink-and-blue plaid bow Mike had given her when she was pregnant years before. It had survived even if the baby and their marriage hadn't. The chaise lounge was once upon a time Kassie's favorite chair, especially when losing herself in a murder mystery. After she'd adopted Topher, saving him from almost certain death, he in turn adopted the chaise. She nudged him and swiped her jeans and the black turtleneck she'd thrown there after dinner. Cat hair be damned.

"Do you need help getting downstairs?"

"No, I don't think so. Don't forget your phone."

Kassie unplugged it. Though fully charged, she took the charger anyway and headed downstairs to her office. She grabbed her wallet from her purse and threw everything in her black leather briefcase.

Almost on autopilot and without checking the "Topher's care" list she'd posted on the inside of the pantry, Kassie went into the eat-in kitchen and filled Topher's food and water bowls. They should be back home in time to give him his meds.

She filled a water bottle for herself and shouted to Mike, who had begun his measured descent.

"How about a bottle of water for the road? Might that help?"

"You're kidding me, right?"

"No, I'm not. How do you expect to pee if you don't have enough fluids in you? Less soda and more H2O might do you some good."

"Whatever. Which car we taking?"

"Mine. Does it matter?"

"Sure. If I'm gonna puke again, I don't want to be in my car!" He laughed alone. Not quite a Mike-ism, but typical Mike, a side of him Kassie came to ignore with practice.

She tossed her briefcase into the backseat and helped him into the car.

"Planning to drop me at the hospital and then go to the office?"

"No, but I might as well work on my Georgetown presentation while I'm waiting for you to be examined. Remember I'm heading down there this weekend?"

Kassie bit her lower lip at the lie and backed the midnight-blue Mercedes out of the oversized two-car garage. She checked the gas gauge. Half full? Half empty? Didn't matter. She had plenty to get them to the hospital. The trip from Newton to Boston on I-90 should be quick at that hour.

"Where's your transponder?" Mike said in between heavy breaths.

"Right here on the visor. Hang in there, Mike." She touched his arm with assurance. "Not much traffic at this hour."

And she was right. Kassie wheeled the Mercedes into a familiar parking spot in front of the ER as if it was reserved for her. She leaned toward the steering wheel and kissed it. "Good girl," she whispered. At least the car could be called that.

3

Lady in Waiting

Kassie peered into the ER lobby that was lit up as bright as a highway construction site at night trying to anticipate how long they'd have to wait. If only she were clairvoyant, like her mom swore she was. Though she never claimed to have ESP, Kassie thought it wicked cool her mom had bestowed that superpower on her when she was growing up.

As a child, there were the times when the phone would ring, and Kassie would announce who was calling before her mom answered it. Or they'd be at a restaurant, and she'd predict a waiter would drop a stack of plates, and then before she could count to ten, *crash.*

"What do you think's gonna happen?" her mom would ask ahead of an upcoming family or sporting event. "Will Aunt Emma bring her dreadful pasta to the picnic? Who's gonna win, Yankees or Red Sox? What's the score going to be?"

"I don't know what will happen. It doesn't work that way. I just watch and listen to what people say and do, and then sometimes something inside me stirs. I'm an observer of life, and just lucky in my guesses, I guess."

There were times, though, Kassie shocked herself because the sensations that bubbled up from somewhere deep in her gut were vivid, intense, and foreboding. She couldn't ignore them. Like the day the principal walked into her third-grade class. She sensed he'd call her name even before he did. And when she saw her mother waiting in the principal's office, she knew her father had died. Why else would her mother show up at school on Friday the thirteenth? *Freaky!*

Still, Kassie refused to totally buy into her mother's ESP theory. Rather, she attributed these strange occurrences to a finely tuned intuition fueled in part by reading the Stephen King books lining her bookshelves. As an adult traveling around the country, she'd often track down fortune tellers for a palm or tarot-card reading. Over time, their prognostications scared Kassie shitless because of their similarity whether it was a psychic in San Francisco, Scottsdale, or Seattle. Didn't matter.

Starting in her twenties when each foreshadowed some version of "A younger man will come into your life and turn your world upside down," she interpreted it to mean she'd have a son someday. But when their single-focused prophesy continued unfulfilled into her forties, she halted the useless psychic research into her future. Enough of that insanity. Instead she'd take her chances on her own magical powers to guide her destiny, be it good or bad.

If her mother was right, how did Kassie not foresee this trip to the ER? She inhaled deeply to conjure up whatever inner force she possessed. Squinting her eyes to get a better view, she concluded the ER looked alive but not crazy busy. She took it as an optimistic sign they'd get in and out fast.

"I'll get a wheelchair."

"Don't bother. I can walk."

No sooner had she jumped out of the car to open the door for Mike when a tall good-looking black man in blue scrubs approached their car.

"What have we got here?"

"It's my back, doctor."

"I'm Tommy Thompson. A nurse. Not a doctor. Let me grab a wheelchair."

Kassie leaned into the car, clenched her teeth, and whispered, "Your back? Since when?"

"He's not a doctor. Damn it. I'll wait to talk to a doctor." Mike stared straight.

"Why because he's black? Or because he's a male nurse? Can't you stifle it for once in your life?"

Mike held onto the car door for leverage and settled his rear into the wheelchair.

"It's not too hectic tonight, so I'll take . . . oh, I'm sorry, sir, what is your name?"

"Mike. Mr. Mike Ricci."

"Okay, Mr. Mike, I'll take you right into an examining room. And Mrs. Ricci, please go to the main desk. The staff there will take your husband's information and get him checked in."

Relieved to get away from Mike even for a few minutes, she walked through the sliding glass doors chuckling. Tommy Thompson gave as good as he got. *How do you like them apples, Mike?*

She fumbled through her briefcase to retrieve their insurance information and filled out and signed the paperwork. She noticed the Wi-Fi password on a poster and logged on. No messages yet. The redeye from San Francisco wasn't due for another three hours. Enough time to have Mike examined and back home, she hoped.

"Could you tell me where Mike Ricci is? My husband?" She almost choked. Her words tasted as bitter as a mouthful of kale.

"Just have a seat, Mrs. Ricci. We'll let you know when you can see him. The waiting room's over there. Is that your car outside? You'll need to move it to the garage."

Gulp. She'd recently attended an international travel safety course sponsored by her company where she learned in graphic detail how bad people in this world operated. Parking in a dark, poorly lit garage in the middle of the night especially alone was something to be avoided at all cost. She knew if she were going to divorce Mike and be on her own, she'd have to overcome fears like these, no matter if they were rational or not. She took a deep breath and obeyed the admitting nurse who had the power to make her time there miserable if she was so inclined.

"Excuse me. Would it be possible, I mean, may I leave my case with you, here, while I move my car? Please? I'll just take my keys." Kassie waved her carabiner.

When she returned unharmed, she strode down the hall to the all-too-familiar waiting room. She'd been there before when her mother was ill. She studied the room, assessing her seating options. Something had changed. Wood-framed couches and chairs with complimentary cloth cushions of royal blue and forest green stripes replaced the metal and black vinyl chairs. Hand sanitizer stations stood guard on both sides of the entryway, as well as in the middle and far corners of the room. Germs better beware.

Taking the not-so-subtle hint, Kassie availed herself of the cold gooey gel and chose a seat in the far corner facing the doorway so she'd see when someone came to get her.

But no one came, at least not within the fifteen minutes Kassie allocated as waiting time. She heard sirens approaching, reminding her of her mother's lengthy decline and demise.

"Mom, if you're watching, you better have my back today," she prayed.

Her stomach gurgled in response. *Tea, I need tea. What are my choices?* There were no Starbucks or Dunkin' Donuts on site. The 24-hour coffee shop was in another building. She didn't want to be too far away in case Mike was ready to leave.

"Pardon me," she whispered. "Is there somewhere to get tea around here?" She lifted her index finger and gestured a circle.

The same admitting nurse raised her eyes from the computer screen and peered over her tortoise-shell glasses. "Just vending. Down the hall on the right."

"Oh yes, I forgot. Thanks, any word yet on Mike Ricci, my husband?" Again, that word. Again, that hint of bitterness in her voice and her mouth. Was she being punished with this constant reminder she was about to take steps that would change the whole husband-wife until death do you part thing? She wondered if ex-husband would roll off her tongue any smoother.

"No, I'm sorry," the nurse replied in full voice. "Not yet. The chief resident is with him now. These things take time, especially at night. If they're running any tests, it could take twice as long to get the results, you know."

Another déjà vu moment. Kassie knew all too well.

Tiptoeing down the empty hallway, she tried to silence the *clickety-clack* of her heels. *Should've worn my Skechers.* She imagined the hospital's infrastructure asleep, regenerating itself as the human body did. God forbid she disturbed or slowed down that process.

Kassie found the small windowless room that housed the vending machines. She crossed her arms and stared at them. Who invented these cretins anyway? Did they replace automats she and her mom visited in New York City when she was little? She'd call them food prisons where only exact change could free boiled-ham-and-processed-cheese sandwiches and slices of lemon meringue pies from their jail cells. Or were they another method for the mob to monopolize an industry and make a shitload of money? Maybe a little of both. Didn't matter.

There they were. Three vending machines standing idle side-by-side beckoning her to feed them so they could feed her.

Kassie took the smallest bill she had in her wallet and checked for a change machine. No luck. She stepped back, eye-balling them. Which would take a five and make change? The "Exact change only" light on the candy and coffee machines flashed. Only the one with wimpy-looking sandwiches would take her five. She purchased a turkey-and-cheese on what she expected was soggy, day-old rye bread and scooped up the change she'd need to buy a lukewarm cup of tea. The sandwich found its way into the green trash bin with a loud *kerplunk*, and the tea went down the hatch. On the way back to the waiting area, she swung by the ladies' room.

"I'm cleanin' here," a tiny pretty woman said with a thick accent. Was it Turkish or Greek or Mexican? If it weren't Italian or Irish, Kassie couldn't place it. Didn't matter.

"You should be at home with your family, in bed, asleep!" Kassie teased.

"You got that right. You, too."

"Can I come in?"

"Sure. But be careful. Floor's a little slippery."

A little slippery? That's all she'd need to do was fall on her ass and land in a bed next to Mike. What would happen to her plans then?

As she left the ladies' room, Kassie gagged as cleaning fluid fumes and hospital antiseptic converged up her nose. Stark reminder of where she was. She ambled back to the waiting room, gelled up again, and glanced at the oversized round clock on the wall. She'd been there for an hour and a half already. No word yet, from anyone.

In the time she'd been away, two couples had arrived. From what she overheard as she passed them, one was a car accident, the other was an overdose. Kassie's chest tightened as she maneuvered her way past the families to the same chair she had previously occupied, claiming it as her own, the same way college students did.

The tea may have settled her stomach, but it did little to help her figure out what was wrong with Mike. Was it the lobster he ate? He'd passed on his usual Dewar's and water, which she thought might be a good sign.

Mike had told her that during his last physical his doctor advised him to slim down, shape up, and stop smoking. Even at his age, Mike should be able to improve his health. Kassie took the doctor's advice seriously, but she was never sure if Mike did. She enrolled in a Weight Watchers cooking class, and once a week for six weeks, she left work early and learned how to poach, smoke, and grill foods that would reduce carbohydrates. While Mike had lost about ten pounds, Kassie benefitted more, losing fifteen. Together with her walking, yoga, and weight training, her fifty-four-year-old body had taken on a leaner, sexier shape, which would not go to waste even if Mike turned a blind eye.

Kassie checked the clock again. Almost five-thirty and still no sign of a doctor or Mike. The other couples had already left. Leaning back in her chair and closing her eyes, she inhaled, imagining the rest of the day, starting with getting Mike out of the hospital as soon as possible. She calculated they'd need to head home by ten at the latest.

The pit stop to the ER was not on her agenda. She wanted to get on with the first day of the rest of her life, starting with the Red Sox game. A couple of months ago Kassie was invited to sit in the company box at Fenway. Under the circumstances, she declined the invitation. Instead she'd called her ticket broker and bought bleacher tickets for two.

Truthiness

Just before dawn. Kassie's mind roamed as she slouched in the waiting room seat and struggled between drifting to sleep and staying alert.

At first, lying to Mike was so much out of Kassie's comfort zone, she'd break out into a clammy sweat and call Annie, her BFF since fourth grade, for moral support. Annie, who had dubbed her "Bad Kassie" during the stepfather years, accepted Kassie's deviousness as her survival apparatus. Along with that, Kassie developed and sustained into adulthood a quick wit that caused her to roll back her tongue like Ally McBeal on more than one occasion. The moniker stuck.

"Cinderella may have had a wicked stepmother, but I had a wicked stepfather," Kassie confided to Annie. "He'd beat me for talking back, he'd beat me for not eating Cream of Wheat, he'd beat me just for the sake of beating me. Once, he choked me until I passed out because I fibbed about eating my lunch at school. Wouldn't you think I'd have learned never to lie again?"

After her mother divorced him when she was a young teen, Kassie rarely lied except for an occasional white lie. Yet there she was, a full-grown woman lying as easily as she breathed to her husband for goodness sake. For her sake. What will Mike do when he finds out? Choke her? Not likely. He was more of a Boston bully than a Boston strangler.

Soon after her marriage to Mike soured, Kassie brought her mother into her circle of trust. Much to her despair, her mother often stuck up for him, encouraging her to hang in there and work things out.

"He's a good man, KO. Don't hurt him."

But she hurt, inside. In the last years before her mother died, she complained to her how their marriage was clinging to the edge of a cliff, hanging by a threadbare bungee cord. She and Mike had grown apart. Doing less together. Tending to their own needs, rather than each other's. When did they last hold hands? Five years ago? Ten? It didn't matter anymore.

They'd developed their own interests. Hers mostly centered around her career, and sports—Red Sox, Patriots, of course. His around his business, and . . . what were Mike's other interests anyway? She realized she didn't know what floated his boat anymore. For sure, it wasn't her.

Kassie long held a philosophy about marriage she'd share with anyone who'd listen, especially at cocktail parties after a couple of Cosmopolitans.

"Marriage is work. Hard work," she'd say to a small group of friends gathered around her. "Many of us married folk take for granted we'll be together forever. And if not, that's okay. Divorce is too easy. If, however, marriage was a five-year renewable contract, dissolvable by either party at the end of the term, just think about it, maybe the fourth year would serve as a wake-up call. Either make it or break it."

"What are you a lawyer now?" Mike would interrupt her, rolling his Paul Newman-blue eyes, suggesting to her that he'd given up on their marriage. Sometimes she wished he hadn't.

The waiting room provided Kassie no refuge. Ambulance sirens jarred her back to real time. Sliding doors screeched open and a bell *ding-dinged*. Tommy Thompson rushed a woman past the admitting desk. The woman gripped the arms of the wheelchair as a rather excited man hurried in with a tote bag slung over his shoulder. Kassie assumed it was her husband, but these days, who knew? It didn't matter.

Staring out the window at the twinkling lights of the city, she wondered if their marriage would've thrived if they'd had children. Did she stop trying too soon? Should she have pressured Mike to adopt?

Where was all this melancholy coming from? Hospital-induced memories? The intoxicating influence of a sleep aid? The anticipation and fear of telling Mike she wanted out?

"Mrs. Rizzi."

No response.

"Mrs. Rizzi." And then more sternly, "Kassandra Rizzi?"

She turned toward the voice, rubbed her tired eyes, and saw a short bald man with glasses standing in the waiting room doorway. *He's really short. Shorter than me.*

"Do you mean, Ricci? If yes, it's Ricci, which means curly in Italian, then yes, I'm Mrs. Ricci." She bumbled and rose to greet him.

As this small man approached her, she wondered if they made special lab coats for him. He must be a technician.

"Hello, Mrs. Ricci. I'm Dr. Alexander. Pleased to meet you." He offered his right hand.

"Oh! Doctor! I'm sorry, I didn't hear you come in. And mostly I go by my maiden name, O'Callaghan, but you can call me Kassie."

She continued to babble. "When I hear Mrs. Ricci, I think some-one's talking to my mother-in-law. But that couldn't possibly happen now because she's dead." She giggled. "And you said Rizzi, so I didn't hear you right away."

"Mrs. Rizzi. Kassie. Please sit." The doctor sat down and leaned toward to her. "You're obviously concerned about your husband and understandably you're tired. You've been here half the night waiting to get some news."

"Yes, that's true. Is he ready to leave now?" She resituated her body, taking back her space.

The short doctor continued his long explanation. "I appreciate how stressful this must be, and I know our waiting room isn't as comfortable as your living room."

What's with this guy? Just answer my question.

He droned on about the damn waiting room. "You'd think we could at least get a television installed here. With all the budget cut-backs, we were lucky to replace some of the old furniture. We can barely order Q-tips," he said with a half-grin and raised eyebrows.

Oh, that's reassuring. Let's suspend with the pleasantries already, shorty, and tell Bad Kassie what's going on.

She inhaled deeply and tried to gain control of her tongue before she embarrassed herself.

Switching gears, Kassie noticed his full name on his badge, Dr. Samuel Alexander. Kassie adopted her mother's practice of putting professionals like doctors and lawyers on an equal footing by addressing them by their first name, if and only if, they called you by yours.

She had already given him permission to call her Kassie. The name calling should be reciprocal in her mind. She wondered if he went by Sam or maybe he preferred Alex, which was always an option when a person's surname could also be a first name.

"Dr. Alexander. May I call you Sam?"

"But of course. But most people call me Alexander. Some even call me 'the Great.' You know, Alexander the—"

A smile danced on her lips, though she was frustrated with his dillydallying.

"Seriously, Doctor, where is my husband? What is going on with him? When can I see him and take him home?"

"Well, Mrs. Ricci . . ."

Finally, he'd gotten her name right. They apparently reverted to formalities. This wasn't boding well. The great doctor went on.

"It's possible your husband's kidney disease is progressing. But we're waiting for Dr. Singleton to arrive. We called him, and he said he'd be here after the test results came back. Some results are in, but we expect Dr. Singleton will want to run more."

The waiting room became a whirling dervish. Trying to process his words, Kassie closed her eyes, leaned into his space, and then tilted her head toward him.

"Excuse me? What did you say? His kidney disease is progressing? What kidney disease?"

"Oh dear. You are unaware of your husband's illness, I gather."

"You gather right. Tell me more, Doctor."

"Mrs. Ricci, under the circumstances, I'm unable to continue. The privacy laws, you know, even protects spouses."

Privacy, schmimacy.

"That's hogwash." Kassie stood and snagged her briefcase. Her cellphone dropped to the floor with a *thud*. She picked it up, checked it hadn't cracked, and out of habit clipped it to the waistband of her jeans, covering it with her turtleneck.

"Where is he? I'd like to see him now if you don't mind. I need to get to the bottom of this."

The doctor looked up at her, his forehead furrowed. "Maybe that's not a good idea right now. He's had a rough night. I don't think he's had any sleep."

"He's had a rough night?" Bad Kassie burst onto the scene. "I guess you'd say I was stepping out on the Ritz then, eh, hanging out in this posh waiting room? Let me be the judge of whether or not I should see him."

Dr. Alexander stepped back on his heels, his eyebrows rose above his glasses.

Sensing she may have crossed a line, she consciously switched tactics. "Okay. I promise not to upset him." She crossed her heart and lowered her voice. "I'll stay calm. But I need to know what's going on and what we're going to do about it. When will Dr. Singleton get here?"

"If you promise not to alarm your husband and say anything rash, I'll take you to see him. Agreed?"

Kassie nodded and tweaked her ear lobe.

As they left the waiting room, she noticed the pink sky in the distance. It was a new day. Good Friday. Would it be a good day . . . or a bad day? It mattered.

Kassie was grateful to see Mike was alone in the examining bay. Not a private room. No such thing in emergency rooms. More like a horse stable, with one stall after another.

Mike opened his eyes as the doctor walked in with Kassie close on his heels and half-smiled at her, reminding her of when she'd catch him watching porn. Explaining his porn habit was one thing, justifying hiding his kidney problem quite another.

Abiding by her promise, Kassie softened her approach. "Hey, babe, what's all this about?"

The doctor jumped in. "Mr. Ricci, I think you should know I was unaware you had not shared your health condition with Mrs. Ricci. As is hospital custom and protocol, I intended to give your wife a full update on your situation ahead of Dr. Singleton's arrival. As I was talking with Mrs. Ricci, though, it became apparent that you had not advised your wife of the problems you've been having and the treatments—"

"Treatments, what treatments?" Kassie demanded, her eyes boring into the doctor and then Mike for answers. So much for her promise. It was off the table.

"Please don't be alarmed," Mike said. "I've got everything under control. Sit down. I'll tell you what's going on. Alexander, can we have a few minutes alone here?"

"I'm sitting down. *Alexander* said you have a kidney disease, and that it's progressing. What does he mean? How can that be? It must be a misdiagnosis. Maybe the tests are wrong. He thought my name was Rizzi, not Ricci. Maybe they got the test results crossed."

"There's no mistake. I do have chronic kidney disease. This is probably just a flare up, not a progression. Let's not jump to conclusions."

"Flare up? Progression? Conclusions? What the hell, Mike, I don't even know where to begin."

Kassie put her head in her hands, trying to think fast.

"Look at me, Kassie. I never wanted to worry you. I thought I could take care of it myself. But I'm not the superman you once thought I was. I'm not able to jump buildings in a single bound anymore."

Superman? Who's he kidding? Not even close. She bit Bad Kassie's tongue and refrained from bursting his bubble, giving the short doctor time to wisely leave the scene.

"This is no time to joke. You've been lying to me. For how long?"

As Mike frowned and shifted his weight, the sounds of a strumming guitar reverberated from Kassie's waistline.

"Are you going to get that? Who'd be calling at this hour, and on your day off?"

Kassie stood poker-faced. She didn't have to look; she knew by the ring tone. But she looked anyway. Her caller ID read *Topher*. The redeye from San Francisco had landed.

5

Here's Ricci

The jig was up. Mike waited in the emergency room cubicle alone, staring at the ceiling tiles, counting them one by one. Wearing just a light-green-striped johnny coat, Mike felt a chill, the kind that's difficult to shake unless you had socks on your feet. But no, Kassie insisted he wear flip-flops. With no blanket in sight, he reached around his neck and then his back to be sure the strings of the hospital gown were tied. One was not, so he fixed it. Maybe that would help.

On the positive side, he was relieved that tests done in the ER would take forever. The longer it took, the better. He needed time on his side.

"How will I explain *this* to Kassie?" He shook his head, glancing at the IV the nurse just inserted. He'd succeeded at hiding his illness. Until now.

Getting up during the night to pee without disturbing Kassie was a big challenge for a couple of years. The damn waterbed sloshed with his slightest move. He wanted to get rid of it, swap it for one of those trendy Sleep Number beds, but Kassie wouldn't hear of it. Sentimental value. Great sex; memories of great sex. Distant memories.

How long had it been since the waterbed had seen any real action? How long had it been since he and Kassie had seen any? Three, four, maybe five years? His passion for her had faded gradually, though he couldn't remember exactly when. Didn't seem to matter to Kassie, which was fine with him.

After he'd turned fifty, Mike put on a few pounds here and there. The ol' beer belly many middle-aged men battle, he'd convinced himself. An active lad in his younger days, he played softball, tennis, squash, racquetball. He held his own with a racket in his hand and a ball to hit. Football and basketball, on the other hand, reminded him of hand-to-hand combat. To be honest, he avoided most sports like the Ebola virus, turning Kassie down whenever she invited him to join in her running, yoga, meditation exercise routine.

Laying there shivering, he covered himself with the sterile white sheet so as not to expose himself to the world. With two monitors humming alongside him, Mike focused on preparing to meet the doctor.

He remembered he was looking forward to the long weekend when he'd gone upstairs to bed. Kassie was going to the Red Sox game with folks from work, which meant he'd have the house all to himself. A little tinkering around the house, a little beer, a little porn. Good times.

Kassie had gone to bed a couple of hours earlier. Mike assumed she was already asleep. As usual, she lay facing away from his side of the bed, her breathing measured. She claimed he snored like Amtrak at full speed. Total exaggeration on her part. It couldn't be that bad, could it? Rather, he was convinced she'd turned her back on him in direct response to his tossing and turning and getting up so damn frequently to pee. Sometimes he'd whiz a little, sometimes not at all, despite the ever-present urge to go.

Mike's first appointment with Dr. Singleton, a highly recommended nephrologist in the area, was two years ago. The doctor ordered routine tests. They both thought it was the proverbial prostate acting up, a common ailment and complaint among guys his age. But that wasn't it.

Dr. Singleton ordered more blood and urine tests that revealed Mike had a kidney problem. Nothing to be alarmed about. Drugs should take care of it. Mike decided there was no need to tell Kassie. She needed to stay focused on her career, and her travel schedule meant he could arrange follow-up doctor's appointments when she was out of town. She wouldn't have a clue. He could straighten this out without her ever being the wiser.

That's what Mike thought. Dr. Singleton said his tests showed that he had a chronic kidney disease possibly heredity or caused by his high blood pressure. To his knowledge, no one in his family had kidney problems. It must be a blood pressure issue, he'd decided.

The doctor's initial recommendation focused on medication and diet. They'd monitor him over time and see if he improved. It would help, Dr. Singleton advised, if Mike could lose about forty pounds and by all means, stop smoking. He gave Mike a firm warning and handed him some reading material. But the words fell on deaf ears, and the pamphlets found their way to the circular file at the office. The first two recommendations—diet and pills—seemed reasonable. It would be easy to explain to Kassie. Most men his age needed to diet and take medication, right?

Quit smoking? Maybe he'd just cut back. He'd tried to quit multiple times before, always unsuccessfully. If he tried hard, he could cut down from two packs a day to one.

"Those non-filtered cigarettes will kill you," Kassie used to harp on him day-in and day-out. "You'll make me a young widow if you keep that up."

After Dr. Singleton's news, he succumbed to her nagging and switched to filtered. He still enjoyed smoking, but not as much.

As was his custom, Mike fell short of telling Kassie the whole story. He fibbed when he told her all he needed to do was change some of his lifestyle habits—lose weight, cut back on red meat, eat more veggies, drink more water, put the salt shaker away. That should make her happy.

Kassie embraced Mike's new diet like a challenge, as if she was fulfilling the requirements of a Girl Scout badge. She enrolled in a healthy eating and cooking class and joined Mike in his weight loss program. Of course, she lost more weight than he did.

"Whoever said it's easier for men to lose weight than women wasn't married," Mike would say, letting himself off the hook.

It wasn't long before Mike observed that Kassie was benefitting from *his* diet. For a tiny lady who had always battled her weight, Kassie looked mighty fine, sexy, and inviting. But Mike hesitated to pursue her. His guilt and his lies had caught up with him. He'd hoped she interpreted his distance as a combination of being middle-aged and being married for so long. The bloom was off the rose sort of thing. Mike wanted to believe Kassie, too, was disinterested for the same reasons because she hadn't touched him like she once did in years. There were already so many divides between them. Lack of intimacy was just one more breach.

Most of the time Mike didn't dwell on their sex life; it was ancient history. And he was too busy covering up for himself on multiple fronts. Except for the time he was at lunch with his colleague, Bill, when the subject of how times had changed in the sex department with their wives over the years.

Bill boasted about how he was shocked, yet ecstatic, at the interest his wife, Nancy, had in making love recently. Bill described in great pains the cycles of their love life. In the early years before they married, they couldn't get enough of each other. And they didn't care where they did it. In the backseat of his Honda, in the stairwell of a hotel in the middle of the night after a New Year's Eve party, up against a tree in the park after a concert.

Then, Bill continued, they married and all that spontaneity disappeared. The bedroom became the more conventional venue to have sex. Though occasionally Nancy would turn the television off at halftime of an NFL game and unzip his pants right there on the couch with no prompting from him. Those were the days.

Once the kids came, they both became sleep deprived and just plain old tired, balancing work and family. Sex became perfunctory. Almost always Saturday night. Kind of the date night hold over from their youth. And maybe they'd slip in another go-round on Thursday night, just so they could say they got it on twice that week. Neither of them tried to spice things up. Bill confessed he'd become bored at home.

As Mike was well aware, Bill traveled for work, often to New York City, to visit clients. And that's where he met Stella, a fetching and willing account executive.

"*STELLA!!*" Bill bellowed, mimicking Marlon Brando in *A Streetcar Named Desire*. "Now there's a gal worth risking a flight to LaGuardia."

One thing led to another, Bill explained, showing no guilt or remorse. First, coffee together, then lunch. And finally one night, after dinner and a night cap at her apartment on the East Side, Bill was bored no more. He'd forgotten what igniting a man's passion did for his ego and performance—in the bedroom and at work.

"Didn't Nancy suspect?"

Bill didn't think so. He kept to the twice-a-week-routine at home. His affair with the long-legged Stella went on for a few years. Neither of them made promises or commitments.

"Did you love her?"

He wasn't sure if he did or not. He loved the sex sure enough. But love?

"Would you leave Nancy for her?"

No, Bill never gave it a thought. In fact, it was easy to end it with her. She met another guy, got married, and had a little girl. All's well that ends well.

So how did things turn around for him and Nancy? Mike's interest peaked, feeling himself getting off on Bill's story.

Bill continued. "Our boys are teenagers now. They both drive and are out a lot. We have the house all to ourselves."

It was Nancy that renewed the spark between them. One night, Bill came home from work and when he walked in, she stood there wearing nothing but her leather coat and offering him a gin martini. Bill knew it sounded cliché, but it worked for his libido, so why not? He chugged the drink and peeled open her coat. They dropped right there to the floor and had the best sex he'd had in years, even with Stella. That was just the beginning. Since then Nancy was always hot to trot, experimenting with locations and even toys. Bill admitted he felt nineteen again.

Wearing a big, shit-eating grin on his face, Bill asked, "What about you and Kassie? How are things going in that department?"

Adjusting himself and his seat, Mike was reluctant and embarrassed to say not quite as well as he and Nancy. So instead, he deflected saying their paths were totally different. And knowing words sometimes lie, he crossed his fingers and said no, he didn't have a Stella on the side. Not that he wasn't tempted. And, of course, they didn't have children.

Mike's cover-up continued. He and Kassie were ten years apart, so their sexual appetites and expectations of each other were naturally different; couldn't expect to be on the same plane. And then, their busy careers. Kassie traveled all around the country.

"Stop right there, ol' boy. Did you ever think maybe she's got a stud on the side? You know what they say? If they're not getting it at home, they're getting it somewhere. And that doesn't just go for us guys.

Women have needs, too. I know. Nancy's been whispering all her fantasies, and it's pretty damn kinky what goes on inside a woman's mind."

What was going on inside Kassie's mind . . . right now? With Kassie at the hospital with him, he couldn't continue hiding from her. What would she think? Would she ever forgive him? Luckily Tommy Thompson had whisked him away from the lobby, and Kassie stayed behind to get him checked in. A bright green, blue, and yellow plaid curtain stood between Kassie and the hot mess he'd created.

Reality struck. The silver metal grommets screeched twice in succession as a small man in a white coat pulled open the curtain and closed it again. For a moment, he thought maybe he was having a nightmare. A black male nurse and a peanut-sized doctor all in the same day. Was he dreaming he was in a circus hospital? A sharp pain in his back told him this was no dream.

"Mr. Ricci, good evening, or should I say good morning. I'm Dr. Alexander, the attending," he said, grabbing a small white step stool. Were stools scattered around the hospital for this doctor's convenience?

"Now tell me what brings you in here today? Trying to get out of coloring Easter eggs?"

Mike brushed off the doctor's attempt at a humorous bedside manner. He was in too much pain to care. While the doctor tortured Mike with his icy stethoscope and checked his pulse, he painstakingly downloaded his medical history and that night's events. What concerned Mike the most was the back pain and the swelling in his feet. Couldn't he prescribe something for those two things and send him home?

"A person could contract a terminal illness in a place like this," Mike said.

"Not likely. But I do applaud you for coming to the hospital when you did. When there's a long weekend like this, many folks put off getting life-threatening symptoms checked until Monday."

Life-threatening? Was this life-threatening? *Good grief!* He was only kidding about a terminal illness. Mike's eyelids sweat as he tugged at the plastic admittance bracelet.

"Let's not jump to conclusions. We're running a series of tests and scans. This way when Dr. Singleton gets here, he can review them. It shouldn't surprise you, Mr. Ricci, that your chronic kidney disease is more than likely progressing, which is what has caused you the back pain and edema in your feet. Dr. Singleton will discuss the test results and prescribe the next steps in your treatment. Please don't worry. You're in good hands here." Dr. Alexander snapped off his gloves and pumped the hand sanitizer.

"In the meantime, we'll give you something for your pain. Be sure to drink plenty of water. We'll get you some ice chips, too. You might like them better."

"Thanks, Doc." Mike felt reassured and nervous at the same time. If only he'd read those damn pamphlets.

"Do you smoke?"

Mike admitted he did, but he'd tried to cut back to just one pack a day. He had so few vices left these days.

Dr. Alexander left Mike alone to think about what Dr. Singleton might tell him. Was he ready for bad news? What would it mean for his life, his business, his marriage? In that order. He was confident that his business was in good shape; his marriage not so much.

He laid there enjoying the warmth of the blanket a nurse had draped over him, imagining he was on the warm beach again in Haiti, one stop on a cruise he and Kassie had taken during the good times. What a joy it would be to trade that day for this. But that would not be. He would have to face the music and hoped she could find it in her heart to forgive him, at least for this.

Mike opened his eyes and saw by the jumbo clock on the wall it was almost six o'clock. He'd been there for nearly three hours and had seen no sign of Kassie. The curtain scraped open again sending a shiver up his spine, and at long last Kassie walked in behind the short doctor. The next few minutes boggled his mind, one moment he was in the express lane, the next he shifted into reverse. Questions were asked, but not answered. Neither was her cellphone.

He recalled hearing that ringtone before. The conversation with Bill flashed through his mind. A sourness rose from his gut. He reached for the kidney-shaped stainless-steel vomit dish, and tipped over the blue plastic pitcher. Humpty-Dumpty had better days.

6

Man of the Hour

Finally, it was time. Christopher Gaines scheduled Uber to drive him to San Francisco International Airport. Usually he'd take the BART, but that night he had more luggage than most self-respecting forty-year-old men would have. He scoured his one-bedroom walk-up, making sure he'd left nothing behind he might need before he returned in September. If he'd forgotten something, he could always call his friend Sam whom he'd given a key the night before so he could check the place from time to time.

With the checklist provided by Kassie, Chris approached his departure like a moving pro—emptying the refrigerator, cancelling his cleaning service, and forwarding his mail to the Charlestown post office box he'd rented when he was in Boston the month before. He turned off the thermostat and unplugged almost everything. He left one light in the living room on a timer, just like she said he should.

It took three trips to get his bags down the stairs to the sidewalk. So much for traveling light. He'd ignored the packing list Kassie had emailed him. Besides clothes for work, he had casual and gym clothes, and three pairs of swim trunks. He also had his MacBook and iPad, and all the peripherals that went with them, including various types of headphones. And then there were his shoes. He wore his brown loafers and packed his black wing tips, plus two pairs of running shoes, two pairs of sandals and flip-flops for the pool.

Ten minutes later, a black SUV arrived as scheduled. Chris and the driver loaded nine bags.

"Long trip?"

"Moving east, at least temporarily. Might be back, all depends."

As they made their way to the airport, Chris marveled at the sparkling city lights. The San Francisco skyline took his breath away. Maybe someday he could convince Kassie this was where they should live. Boston had its good points, but to him, there was no place like San Francisco.

Before he knew it, they arrived at American Airlines departures. *I'll need a cart.* The driver was one step ahead and commandeered one as soon as they pulled alongside the curb.

Chris grabbed his black backpack from the rear seat. Better not forget that. It carried everything that was important—his computer, his novel, and the lease to the apartment in Charlestown, which he could move into after the holiday weekend. While he may leave his heart in San Francisco, he couldn't leave his backpack. He slapped the driver on the back, thanked him, and gave him a twenty-dollar tip.

How cool was this? No crowd. Chris rolled the cart toward the check-in counter and unloaded his luggage. As he handed his reservation receipt and identification to the pretty redhead, he noticed her name was Melissa.

"You always wear a suit on the redeye, Mr. Gaines?" Melissa gushed.

"Sometimes. Dress to impress, right?"

"That you do," she murmured.

"You always this perky late at night? Is it *Miss* Melissa?"

"Generally. Depends on the passenger, I guess. How many bags will you be checking, Mr. Christopher?"

"Eight."

"You might want to move to the side and repack a couple. Otherwise I must charge you for at least six," she said with a coy smile.

"Thanks for the suggestion. But that's okay. I knew there'd be charges."

"Why so many bags? If you don't mind my asking, are you moving to Boston?" She fake-pouted.

"Yes, at least through the summer, I hope."

"Let me see. I think I can waive the fee on a few of these. How about I charge you for five? Maybe when you move back, you could look me up and thank me?"

"Sounds like a deal." Chris winked and concluded the financial transaction with his AMEX Platinum card, leaving her invitation floating unanswered.

Chris retrieved his boarding pass and luggage receipts and headed toward security. Behind him, he heard giggling and female voices say, "Was that Chris Hemsworth? No. Couldn't be. Wasn't he *People Magazine's* sexiest man alive? Not sure. Let's look him up?"

He did a one-eighty back toward the counter.

"Oh, Melissa, I forgot one thing. Look me up if you're in Boston this summer. Perhaps we could get a drink some time." Chris handed her his business card.

More giggling as he walked away. He shook his head and stifled a laugh. It wasn't the first time he'd been mistaken for a celebrity, but Chris Hemsworth? Was he Chris's doppelgänger? He'd have to look him up.

There was a good hour before boarding, and he felt a pang in his stomach. Nerves or hunger? Not all the restaurants were open this late. He found his way to a new pub he'd heard about and found a two-person table open. He settled in and ordered a Corona and a chicken quesadilla. That should hold him until morning.

He checked his phone. No call or text from Kassie. It was after one in the morning in Boston. He hadn't expected to hear from her. She'd said she and Mike were going out for dinner. The last supper? How appropriate and kind of surreal when he thought about it. Chris decided not to point out the irony to Kassie, afraid she might think it a bad omen, change her mind, and delay her well-planned escape once again.

Kassie had agonized about how Mike would take the news. Would it be like a bomb coming out of left field, Chris wondered? Or maybe her husband had sensed her infidelity all along? Did Mike consider Kassie's frequent business trips normal, or were they red flags? Did he accept late nights at the office as part of her job? Kassie had assured Chris she had covered her tracks, and Chris had assured her that he would be there to support her.

Chris's meal arrived. The sweet smell of peppers took him back to the Mexican dinner he had with Sam the night before.

"So, buddy, you really gonna do this, huh?" Sam had quizzed him.

"Yup. What's it to ya?"

"Do I need to state the obvious? She's a lot older than you. A cougar and a married cougar at that."

"Jealous?"

"Depends. Honestly now, is she that good in the sack?"

"None of your business."

"You think it'll last?"

"We'll see. Taking one day at a time. Tomorrow's day one."

"Day one? What's happening tomorrow?"

"Didn't I tell you? Kassie's telling her husband she's filing for divorce and moving out of the house. We're moving into a furnished apartment next week."

"Wow! This is more serious than I thought. I figured you were just going out there for a few months to get laid more often than you do here."

"There's that too. I could've stayed here, out of the possible line of fire. Her mother died last year. She could use some support. And, living together for a few months should give us an opportunity to see whether it's real or just the excitement of a tryst and unbelievable sex."

"Rubbing it in, huh? Think Kassie's got a friend just like her? Can't say I've been with an older lady. I hear they've got all the same parts as their younger sisters, yet with all their wisdom, they leave all their inhibitions behind."

"Is that what you hear? I don't kiss and tell. I'll just say with Kassie we take it up a notch." Chris winked.

Sam asked about whether Kassie's husband knew or suspected anything? Did Chris think he'd shoot him?

"Hope not! That would be a waste of two good lives. Wouldn't want that to happen."

Chris told him that in all the time he'd been seeing Kassie, there'd never been a close call. They took measures to keep their affair a secret, traveling mostly away from Boston to meet or timing their visits for when Kassie had a good excuse to be out of the house. They never met at her place, avoiding gossipy neighbors or the accidental toothbrush left in the bathroom. No husband barging in unannounced.

"If she's been unfaithful to her husband, what makes you think she'll be faithful to you?"

Chris raised his eyebrows and explained to Sam there were no commitments between them. Not yet anyway. Over the last few years, Chris continued to date either gals from work or someone he'd met at the gym or at a bar. They were mostly one- or two-night stands. Nothing serious. He always gravitated back to Kassie.

"Did you tell her about the others?"

"Sometimes. She's married, so I thought I should keep my options open. I don't think she much appreciated it, but she understood, I guess. Maybe filing for divorce is her signal she wants me to stop fooling around."

"What about her? Were you her only lover all this time?"

"I don't know. Haven't given it much thought." Chris gazed around the restaurant. "She's got enough baggage already with a marriage, a career, and a long-distance affair. God bless her if she found time for someone else; but I doubt it."

Chris had paused, tapped his fingers on the table, and turned his eyes to the ceiling. "Thanks, Sam, for bringing that up. What a pal."

Changing subjects, Sam asked, "What about your job here? What are you gonna do about that?"

"That was easy. I quit."

"What? Are you crazy?"

"Nope. I've saved enough money to carry me for a while, and I have an interview at a marketing firm in Cambridge next week to do some freelance work."

"What if things don't work out as you plan with your lady friend?"

"I'll come back here. You know, I am keeping the apartment. You're watching it, remember?" Chris slid the keys across the table. "I've kept my options open at the office to come back if I want to, and I always have my great American novel to finish."

"Right. Like you'll have a lot of time to work on that. Sounds like you've got it all figured out. One lucky dude."

Yes, I hope I am. Chris gulped a last swig of beer, left a ten, and headed toward tomorrow.

7

Christopher's Mettle

C hris settled his long lanky swimmer's body into his exit row aisle seat. He'd sized things up as he boarded. The flight didn't appear full and, so far, no evidence of cranky, screaming babies. One positive reason to fly the redeye cross-country. Another was the middle seat was unoccupied.

He unzipped the case that held his Bose noise-cancelling headphones, a gift to himself a few years back when he realized the amount of flying he'd be doing if he wanted to see Kassie on a regular basis. The headphones were pricey but worth it for the peace and quiet they provided.

When it came to his preferences in tunes, Kassie accused Chris of having a midlife music crisis.

"Look who's having a midlife crisis?" Chris would tease her. "I'm just an old soul."

The week before he'd left home Chris uploaded songs for his pleasure and for theirs. Norah Jones for foreplay. Barry White for the deed itself. And a healthy dose of Stevie Wonder for post-coital cuddling. Mood music for sure.

Not that they needed it. From their first time together in Venice, they had what he thought was the unique capacity to make symphonies of their own. And did they ever. He wiped his eternal, internal grin off his face.

As the plane ascended above the clouds that resembled puffy white cotton balls against the midnight-blue sky and the obligatory ten thousand feet, Chris put on his headphones, pushed his seat back, and closed his eyes. He was excited about his first trip to Fenway. He loved baseball. So did Kassie. Even though he wasn't a Red Sox fan, he looked forward to sharing the experience with her the next day. And he'd fantasized about making love afterward. It'd been thirty long nights since they'd last been together. But who's counting?

Chris tried not to stress thinking about what Mike's reaction would be and prayed Kassie would make it through the ordeal. They'd practiced what she'd say many times. Something like, "Mike, it's obvious you and I have been growing apart for a very long time. I'm very sorry. Neither of us seems eager to take any action to make things better. It's about time we open our eyes and our hearts and agree we both would be happier if we go our separate ways."

Then, she said she'd stop, take a breath, and let Mike absorb it all before she'd go for the jugular. Kassie believed it was important to pace the delivery of bad news rather than just blurt it out.

"Mike," she'd continue, "you need to know I've filed for divorce. The legal papers are scheduled to be served to you next whenever. I'll fill in the blank. I need you to decide whether you want them delivered to you at home in the evening, or during the day at the office, which could be icky."

Oops, Chris told her to stop right there. She can't tell him it could be icky. She's a marketer, for chrissake. She should know Mike would not take her seriously, and then where would she be?

Chris would make her go through it all over again. She'd get right to the end and freeze, confused on how best to end it without passing judgment on the process with some expletive deleted like, "Oh Mike, just sign the frigging papers."

He recommended she stay calm and just ask Mike where he'd like the papers served and leave it at that.

"What if he asks you why you want a divorce?" Chris asked more than once. Would she tell Mike about him? Wouldn't she have to if they were going to move in together?

Every time he'd ask her those questions, which was often, especially when they were spooning, Kassie would say, "It's not about you, Chris. You know the marriage was doomed and over long before I met you. You are an unintended consequence. In a good way." She certainly had that response down pat.

Chris felt a soft nudge on his shoulder.

The flight attendant leaned close to his ear and whispered, "Sir? Anything to drink?"

"Sure, water. Flat, no ice." Chris grinned at her and returned to Kassie.

Unintended consequences. What had she meant by that? Was he an accident? Was he her exit strategy from a bad marriage? How long would she stay with him? Kassie always gave him the same answer.

"Stop that, Chris, your insecurities are showing. What I mean is that I never intended to fall in love with you, or anyone else for that matter. But I did. And you've got me whether you like it or not. Hence the consequences."

That made little sense to him, but his being in love with an older woman didn't make a whole lot of sense either.

In love? Was he really in love with her? He had never told her or any woman, other than his mother, he loved them.

Dear God. Right on cue, Stevie Wonder sang "All is Fair in Love" in his ears. One of Kassie's favorites. Chris's mouth went dry as sandpaper. He took a large gulp of water. He'd thought Kassie liked the song because the lyrics were apropos to her and Mike's relationship.

But now, as his flight streamed toward a woman with expectations he was uncertain he'd be able to fulfill, he feared those words would come back to haunt them and reflect on their relationship as well.

Enough of Little Stevie Wonder. He'd save him for better times. He scrolled his iPad to his meditations app, clicked the track labeled "Sleep."

"Good morning, folks. We're about twenty minutes west of Boston, so I'm going to ask the flight attendants . . . blah-blah-blah . . . " was what Chris heard as he stretched the kinks out of his body and rubbed the sleep out of his eyes.

Well, that was fast. Now the fun begins.

He cringed at the prospect of retrieving all his luggage, a nuisance that had to be done. Kassie arranged for an SUV from Boston Coach to meet him and take him to the hotel. And he reserved a Hertz car to pick up later, away from the airport where it would be cheaper. As Chris came down the escalator, he spotted the "Gaines" sign and was grateful the driver was already there. Since it was early morning, it didn't take long for the luggage to make its way to the carousel. One by one, he grabbed each bag while the driver loaded not one, but two luggage carts.

As they each grabbed a cart and pushed them out to the curb where the car was waiting, the driver couldn't help himself.

"All this for one guy?"

"Yes, sir. Sorry about that." Chris played along and chuckled. It didn't matter which coast. The reaction was the same.

"No problem. You moving here or just passing through? You can't have all this just for vacation?"

"Here until September to start. We'll see," he said determined to keep his options open. Chris counted each bag. All made it. Thanks Michelle, or was it Melissa? Didn't matter.

Chris climbed into the back seat and pulled out his phone. It took a second or two for it to adjust to East Coast time. Four voice mails and three texts popped up. His mother called, of course. She knew he was moving to Boston, but he hadn't told her the whole story. He figured someday he'd have to come clean about being involved with a married woman. Someday would have to wait.

The other messages were from friends wishing him luck and hoping he'd find his way back to San Francisco. Some warned him that becoming a Red Sox or Patriots fan was like selling his soul to the devil. Remember his San Francisco roots.

As the car proceeded away from the airport and through the tunnel, the blue sky sparkled with the morning sun. Roots, huh? Growing up, his family moved several times. Chicago, Phoenix, and then back to Chicago again. It wasn't until he graduated college that he found his way to San Francisco in search of the perfect job. Not sure where his roots were. Maybe here, maybe there. Perhaps somewhere else.

No matter what, Chris felt free and unencumbered. Kassie made him feel that way. She wanted them to live together with no intention of marriage. She wanted to be free of that institution. Her word was good enough for him.

"Mind if I make a phone call?"

He clicked on her personal number. It went to voicemail. "Hi, this is Kassie O. I missed your call, but you know what to do. Talk later."

Not satisfied, he called her business cellphone. "Hello, you've reached Kassie O'Callaghan. Your call is important to me. Please leave a message and I'll get back to you asap. Thanks and have a great day."

Strange. No answer on either phone. WTF? He chose not to leave a message. She'd be able to see he'd called.

Chris gazed out the window as they made their way through

Boston on I-90, just passing the Citgo sign next to Fenway. Suddenly, things weren't going according to plan. Great day? Or a harbinger of the future? There was only one way to find out. Game on.

8

Bowed Vows

Dr. Alexander returned to Mike's exam room and with few words gave them a heads-up Dr. Singleton was on his way. He then left Mike and Kassie alone to wait. Kassie turned off her cellphone and sat rigid, as if she was mummified, in the forest-green vinyl chair alongside Mike's hospital bed.

All around her the hospital breathed to life. Equipment silenced overnight clicked on and purred, providing a fair amount of white noise. Not enough though to mask conversations among staff that ranged from medical-speak to what plans they had for the Easter weekend. Kassie wasn't convinced her plans were in jeopardy just yet. There was still a chance Mike's tests would come back fine, and they'd head home shortly. One could hope.

Mike and Kassie shared proverbial silence. If the hospital furniture and medical equipment could talk, they would say an emptiness hung heavy like the fog on a damp night at Fenway Park. As the minutes passed, a feeling of dread filled the void. Their breathing became heavy, in unison, as each waited for the other to speak. Whoever speaks first loses, right?

Mike bowed his head and fiddled with his gold wedding ring, which he had enlarged twice over the years as he'd gained weight. Kassie stared at the heart monitor; at least he wasn't flatlining.

"So, what now?" they said together, eyes meeting.

"You tell me. Seems like you've got some explaining to do."

"Let's wait," he said, rotating his ring again and again.

"Wait? For what? What are we doing here?"

"You know why we're here. You saw me last night. I can't pee. I'm nauseous. And my back is killing me."

"Don't forget your swollen feet. And your bad attitude."

"Really, you gonna go there now?"

"No, I guess you're right. That can wait 'til later," she said, willing Bad Kassie back inside. Trying to get back on topic, Kassie asked about the treatments the doctor mentioned.

"Well, I'm not receiving treatments exactly, like in a hospital or anything. I think he meant treatments in general—my blood pressure medication and watching what I eat."

"You've been taking your meds, right? And I tried to work on your diet. Maybe you'll need to tweak that a bit. And what about smoking? Shouldn't you stop?"

Kassie refused either to accept responsibility for Mike's current condition or to commit to solving whatever his pending diagnosis. She recalled her lawyer's warning as they discussed the pros and cons of divorce.

"Don't wait too long," her lawyer had said. "You know what you need and want to do. Mike's ten years older than you. I've seen this with other couples. He could end up with health issues that make it difficult for you to leave him. Then you'll be stuck."

This can't be happening. "Stuck," she thought out loud, looking down at the beige floor tiles flecked blue and green.

"What did you say?"

Kassie was spared from answering as the privacy curtain screeched and two handsome men—one short, one tall—walked in. She knew the short one and assumed the tall gent was Dr. Singleton.

"Hello, Mike. Sorry to see you here this morning. This must be Mrs. Ricci."

"Dr. Singleton? Call me Kassie."

"Glad to meet you, Kassie," Dr. Singleton said with a strong handshake and a warm disarming eye-to-eye hello.

Kassie hadn't met this doctor before. She had her doctors, Mike had his. She asked him if he was a general practitioner or a specialist.

"I am a specialist, Kassie, a nephrologist."

He seemed to give her a moment to let that sink in before adding, "A kidney specialist."

It appeared not to faze him he had to introduce himself and explain his role in her husband's healthcare. Were they in cahoots? Was he complicit in Mike's deception?

The doctor asked Mike what had happened. Mike related the events, the dinner, the bathroom scene, all from his perspective. To Kassie, Mike's version sounded accurate. All she could add was how shocked she was when she heard him throwing up in the bathroom, how pale he looked, and that his feet were so swollen she didn't think he could wear shoes to the hospital so she found flip-flops for him to wear.

Then softly, but still loud enough for all to hear, Kassie looked squarely at Mike and said, "I didn't know about your kidney problem. Why didn't you tell me?"

With a nephrologist in the room, Kassie feared the situation could be more serious than she thought.

Dr. Singleton raised an eyebrow at Mike.

"As I've discussed with Mike, chronic kidney disease doesn't develop or even progress overnight. Most often it creeps along.

Symptoms can be nonspecific, like fatigue or loss of appetite. High blood pressure, like Mike has, is also a symptom, but it too can be a symptom of other illnesses. So, in the early stages we treat the symptoms and try to get things under control. I need to see what else Mike may have going on here before we decide on next steps or further treatments. No need for alarm."

Kassie nodded as if she understood, but she didn't. She knew nothing about chronic kidney disease and struggled as much with Mike's dishonesty as she did with this news. *For better or worse, in sickness and in health, 'til death we do part* echoed in her mind. She'd experienced for better or worse with Mike; she gathered this was the sickness part.

"Now, if you don't mind, Kassie, I'd like to examine Mike alone for a few minutes. Why don't you give us ten? The café should be open by now if you'd like to get coffee and something to eat."

"Tea, doctor. I drink tea, and I know where it is. I'll be back," she snapped, unhappy at being summarily dismissed. Bad Kassie snagged her bag, swept the curtain aside, and stormed out.

"Forgive her. She's not herself today. This isn't easy. Her mom died here last year." She heard Mike explain away her alter ego.

That's right. My mother's not here when I need her. But then again, she never was.

Desperate for some real, non-vending machine tea, Kassie found her way to the cafeteria. The tall doctor was right, it was open. But then she knew it would be. She felt a stabbing pain in her gut. Hunger or fear or just plain fatigue? She didn't know. She'd start with tea and go from there.

Scanning the seating area for somewhere quiet, she spotted lots of scrubs in various faded colors occupying the tables, feeding on carbs for a long day ahead. Kassie chose a small table with a bench seat in a corner. The tea was too hot to drink right away. Why was coffee instantly consumable, yet tea was scalding and undrinkable for an hour? What's with that? Didn't matter.

God, she was exhausted physically and mentally. She worried she could become so tired she wouldn't be able to think straight or keep her wits about her. Kassie crossed her arms on the table and rested her forehead on them. After a few minutes, she raised her head with a big yoga inhale and tried to shake the cobwebs. What time was it anyway?

"Oh, no. Chris." The phone call. She turned on her phone. No message, but she could see in her *Recents* file he'd called. She checked her office phone. Same deal. She looked around, recognizing no one. It should be safe for her to call him from there.

No answer. She hung up exasperated and took another deep cleansing breath. Chris was probably tired and asleep. She had to leave him a message. He'd wonder where she was. What could she say at this point? What should she say? She had nothing definitive to tell him. Would Mike be released that morning? Could they still make the game? What about all their other plans?

Time to control what she could. Voicemail again.

This time Kassie put on a happy voice. "Hi, lover. You will not believe where I am. At the hospital with Mike. Long story, long night—"

An incoming call interrupted her.

"Hey, KO. I made it!" Only two people ever called her that, Chris and her mom.

"Welcome to Beantown!" She paused, before changing her tone. "Hey, I was just leaving you a message. You'll never guess. I'm at the emergency room with Mike. Long story, long night."

"What the hell?"

"I know. Don't worry. I think things will be fine. He got sick during the night, and I had to rush him here to Boston Clinic. The doctor's examining him right now. Hopefully he'll be released soon."

"Guess I shouldn't ask how dinner was. Gee, babe, you okay?"

"Kind of. I'm not sure what's going on with him. Some kidney thing. Great timing, huh? I'm glad you're here. Fenway is probably out. Sorry. We'll get there another time."

"That's too bad. All of it."

"I need to get going. I'll keep you posted. And I'll see you later. No matter what."

"You gonna tell him about the divorce?"

"I don't know. Hope so. We'll see. I don't want you to worry. This is my problem."

"Right," Chris said. She could hear the heavy emphasis on the 't'.

"Listen, stay there. Leave me a key at the front desk in case you fall asleep. Get some rest. You're gonna need it."

"Make it fast."

"You got it. Don't start without me." Kassie ended the call reinvigorated somewhat.

She tried to sip her tea. Still too hot. With her elbows on the table and her hands interlaced, not good form according to her mother, she chewed the lavender polish off her left thumbnail. Really bad form. Before she headed back to Mike, she needed to find out about chronic kidney disease.

Google, of course. Forty million posts. *Are you shitting me?* She opted for the short form description provided by Yale and others. She'd search for Boston Clinic's description later.

In the meantime, she learned chronic kidney disease, a.k.a. CKD, is a common disease with over two hundred thousand cases diagnosed in the United States each year.

All right, it's common. Probably means Mike could lick this thing. Kassie read on:

> *Treatment can help, but this condition can't be cured.*
> *Requires a medical diagnosis.*

Lab tests or imaging always required.

Chronic: can last for years or be lifelong.

The kidneys filter waste and excess fluid from the blood. As kidneys fail, waste builds up.

Symptoms develop slowly and aren't specific to the disease. Some people have no symptoms at all and are diagnosed by a lab test.

Medications help manage symptoms. In later stages, filtering the blood with a machine (dialysis) or a transplant may be needed.

Besides needing to adopt the jargon, four things jumped out at her—CKD can't be cured, can last for years or be lifelong, and in later stages . . . dialysis or a transplant may be needed. Kassie interpreted that to mean Mike had this CKD-thing and hid it from her for quite a while. *When was he diagnosed?* It is chronic. *He'll have it forever, however long his forever may be.* May not be immediately life-threatening. *Good thing.* It has stages. *Stages? What stage was Mike in?* At some point, dialysis or a transplant may be needed. *Oh crap.*

Kassie leaned back, her knees jittering. The tea was finally drinkable. She knew nothing about dialysis. What kind of care would dialysis require? Where in God's name would Mike get a donor for a transplant if he needed one? No kids, one elderly sister. Would he get on a list? How long would he have to wait?

Bad Kassie kidnapped her thoughts, jumping to conclusions before she had any facts at all. *Down girl, let's not get out over our skis.*

Time to get answers and get Mike home. On the way back, she swung by the same restroom she'd visited earlier. She navigated around the squat, bright yellow caution sign in the doorway. It was being cleaned . . . *again.* If nothing else, the hospital sparkled. She leaned over the sink and stared into the mirror. She looked like hell.

Kassie found Mike sitting upright with his eyes shut when she clickety-clacked into his exam room.

"That was more than ten minutes. I figured you went home without me."

Kassie recognized that tone and decided not to engage on Mike's level. Instead, standing at the foot of the bed, she asked about Dr. Singleton's whereabouts.

"You missed him. If you'd been here, you would've heard it for yourself. Looks like I'll be spending Easter right here in the goddamn hospital."

"What? You're being admitted?"

Mike told her the tests were inconclusive, and more were being ordered. It was possible last night's dinner was too rich for him and had caused a flare up. Dr. Singleton wanted to keep an eye on him for a few days, and since it was a long weekend, the easiest way to do that would be to keep him in the hospital. That way they could control his meals, monitor his blood pressure, and track his urine output.

"I know you don't like the idea, neither do I. But you didn't have any big plans for us for the weekend, right?"

Kassie swallowed hard and felt her throat dry as she processed this major turn of events. She babbled about having to call her boss and her friend to cancel their plans to go to the Red Sox game, and she'd have to figure out what to do about her trip to Georgetown.

"So, what are you going to do now?" Mike asked.

"About what?" Kassie stammered taken a little off guard.

"I think you should go home, get some rest. You look a little flushed."

"It's been a long night. I'm worried."

"Don't get all weird over something you know nothing about and have no control over. Now, go make yourself useful. You're good at that. Bring me back my robe and pajamas. Hate this hospital gown. And check my slippers. If they're too worn out, you'll need to buy me new ones. And something to read. There's a book on the round table in the family room. Bring me that."

Kassie turned away and gave him the finger.

"You gonna write that down?"

Kassie fished for her notepad. "Anything else?" She gritted her teeth. Relieved Mike was focused on himself and not her, she was still pissed at his tone, his lies, and how he'd screwed up her plans. Royally.

"I'm not sure what time I'll be back. You're right, I'm exhausted." She needed to buy herself time.

"I'm tired, too. Wish things were different."

As she turned to go, Kassie stopped and looked him in the eye. "What stage, Mike?"

He bowed his head, twisted his wedding ring, and said, "Three."

9

Box Scored

Kassie bypassed the elevator and mounted the garage stairs two at a time. She climbed in her car and let it all out. A primal scream. "Stage Three?" She pounded the steering wheel, just missing the horn.

While she wasn't sure what that meant exactly, it did mean Mike had gotten to that point without telling her, without sharing something as intimate as his health. "I'm his wife for God's sake," she shouted not caring if anybody heard her.

She dried her tears with the back of her hands and headed home. Ugh. Morning rush. When had Good Friday ceased being a holiday? Luckily, she was headed in the opposite direction of the heaviest traffic, though it would thicken up near Newton and the I-95 interchange. With a deep breath, she tried to focus on her driving as much as she could.

But something gnawed at her. Before she left his bedside, Mike asked her what she was going to do now? Where had she heard that before? Surely he meant what was she going to do next, this morning. Right? He couldn't possibly have meant what was she going to do now, about the divorce, about Chris? She scratched her head. Paranoia or intuition?

The traffic halted before the interchange just as she predicted. The car in front of her was a light blue VW beetle, or bug, which they were called when she owned one in college.

That was it! College . . . where she met Mike, the tall, dark, and handsome Italian professor with sparkling blue eyes. In class he'd made her feel self-conscious, but in a giddy way, for her slight Boston accent, which by the way she successfully suppressed as a professional adult. It was natural for her to gravitate toward him then as he too was a Massachusetts native, without an accent for some reason. They had something in common. Few folks from New England went to the University of Missouri, and those that did often hung out together.

Kassie struggled with foreign languages, barely passing three years of French in high school. She'd dreamt of visiting Italy some-day, so taking Italian was a step in that direction. It didn't go well, at least at first. Professor Ricci had suggested it might help if he tutored her privately. And so began their teacher-student relationship.

Things didn't get serious until the fall of her sophomore year. After not seeing each other over the summer, they were like young puppies in heat when classes resumed. When Mike invited her to his apartment under the pretext of studying, she figured he didn't mean Italian.

He wasn't her first, but Kassie was still very much a novice in the sex department. Mike tutored her on how to turn him on and take care of his desires, and she was the willing student. In turn, he took her to places she'd only read about.

They spent all their spare time together, yet they tried not to be seen as a couple in public. If they attended the same events, including football games, they refrained from public displays of affection. They found it hard to hide a flirtatious glance or horny smile. They were in love, she believed.

That spring, the department head summoned Mike to his office. Despite how careful they were, rumors had spread about their relationship. Was it a dalliance or something more serious? Mike would have to decide. Either way, he'd violated the university policy prohibiting professors from fraternizing with the coeds. He was given a warning. If he didn't handle it, he'd be asked to leave.

Mike dropped the news and responsibility in Kassie's lap.

"What are we going to do now?" Kassie asked.

"We? If it were up to me, I'd tell them to go shove it. But I need my job, Kass. You know I'm close to getting tenure and my MBA here. I can't leave. I think it's up to you." And then he'd said, "What will *you* do now?"

Kassie was devastated. How was it all up to her? They argued. She cried. For two weeks she skipped his class and didn't answer his calls. Finally, she offered Mike a solution. She'd leave the university at the end of the term and transfer to a school back home. Maybe UMASS or Simmons. Her grades were good, especially Italian. Transferring shouldn't be a problem.

Mike appeared relieved. He assured her that if she enrolled at another school, they could be together openly. So that's what she did. She saved his career and their relationship.

Now, as Kassie pulled into the driveway, she shook her head realizing Mike's dominance over her had started before they married. And throughout their lifetime together, she'd put his needs ahead of hers. The time had come for her to turn the tables. She prayed her lawyer was wrong, and it wasn't too late.

In her haste to get Mike to the hospital, Kassie had forgotten to lock the kitchen door or turn on the security system. Didn't matter. Topher was there to attack any would-be burglars. Not really. He was a pussycat. Really.

Topher, who had been curled up on his blanket in the kitchen waiting for her arrival, greeted her with loud meows and leg brushes. He flopped over on his side demanding a tummy rub.

"You men are all the same." Kassie stroked and teased him.

She spent a few minutes taking care of all of Topher's needs without checking the list. She made a cup of strong black tea and tried to relax at the kitchen table staring out the bay window, the sun shining, promising a lovely spring day. If only they could've gone to Fenway.

Though her original plans had gone up in smoke, she was hopeful. With Mike in custody for the weekend, she was free to come and go, except when she'd have to make a showing at the hospital.

Kassie pulled out her laptop and booted it up. She googled Stage Three chronic kidney disease. Results: 549,000. She clicked the first one. Some symptoms listed matched Mike's. Fluid retention, pain in the back, sleep and urinating problems. And he had high blood pressure. Of course, to complicate matters, there were two stages within Stage Three. Nothing's ever simple.

Another article explained Stage Three could last years, with proper diet and medication. It was up to the patient to work with the doctor and a dietitian. Mike already had Dr. Singleton. He might need to get a good dietitian and change his dreadful eating habits. Would he be able to do that? She might need to postpone her divorce plans once again, for a week or two until Mike stabilized and had a regimen in place.

At the moment, she needed to get this show on the road. On her way upstairs to the shower, she walked past the family room. She picked up the Ernest Hemingway biography she'd given Mike last Christmas and left it at the foot of the stairs so she wouldn't forget it.

She shed the dirty and sweaty clothes she'd worn to the hospital. The shower's warm water comforted and relaxed her. She bathed in vanilla bath gel, Chris's favorite. Not hers. It reminded her of breakfast. She preferred citrus or floral scents, which supposedly made one seem younger. Or so they said, whoever they were.

The shower's hot steam shifted her mood and aroused her. Kassie massaged her body with a loofa and found the sweet spot between her legs. It felt good. No time like the present. She pressed her left hand against the shower wall to steady her silken body and let her right hand methodically take care of business. Soon it would be Chris who would do the honors.

Yum. Kassie wore a Cheshire-cat grin as she stepped out of the shower. She had perfected her technique because of her long-distance affair with Chris, which required either regular phone sex or going it alone. It was never part of her repertoire with Mike, probably because she was young and naive when they first started screwing around, and it was all about his satisfaction, not hers.

She wrapped her damp, sated body in a long, white terry-cloth robe and her hair in a matching towel like a turban. She looked at her face in the mirror, hoping she looked better than she did in the hospital. Luckily, she'd inherited her mother's supple skin, continuing to look ten years younger as she aged. Moisturizer and a little makeup should help any lines or dark circles that had cropped up. Though Chris voiced no concern about their age difference, Kassie refused to let her looks be a factor, or a deal breaker.

The white Red Sox jersey with Pedroia in red letters on the back she'd intended to wear to the game draped the back of the chaise lounge that Topher now occupied. She hung it up for another day. She retrieved the new, red, lace bra and thong out of hiding in her bureau and put them on in front of the full-length mirror in the bathroom. She dried her thick just-below-the-chin-length blond hair, pulled it up in a knot, and then applied enough foundation, eyeliner, and mascara to make her look alive. No perfume required. The vanilla shower gel provided all the pheromones she'd need to entice her man. She found her skinny jeans and a black, scoop-neck, long-sleeved shirt and finished dressing. Her only jewelry was a pair of silver hoop earrings and her diamond engagement and wedding rings.

Next, Kassie pulled two suitcases she'd pre-packed for her great escape out of her walk-in closet. One contained casual clothes, the other clothes for work. With the sudden change in plans, she wouldn't need both. She repacked them with what she thought she'd need for about a week, putting one back in the closet, the other at the top of the staircase.

She found an LL Bean medium-sized royal-blue duffel bag in Mike's walk-in closet. What was it again he'd asked for? The list remained untouched in her bag in the kitchen. She relied on her memory. She got his robe out of the closet, folded it, and placed it in the bottom of the duffel. While in his closet, she grabbed his slippers and took a swift sniff. *What wives do for their husbands!* They smelled like worn slippers, but not too bad. They'd pass. She had no desire or time to go shopping. He also had the flip-flops he'd worn to the hospital if he turned his nose up at the state of his slippers. She placed them on top of the robe.

Next . . . pajamas, underwear, and socks. Mike hadn't asked for underwear or socks, but Kassie knew better. She stood paralyzed in front of his tall bureau. Previously off limits to her, she suddenly had permission to enter his domain. She had a premonition she was about to venture into dangerous territory.

The night before she'd learned his t-shirts and boxers were in the second drawer. So, that was easy. She pulled out half a dozen of each and put them in the bag. Too many? You can never have too much underwear. She took a chance his socks would be in the top drawer. Right on. White or black? Probably white. For safe measure, she took three pairs of each. Should suffice until Monday.

Pajamas. Probably in one of the two large bottom drawers. She opened the very bottom drawer. Sweaters and long-sleeved t-shirts. She opened the drawer above. Eureka. She lifted two pairs out of the drawer, one striped, one solid blue. Mike could mix and match them if he wished.

As she removed the pajamas, a steel gray metal box caught her eye. *What's this?* Kassie pulled it out gingerly as if its contents were explosive, placed it on the waterbed, and stared. *Should I open it?* Permission to get his clothes did not necessarily extend to snooping.

But Mike had hidden his kidney problems from her. Was he hiding something else? She tried to open it. Locked. *Shit.* She shook it, nothing rattled inside. She sniffed it. Not pot. *Silly girl.* Mike would never let his pot stink up his clothes. Anyway, she knew where he kept his stash.

She left the box on the bed while she got toiletries for him, zipped up his bag, and put it alongside hers in the hallway. The sound of bells jingling and banging against the inside of the front door startled her. Of course. It was Friday, cleaning day.

"Teresa, is that you?" Kassie shouted.

"Yes, Miss Kassie. You going somewhere?" Teresa almost certainly spotted the luggage from the bottom of the stairs.

"Yes. Um." Kassie stood hands on hips, shifting from one leg to the other. "I took Mike to the hospital early this morning. Looks like he'll be there a few days. I'm going to stay with a friend," she said, providing an excuse for the multiple bags.

"Oh my God. Mr. Mike okay?" Teresa blessed herself.

"Nothing too serious. Just there for observation."

"What about the cat? Do you want me to check on him until you're back?"

"Well . . . um . . . no. Thank you. I already asked a neighbor to do that." She crossed her fingers behind her back.

Kassie retreated to the bedroom and finished dressing. She looked at the clock on her nightstand. Getting close to noon. Time to leave. She returned the metal box to the bureau drawer. She'd tend to that later.

A naked man awaited.

10

Guilty Pleasure

For the first time, Kassie walked into a local hotel to meet Chris without caring whether anyone recognized her. From her perspective, Mike's hospitalization was a temporary setback. Divorce papers would be served as soon as his meds and diet were squared away. She sauntered into the lobby with an air of accomplishment as if she'd won a gold medal.

The attendant at the Westin's front desk handed Kassie a gray envelope containing a keycard and a note written in red, apparently the color *du jour*.

My desire to be part of you is surpassed only by my longing to be with you for eternity.

Oh, my! Chris was the romantic Mike never was. Chris had a way with words, but then again he was a professional scribe.

As the elevator doors opened to the dimly lit eighth floor, Kassie detected a tingling between her legs. The mere thought of Chris did that to her every time. She spotted his room down the hall, the one with the *Do Not Disturb* sign even though it was the middle of the day. Figuring he'd be asleep, Kassie snuck in, slowly clicking the door shut.

Sure enough. A sliver of sunlight peeked through the heavy full-length lined drapes, directing her eyes to Chris who was covered in a bright white sheet facing away from the door. She stepped out of her shoes, stripped down to her bra and thong, and without a word slipped in alongside him.

Hoping not to jar him, Kassie kissed his back and stroked his smooth naked bottom. Chris responded with a low moan, but didn't rouse.

She nestled her nose between his muscular shoulders and his signature fragrance of tart green apples quieted her mind, but not enough to nod off. At times like these when it was hard to fall asleep, she'd relive how she and Chris became she and Chris.

It was late May five years ago in Venice and the evenings had just begun to hold the warmth of the day. She sat alone at a café in St. Mark's Square, reflecting on her journey there.

"Let's go to Italy again," Kassie had suggested to Mike. "It'll be like a second honeymoon."

"Let's not go there."

And that was that. He refused to talk about Italy or how their marriage could benefit. He probably thought she'd forget about all of it.

"You have to live your life with or without Mike," her therapist said. "It's your choice."

When she persisted and told him she was going without him, he didn't try to stop her. He showed no interest in her itinerary, didn't offer to take her to the airport, or even say bon voyage.

The white lights strung around St. Mark's Square twinkled like stars in the sky as tourists, conversing in unrecognizable languages, strolled lazily to music so romantic, Kassie yearned to share the experience with someone she loved. Instead, she settled on a twenty-euro glass of pinot grigio to keep her company. If you can't get a great glass of pinot grigio in Italy . . . ? Echoes of Mike eroded her mood.

Kassie loved to people watch. She'd make up stories about them. Given this was Italy, and Venice no less, she imagined most people, couples anyway, were there with their significant others. Except for her. If the other folks there were people watching too, what stories would they make up about her sitting all alone? She sipped her wine politely on the chance someone might be watching.

Gino, the handsome waiter in black tie, placed a second glass of pinot grigio on the small round table with a white tablecloth. "Grazie, *Gino, but I didn't order—"*

"No, signorina, signore." *He gestured toward a fellow sitting at a table about thirty feet away. Kassie bowed her head toward him in gratitude he apparently interpreted as an invitation.*

"Buono sera, *may I join you?"*

"Looks like you already did." She laughed as she absorbed this tall stranger with thick medium-length chestnut brown hair and a slight, yet attractive, afternoon shadow. He wore a smile reminiscent of someone she once knew, a crisp, white oxford shirt with sleeves rolled up displaying a Rolex watch, and gray slacks that hung on him as though he were a model from Milan.

"I'm Christopher Gaines," he said, offering her his hand.

"Buono sera, Christopher, *I'm Kassandra O'Callaghan. Kassie for short."*

"Well, Kassie. I was over there enjoying my night cap and the mystery and magic of Venice, and I noticed this beautiful woman . . . you . . . soaking in the finest sights of Venice. So I decided to take a chance. Hopefully you're not waiting for someone?" He scanned the area.

"No, I'm very much alone," she said, sounding embarrassed and encouraging at the same time.

"That can't be. I aim to change that, if you don't mind."

As the sounds of the bands in the square faded away in the background, Chris and Kassie altered their status quo.

First, they shared the basics in fewer than eight minutes. They were bi-coastal; she lived in Boston, he in San Francisco. She'd graduated from Simmons College; he from the University of Illinois. Coincidentally, they had similar careers in marketing. She was an executive at a mid-sized ad agency; he was a senior copywriter at a large agency. Maybe she could solicit his services someday. Italy was a pleasure trip for her, first Venice, then onto Florence and Rome; he was in Venice attending a client conference. Wasn't he lucky to be there on somebody else's dime?

Then, opening the door further . . . she was kind of married, no children; he was totally single, no children. Ah-hah, something else in common.

She was born and raised in Massachusetts and had a rough, only child, childhood. Her father died when she was young, and she had an abusive stepfather whom her mother eventually and thankfully divorced. He was born in Illinois, an only child, too; in fact, he was adopted.

"Oh, how do you feel about that?"

"What? Being adopted? Great. A non-issue for me. I'm blessed. My folks gave me a wonderful life, and now they're semi-retired and enjoying theirs. I must tell them to visit Venice before it sinks."

Kassie swayed in her chair to Carlos Gardel's well-recognized tango, "Por una Cabeza."

"Would you like to dance?"

"Si, si." She couldn't remember the last time she and Mike had danced, but she was sure they hadn't danced in St. Mark's Square when they were on their honeymoon. He was too self-conscious to dance out in public in front of strangers.

Kassie gave Chris her hand and let him weave through a group of about a dozen couples who had the same impromptu idea until he found a small piece of marble landscape to claim as their private dance floor. She let this Roman-godlike creature, with penetrating Daniel Craig blue eyes, wrap her in his arms. He led her through the intricate tango steps with the skill of someone who knew his way around the dance floor, and she expected the bedroom. Captivated, melting, she didn't care if anyone in the crowd was watching.

They danced their first dance. When the music stopped, Chris held her close, and they swayed in their special place. Was that apples she smelled?

"It's getting late," he said, breaking their embrace. "Can I walk you to your hotel?"

Though surprised by his overture, she accepted it readily. She was staying at the Pensione Guerrato, a historic, boutique hotel near the Rialto Bridge tucked away in a dark, narrow alley. Was that too far to walk? Chris knew the way to Rialto Bridge, if she could guide them from there, they'd be golden. Chris offered his arm; she took it. They strolled aimlessly through the back alleys of Venice accompanied by other tourists also calling it a night, most likely, as most of the stores had closed. They arrived at the hotel faster than she would've liked.

But then . . . could he see her tomorrow? Si. Could he kiss her? Si. Si. The first kiss was cordial and polite as though they were teenagers after a first date standing on her front porch. The second? Well, let's just say Chris lifted her off her feet, pressed her body against the ancient alley wall, and kissed her in a way the nuns who once owned Pensione Guerrato would've considered highly indecent. And then he was gone. Dazed, Kassie staggered up the stairs to her room. Oh, what a night.

Promptly at 1400 hours the next day, she arrived on the Rialto Bridge. So many tourists. Would he show or stand her up? Maybe in daylight he wouldn't think of her as that "beautiful woman" sitting alone in St. Mark's Square. She'd changed her outfit three times until she was satisfied a spring floral skirt and lavender V-neck knit top were more flattering than the other utilitarian, pockets-galore, travel-wear she had packed. The day was sunny and warm again, but she brought a light sweater on the chance her time with him flowed into the evening.

Kassie didn't have to wait long. She saw him walking toward her, briskly, zigzagging between tourists. He was more casual than the previous night, wearing jeans, a deep blue Izod shirt, sunglasses, and a red Red Sox hat. If he were trying to disguise himself, it wouldn't work. She could've easily picked him out of the crowd. He was a tall drink of water, maybe an inch or two taller than Mike. Besides, she'd noticed the night before he had a unique left-leaning swag to his stride. When she asked about it, he explained he had scoliosis as a child. Years of swimming helped but didn't totally straighten him out. And then there was that disarming smile.

He must have recognized her too. He walked right up, placed both hands in the middle of her back, and pulled her in tightly. His kiss was hotter than the second one the night before if that was even possible.

"Oh, it is you! Just wanted to be sure."

"Where did you get that hat?" She giggled and staggered simultaneously.

"At a kiosk near my hotel. Like it?"

"You come all the way to Venice and all you get is a Red Sox hat?"

"Not quite. Sei il mio piu bel ricordo."

"Which means?" she said, acknowledging her Italian was rusty.

"You are my most beautiful souvenir."

This time, Kassie kissed him starry-eyed. What was it that Renee Zellweger said to Tom Cruise?

Chris took her hand in his. "Let's go have fun. You hungry?"

He whisked her away from the overcrowded Rialto Bridge deep into the obscure back alleys of Venice. They cooked up a mission to try as many pubs as possible in two hours, branding it their own "pub and grub crawl." They tasted whatever wines the proprietors recommended and sampled the variety of cicchetti served on small plates. Kassie recognized some, but not all, of the little appetizers and observed that his palate was more adventuresome than hers. Cucumber and crab meat sandwiches. Calamari. Fried mozzarella. All toothpicked for easy handling. And they feasted on crostini and olives too. She drew the line when it came to uncooked fish and vegetables she could neither recognize nor pronounce.

"It's a never-ending smorgasbord."

"Wrong country," Chris teased as he kissed her between nibbles. . . or did he nibble her between kisses? She wasn't sure. Didn't matter. It's her memory after all. She'd recall it the way she wanted.

"Let's go to the Doge's Palace. It's huge. We can get lost in there," Chris said.

"Yes, let's."

Late afternoon. They hopped on a vaporetto now crowded with Venetians returning home from work and tourists with their maps trying to figure out where they were going. The brisk breeze on the open canal was a welcome departure from the dark, confined pubs and alleyways. The sun dipped between wispy white clouds against a sky as azure as Chris's eyes. Was it the sun that was falling, or her?

The immense and gilt-drenched Doge's Palace overwhelmed her, and she was grateful to have Chris to share it with. She clung to his arm memorializing her time with him.

It was evening when they left the palace and were right back where they started the night before at St. Mark's Square.

"Boy, I'm thirsty. I could drink a whole lagoon," she said as they sat side-by-side at a café and had a Coca-Cola. "What a wonderful day, Chris. Can't believe I leave for Florence day after tomorrow. What about you?"

"I have two more nights here."

He leaned in and kissed the small of her neck. His right hand snuck inconspicuously up her skirt, and he gently caressed her inner thigh. "It has been wonderful, you're right. Let's not let it end."

She didn't object.

Chris put his arm around her, and they boarded a private gondola. He draped her sweater around her shoulders and pulled her close against his broad chest. They moved through partially lit back canals as the gondolier serenaded them. They passed other boats along the way, and Kassie's people watching began.

Some boats had small groups of tourists laughing and trying to sing along with their gondolier. What fun! Some had couples who sat opposite one another, enjoying the ride but not the romance. She felt their pain. She supposed that's how it would be if Mike was there instead of Chris.

When they passed a boat with a couple in an embrace like she and Chris, he'd squeeze her waist tighter and kiss her cheek as if he knew what she was thinking. This wasn't Mike, and it wasn't Boston. This was Chris and Venice. She couldn't ask for more. Could she?

The gondolier glided the boat alongside the dock. Chris lifted her out of the black boat and without a single word between them, they walked hand-in-hand two blocks to his hotel where he gave her more . . . and more . . . and more . . . as the early light of a new day rose over the Grand Canal.

Kassie was on the edge between sleep and wakefulness, cherishing the memory. She felt herself being rolled onto her back. Warm hands slid her thong down her legs. A wet tongue and light kisses explored her thighs. She lifted her torso hungry and begging for more. He obliged. She grabbed the side of the bed and moaned softly. Her hips and his talent moved in unison. "Oh, God." Her body released. He rested his head on her throbbing mound.

Fully awake now, all Kassie saw was a white sheet with a lump on top of her.

"Oh, it is you!" Chris peeked out from under the sheet.

She reached down with both hands and pulled his long hot body on top of her. He kissed her voraciously.

"French toast," he exclaimed.

Incessant giggling ensued. So did the sex. And why not? After all, now it was her turn.

11

Excuses, Excuses

Meanwhile, back at Boston Clinic. "Deep breaths, Mr. Ricci. Again. Good. How much do you smoke?"

Mike gave a just-a-little sign with his fingers, being his usual, less-than-cooperative, less-than-honest, cranky self. Who wouldn't be? No sleep. No food. Hadn't they poked and prodded him enough in the ER? Now another doctor checked his vitals. Could they really have changed in the five minutes it took to roll him to his private room?

"We're responsible for you now, Mr. Ricci. We'll run a few more tests. After that, we'll order lunch. Maybe filet mignon. How does that sound?"

"Make it snappy. A man could die of starvation here."

"Not likely, sir, but it's a good sign you're hungry. We'll take care of it. You'll see."

An hour later, a technician removed the IV, and like magic, a young man arrived with a tray with his name and room number on it. Special delivery!

"This is food?" Mike whined lifting the plastic cover and staring at shriveled green beans, colorless applesauce, and crackers so dry they'd disintegrated in the package.

"Oh, and look here. Clear chicken broth," the fellow chided. "Low sodium. Just what the doctor ordered."

A nurse arrived at the same time and had apparently overheard the conversation. "Mr. Ricci, you're here to get better. It would do you good to remember this is a hospital, not Davio's."

"You can say that again," Mike griped, not happy with her attitude.

"If you want me to, I will. Or you can try to eat something. We'd like to see if you can keep it down. If you don't eat, we'll have to reinsert the IV. Your choice."

Did he have a choice? Not a good one anyway. So Mike, outnumbered and defeated, grabbed the TV remote, clicked on Andrea Mitchell, and ate his lunch; one bland spoonful after another.

Not half bad. Not half good, either. Is this what I have to look forward to the rest of my life? Good grief.

Soon, Mike surrendered his mood to sleep. At last.

Three hours later, Mike lifted one eyelid. And then the other. The pungent smell of antiseptic was his first clue. The monitor next to his bed was the second. Oh crap, it wasn't a dream. It was a living nightmare. He was indeed in the hospital. *Un-believable.*

A small tray holding a cup with a red flexible straw like they give two-year-olds replaced the lunch tray. He sipped tentatively. Ginger ale. Not his favorite. At least it was something to rinse the rancid taste in his mouth.

What time was it anyway? He searched the small cabinet next to the bed for his things. What things? No watch. No phone. Still wearing the not-so-attractive or functional hospital gown. He turned on the television. Again. Who turned it off? Kind of creepy to imagine strangers coming and going while he slept.

The little red-and-white time tracker in the bottom right corner of MSNBC read 3:50 p.m. *That wasn't much sleep.* He felt the urge . . . to pee.

Mike remembered a nurse earlier telling him to call when he needed to use the bathroom . . . for two reasons. In case he was woozy, they didn't want him to fall, and because they wanted to collect and measure his urine. *Oh great. Where's that buzzer?*

Unlike last night, this time Mike peed with no problem, most likely the result of the obscene amount of fluids they'd pumped through his system. He put up a ruckus, but agreed to let the pretty nurse help him to and from the bathroom, all the while clinging to the back of the gown for privacy. He sat on the elevated hospital bed and tried to resettle without embarrassing himself.

The TV showed it was four fifteen. Where was Kassie? Shouldn't she be there by now? What's keeping her?

Maybe she's still sleeping. Or did she go to the game after all? Mike wouldn't put it past her. When was the last time she gave a damn about him?

Bored, Mike stared out the window at windows in the hospital wing opposite his. What goes on behind those? All kinds of things he imagined. Good news, bad news, surgeries, babies being born. Babies. It'd been an eternity since he'd thought about kids. Why think about them now?

Maybe he shouldn't have lied to Kassie that morning. It wasn't a total lie, really, just a postponement of the truth. He'd been in Stage Three for several years, had controlled it, and never saw the need to tell her. Now Dr. Singleton feared he may have moved to Stage Four. Mike feared it, too. They both hoped getting some rest and care in the hospital would provide better test results by Monday. If not, he'd have to come clean and be honest with Kassie. *Shit. A Pandora's box waiting to explode.*

Though he was never proud of it and knew he was a dick, Mike had turned postponement of truth into an art form he'd learned from his late father. A drinker and a womanizer, Mike's father lied as easily and as often as he breathed to keep his marriage, family, and job together. Mike learned early how one lie leads to another and justified his own behavior as vital to his survival. Sometimes he amazed himself that he was successful in business, yet such a failure at home. Problem was Mike never considered the latter long enough to do anything about it.

With Kassie, his lies started when he told her about receiving a warning about his relationship with her at Mizzou. The truth was Kassie wasn't the first affair he'd had with a student, nor was she the last. In his first year of teaching there, he slipped up with a pretty little thing from Joplin. That's when he'd received the first warning, and what's-her-name left the school. The second time, with Kassie, he received notice to leave the university. But he begged forgiveness and promised to send her packing. Because he was their sole Italian professor, he kept his position. At least for a while.

Mike had the best of both worlds. Kassie transferred to Simmons College in Boston, so he'd see her during semester and holiday breaks. Except it wasn't long before he couldn't control his hormones and got involved again with one of his students. His time teaching at Mizzou came to a predictable, not-so-abrupt, end.

No way could he tell Kassie what happened if he expected to have a place to live if he returned to Boston. He wouldn't lie. He'd just postponed telling her the truth until such time the lie became a threat to his personal well-being. If it ever did. It was a risk he was willing to take. He concocted a cock-and-bull story, telling her he'd given up his teaching job to be with her. He loved and missed her that much. It worked. She swooned.

Kassie was about to graduate from Simmons with honors and had accepted a junior account executive position at one of Boston's largest advertising agencies. She was ecstatic at the prospect of having Mike in town for good. What twenty-two-year-old wouldn't want to bed her ex-college professor?

"You could teach at one of the colleges in town? Or maybe do something brand new? You have your MBA now," Kassie urged.

She had the right idea as she liked to remind him. But only kind of right. He had no intention of seeking another teaching gig. His reputation would precede him, creating a mess he refused to address with either a potential school or Kassie. Avoiding the truth altogether, he relied instead on his MBA and multi-lingual capabilities and landed a position at a Cambridge marketing agency as a translator. Did they check his references? Nope. He convinced them his time teaching wasn't relevant to the job, and they bought it.

When he started at the agency, Mike was skeptical about how he'd adapt to the whole Monday-to-Friday, nine-to-five routine and the lack of interaction with students, which he'd thrived on. Yet, he had to be honest with himself, if not with Kassie and prospective employers, it was the interaction with female students that catapulted him into his current predicament. So, maybe, it was better for him this way.

Being back in Boston was great, he had to admit. He moved into a roomy loft near Fenway Park with Kassie. Despite his philandering, Mike was crazy about her. He was drawn to her immediately at Mizzou. She was just too cute when she tried to pronounce Italian words with a slight Boston accent. An excellent and willing student, tutoring her was highly gratifying. Not too experienced in the bedroom. Just as he liked. She'd earned her good grades.

Kassie, his total opposite, intrigued him. He was Italian, she was Irish. There was that. He was serious, she was playful. She loved Boston sports, he could take it or leave it. His father never took him to a Red Sox game, never ever. Mike was a fusspot; she needed some taming.

It didn't take long. In the early years, she delighted him and attended to his every daily need. She cooked, cleaned, and did his laundry the way he liked it. With regular practice, she'd even become quite the minx in the sack. She'd be the perfect wife.

Attractive, intelligent, sociable, and able to talk baseball, Kassie made Mike look good. Having her, ten years his junior, by his side benefitted his new career and the business he launched. Not quite the age difference to qualify as his trophy wife, he reckoned he was a winner for settling down with her. A solid decision on his part.

He'd sowed his oats long enough before moving in with her and making a commitment. Was she the love of his life? Probably not; there was his college sweetheart, whom he thought he was in love with back then. She was Jewish. He was Catholic. Neither of their parents approved, especially her parents and his father. His mom thought she was darling. When her parents realized things had gotten out of hand between them, they withdrew her from school and whisked her far away from him. So that was that. But it didn't matter.

Mike's philosophy was there was always another gal out there. He espoused a saying he'd heard: men don't marry the love of their lives, they marry the one they are with when they decide it's time to settle down. So, just a couple of years after leaving his wandering ways in Missouri, Mike took the plunge. Kassie jumped up and down when he proposed. No, literally, she jumped up and down. He thought she'd hurt herself.

Planning the wedding fell into the able and excited hands of Kassie and her mom. Before it exploded into a major motion picture, he hustled them into keeping the wedding small. Instead of spending, or better yet wasting, their limited resources on a huge one-day production, he advocated for a small wedding and romantic honeymoon. Kassie bitched and moaned about not having the wedding she'd always dreamt of, but he knew she'd give in, which she did. She always did.

Take the honeymoon destination. She wanted to go to Ireland in honor of her father who had died when she was a little girl, but Mike had no desire to go there. Boring! Wouldn't they have more fun in Italy where he spoke the language, and she could practice in real time? She suggested they do both, Ireland then Italy. Nope. That wouldn't work either. He couldn't take that much time off from work. Italy it was. In retrospect, Mike would label their honeymoon, *fantastico*. Good food, good wine, some sightseeing, lots of sex.

When they returned from Italy, they settled into routines of married life and budding careers. Children were not on the agenda. At least not on his agenda. In fact, he never remembered them talking about having kids. Nevertheless, Mike feigned his happiness when their birth control failed and Kassie got pregnant, and likewise his despair when she miscarried. *Poor Kass.*

Kassie's close call shook Mike to the core. What the hell was he doing? He didn't want kids. He couldn't visualize himself as a father, especially if he was anything like his own. And he couldn't tell Kassie now they were married. What an ugly confrontation that would be. Time for him to be proactive and covert if he was to prevent World War III.

He planned it carefully. Once when she was out of town for a week on a business trip, he had a vasectomy. After that he played along with the game of trying to get pregnant again. Kassie was tested and everything was fine with her plumbing. Mike refused to be tested. No way he'd jerk off in a cup.

"Let's keep trying. Isn't trying the most fun anyway?" he'd say.

Kassie didn't share his humor and reminded him oral sex wasn't the answer. Maybe not, but at least it was sex.

He watched her sadness deepen into depression but was hamstrung on how to help. It seemed there was nothing he could do to get her out of her funk short of telling her the truth, but that could be a death knell to his marriage.

"What about adoption?" Kassie pleaded.

"Don't even go there. End of discussion," Mike said, unwilling to explain his reluctance.

Instead, Mike had a brilliant idea even if he said so himself. He was tired of working for someone else. He would start his own marketing firm, and she should be his partner. Ricci and O'Callaghan. Didn't that have a phenomenal ring to it?

"Kass, your strengths would complement my weaknesses." *Whatever those were.* "We could create something special together and watch it grow." He deflected from the real issue.

"I'm sorry, but starting a business is no substitute for a having child. Maybe for you, not for me." She'd argue until she wept. He launched the business without her.

Mike reached out to Kassie's mother for divine intervention. She'd always been a vocal supporter of his. Fortunately for him, she interceded, encouraging Kassie to seek counseling. The shrink must've worked as Kassie went back on birth control pills, which she didn't need, and she never raised the prospect of having children again. Mike was good with that. Thank you, Patricia O'Callaghan.

Too bad she'd died last year. She could've been an advocate for him if this diagnosis was discouraging. He feared he'd need all the help he could get with her daughter.

When he returned from another escorted, yet successful trip to the bathroom, Mike's dinner tray was waiting for him. Mac-and-cheese with peas, lime Jell-O, dry crackers again, watermelon cut into one-inch squares. He hated the pits. Water and milk. No coffee or even tea. Not quite an appetite inducer, more like an appetite depressant—to match his mood.

Oh, how he longed for a cigarette. Not going to happen that day. Had he had his last? Not if he had anything to do with it.

12

It's Complicated

"Thanks for saving a towel for me." Kassie teased Chris as she turned on the water for what would be the second shower of the day for both of them. "You used three! You're worse than a teenager!" They laughed as they climbed into the tub.

"Wash my back, Chris."

"I'd rather you wash my front."

Kassie turned to comply and saw the reason for his request. She followed the flow of the warm water streaming down between them, kissing his sweet wet lips, his slightly hairy chest, and so on, and so forth.

"Again, my dear?"

Just as they wrapped themselves in the hotel's thick, white terry robes, there was a knock on the door. "Room service."

"Perfect timing," Kassie said as she sat on the disheveled bed towel-drying her hair.

"*You* are perfect, KO." Chris leaned down, lifted her chin and kissed her on his way to answer the door.

"Great. Thanks. No, I'll do it," she heard him say.

"Do what?"

"Open the wine. Pinot grigio, okay?" Chris wheeled in the dining cart.

"Sure. Just a smidge for me. I have to go see Mike."

"You certainly know how to take the wind out of a man's sails."

"Sorry about that. Let's eat. I'm famished. What did you order for me?"

Somewhat satisfied in one way, they ate the Caesar salads Chris had ordered, his with chicken, hers with shrimp, in almost relative silence. A toast to his arrival in Boston and to their future, more kisses and touching, her breast, his thigh.

"I think you were right," she said.

"About what?"

"Your note. The one you left at the desk. You are one horny toad."

"Me? Look in the mirror. I meant it. I love being part of you, and it's been a month. What do you expect?"

"I wouldn't want you any other way." She leaned across and kissed him long and hard.

"So you're gonna go home and give him the news?"

"No. Not today. They admitted him. He's there 'til Monday, I think."

Kassie stood and paced around the room. She'd wanted to give Chris the *Reader's Digest* version of events, but as the story poured out of her for the first time, she realized how outraged she was.

"Mike said he's got Stage Three chronic kidney disease. What the heck is that? I looked it up."

"And?"

"I read the symptoms and I'm no doctor, but it sounds like him. I think he's right."

"Why'd they admit him?"

"Good question. Observation, monitoring, more tests, I guess. From what I've read, Stage Three can last for years and be managed through diet and drugs."

"So what's your plan now? I'm here for you, babe, because of you," Chris said, gesturing toward his bags lined up against the wall blocking the door to the adjoining room.

"Well, I have to go to the hospital. I promised to bring him some of his things. Then I'll come back here for the weekend," Kassie said, gesturing toward her bags in the living room area of the suite.

"And the divorce?"

"I'm not giving up on that. Neither should you," Kassie said as she dressed. "Just a temporary delay. Once he's stabilized, I'll tell him."

"Are you sure?"

"Yes, I am. Mike and I are done. Don't you see this whole kidney thing personifies what's wrong with our marriage? He lied. And it sounds like he's been hiding this from me for what a year, two years, more?"

"Listen to yourself." Chris paced.

Kassie zipped her jeans, swung her hair back and out of her eyes. "What? I'm his wife for chrissake."

"Come on, haven't you been lying to him? Hiding me, us, from him?"

"That's different."

"How's that?" Chris poured himself another glass of wine. Kassie refused his offer of a refill.

"There are certain things husbands and wives are supposed to share . . . in sickness and in health, I think that's how it goes. Had he told me he was having kidney problems, maybe there would've been something I could've done to help. Before now."

"What about for better or worse?" Chris challenged her thought process.

"Don't do that. Don't twist my words. I didn't tell him about us because WE weren't ready until now to do anything about it. You know that. Why would I hurt him if WE weren't for real? If Mike had been honest with me about his health sooner, maybe I could've been honest with him sooner. Now he's made it more complicated. Don't you, too."

"I'm not. Just pointing out the obvious."

"Since when did you become so moral? Seems you're breaking a few rules here. Adultery, coveting your neighbor's wife?"

"He's NOT my neighbor."

"I know," she said, backing down. "It's not about you."

"Let's keep it that way. Okay?"

"That's my intent. I'd divorce him even if you weren't in the picture."

On the verge of tears, Kassie moved into his comforting arms and buried her face in his chest. Was that applesauce she smelled? She scooped up her purse and waved the room keycard at him.

"I'll be back. Please don't judge me. And call housekeeping. We'll need fresh towels, lots of them."

13

Real Friction

There was just enough drive time between the hotel in Waltham and the hospital in Boston for Kassie to reprogram her brain from lover to wife. Once upon a time they were one and the same. Life was simpler then.

Their honeymoon period lasted about three years. Climbing the ladder at work, they'd saved enough money to buy their first home in Cambridge. A small, two-bedroom, white cape with black shutters, a one-car garage, and central air conditioning. Nothing could be finer. When they weren't working, they spent their downtime together, furnishing and decorating their new home, and luxuriating in their most favorite purchase, the waterbed. It was always warm; they were always hot.

Kassie got pregnant in their third year. She was over the moon at the prospect of having a child and, by all appearances, Mike seemed to be as well. While in the bathroom coping with morning sickness, she'd overhear him on the phone bragging to his friends at the office. Later in their marriage she'd wonder whether he ever wanted a child, or was getting her pregnant years earlier mere confirmation of his manhood?

Devastated when she miscarried in her fifth month, Kassie learned something she never suspected about Mike while they were dating or in their first few years of marriage. He wasn't there for her. Oh, he did husbandly things like taking her to the doctor's and the hospital for a D&C. He bought her red roses and stocked the kitchen with comfort food while she convalesced, but Kassie did the cooking and cleaning.

"I'm sorry I lost our baby, Mike."

"Don't be."

"I miss the baby fluttering inside me," Kassie said, massaging her tummy and expecting some level of consolation in return.

"That will pass," he'd said, leaving the room without validating Kassie's grief or giving her any reassurance they would try again soon.

For Kassie, the emptiness didn't pass, and before long she slipped into a deep depression.

"Both of them abandoned me," she cried to her mother.

"Both? Who?"

"The baby and Mike."

"Poppycock. You can't fight Mother Nature. And Mike loves you, you know that."

Kassie once thought that was the case; after the miscarriage she wasn't so sure. And why did her mother often take Mike's side? She'd even taken up his mantle encouraging her to seek therapy.

"You need to snap out of this funk, KO," her mother mothered. "Mike needs you to get on with your life." No one asked Kassie what she needed.

So she gave in. She couldn't fight them both. Off to therapy, for years, even now. Kassie had a lot to work out besides Mike.

Once her doctor told her she could try again, Kassie wanted

to get down to business, half expecting this would help lift her out of her blues. Mike accepted the invitation back to the marital bed, but seemed more interested in the physical act, not the potential baby-making outcome.

Where had Mike's passion gone? He no longer caressed her thighs or whispered in her ear what he wanted to do to her. They had sex, but they didn't make love any longer. She recognized the difference. One satisfied the body, the other the soul. Her soul starved to near death.

Maybe that's why she had trouble conceiving again. She believed lovemaking and baby-making were synonymous. You can't, or shouldn't, have one without the other.

"What's going on with us, Mike?" Kassie asked one night after having sex with the lights out for the first time ever.

"Nothing's going on. We had sex. What do you want? I'm doing my part. It's all up to you."

As she rolled away from him, facing the wall, she wondered whether Mike was the one who needed therapy.

The effect of Kassie's miscarriage on their relationship was like a crack in the arctic ice. An irreparable fissure occurred between them that widened with time.

Mike turned his attention away from Kassie and launched his consulting business. He spent hours traveling with realtors searching for the perfect office location, which he discovered nearby in Cambridge. He spent weekends away from the house, driving all around New England looking for an antique oak desk they could ill-afford, and he stayed up late at night creating spreadsheets and a business plan and went to bed long after Kassie fell asleep.

With her therapist's counsel, Kassie refocused her energy away from building a family to making a life and a career outside their home and marriage. She took on more clients around the country, practiced tai chi and yoga, volunteered during telethons at the local

PBS station, tutored second graders, and sold pies for Thanksgiving to support a not-for-profit food and nutrition program.

Though married, they separated. Looking back, it pained her to think they had failed to live up to the basic responsibilities of a married couple, and they hadn't even made it to their first five-year mark. Her marriage disappointed her. She assumed the feeling was mutual.

"I'm not sure he even likes me," Kassie confided to her therapist.

"Is there anything you could do?"

"Short of divorce, no, and that's out of the question. We're Catholic."

So Kassie stayed put. She continued to do her wifely duty. How many ways could she fake orgasm? She figured as long as his urge was satisfied, he'd never care about whether she was, or be the wiser. Time took care of ending that illusion.

It started about ten years ago when neither of them instigated sex any longer. A week without sex turned into a month, into two months, into six months, into a year. Then two years, three and so on until their sex life was a memory that couldn't be jump-started.

Relieved, Kassie needn't pretend to be Mike's lover any longer; she was only his wife according to the laws of the Church and of Massachusetts. Thankfully they lived in a no-fault divorce state now that she was ready. She'd deal with God and the Church later.

The hospital's parking garage was more crowded than she'd expected. Maybe the holiday was the culprit. Round and round she drove until she found a spot on the top level. She flipped on her car's interior light and checked for any evidence of Chris. Her makeup appeared in place, no black mascara smears. And no hickeys on her neck, like she had after their first encounter back in the states after Venice.

Kassie took a deep breath, put on a happy face, and walked into Mike's hospital room.

"Hey, there." She dropped his duffel bag on the floor and her purse on a chair. She didn't approach him to give him a kiss. He didn't appear to expect one.

"Oh, there you are. It's about time. What took you so long? Thought you were going to leave me here to die alone."

"You're not going to die. I told you I didn't know what time I'd be back. Did you sleep?"

"Who can sleep in a hospital?"

"You need to try. I need you to get better."

"Looks like *you* slept."

Kassie looked away and stalled. "I tried, but I think I tossed and turned a lot," she said, not lying. "I'll sleep better tonight knowing you're in good hands here."

"Where did you go? The gym? You look flushed. Your hair's wet. Boy, I could sure use a shower."

Ignoring his reference to her afterglow, Kassie went out to the nurse's station and returned with good news.

"Your wish is granted. Let's get you in the shower." She helped him into the bathroom, and she unpacked his toiletries and clothes. Maybe he'd have an attitude adjustment once clean and out of that hospital gown.

"How do you feel now? Better?" She steadied him as he climbed back into bed.

"I'll be better once I get out of this hellhole."

"Any news about that from Dr. Singleton? Any test results?"

"Nope."

"I read about Stage Three."

"Where?"

"Googled it."

"Oh. Terrific. I thought you were smarter than that."

"I needed something, Mike. You've told me nothing."

"Listen, let's just see what happens Monday and go from there. I'm not worried. Don't spend your weekend fretting over me."

"I'll try not to," she said as she told him how she blew off the game and postponed her trip to Georgetown. She wanted to be there on Monday to hear what Dr. Singleton had to say before he was released.

"You know, if you had told me what was going on, maybe I could have helped."

"I don't think there was anything you could've done. It is what it is. I'll figure this out when I know what's happening."

Kassie was quick to pick up his use of "I" instead of "we." In her mind, there was no "we" in their future either. Time to change the subject.

She asked if he'd eaten. Oh dear, another touchy subject. He railed for five minutes about the crappy food and the rude nurse who threatened to put him back on an IV. But he ate, right? Mike rarely missed a meal no matter how unappetizing.

She racked her brain for a non-controversial subject, some common ground. How about the news? What's going on in Washington? He didn't know. He thought he fell asleep when the news was on.

"*This* is a waste of my time. I thought you'd be away this weekend and had planned to go into the office. You need to go there and bring me some things. I've got work I could be doing right here chained to this bed."

"You're not chained. I'm sure you can get up and walk around."

"What in pajamas?"

"Oh Mike, grow up."

Silence. Not the quiet serenity that followed the sexual gratification she'd shared with Chris earlier in the day. Their silence spoke the truth of their corrupted marriage.

"I have to get some tea." She escaped.

When she returned, she didn't take a seat. With little else to say, she had no desire to hangout and chitchat with him any longer than necessary.

"I'm tired, Mike. I think I should go. I'll come by some time tomorrow. Is there anything else you need?"

"You're going? You just got here. Shit. Go."

Kassie turned to leave.

"You gonna stop by my office before you come tomorrow? The key's in my briefcase. There are three manila folders on my desk. Bring them here, okay?"

"Sure, Mike, anything else?" She prayed for a quick getaway.

"And since I'll be here for a while, bring me my goddam phone and charger. You should've thought of that."

"I had a lot on my mind." She turned to leave again.

"Where's my book, Kassie? You brought it, right? It was on your damn list."

She halted and opened his duffel bag. "Damn, I remember getting it and putting it on the stairs. Teresa must've moved it. And I forgot it. I'm sorry, Mike."

"I don't know about you, Kassie, sometimes you're just plain useless."

14

Chronically Romantic

" I missed your beauty marks."

Kassie rolled toward Chris as he applied delicate kisses along her back, her neck, her breast.

"Good morning," she whispered, kissing his nose. "You were saying?"

"I've committed the pattern of your beauty marks to memory, and when I'm horny—"

"You do what? Get off imagining them?"

"As a matter of fact . . ." He pulled her on top.

Stepping out of the shower an hour later, Kassie confiscated the only fresh towel remaining and wrapped it around her waist.

"What are you humming in there?" Chris shouted.

She peeked out at Chris sprawled on the couch in the sapphire-blue silk boxers she'd given him during their first rendezvous when they were back in the states after Venice.

"What a difference a day makes. Tis true, *si?*" Kassie joined him on the couch. "Nice shorts."

Chris switched places with her, unwrapping her towel. Her nipples beckoned him. His tongue traveled along an invisible but previously traveled pathway starting at her navel, around each breast, along the sweet spot between her neck and shoulder and ending at her right ear.

"Better put something on. Food should be here soon," he whispered, as his long fingers stroked her thighs for good measure.

"Spoil sport," Kassie said as she hunted through the suite that mirrored a baggage claim area. She pulled out clean clothes and darted for the bathroom just as room service arrived. The mashed-up aroma of coffee, eggs, and bacon made her stomach gurgle. She'd only had one piece of the pizza they'd ordered in the night before, falling asleep in Chris's arms watching a movie they'd rented.

"Yum," she said, returning to the living area of the suite, this time wearing only a black thong. "How's this?" Kassie stood legs spread with her arms across her chest, moistening her lips.

"The fashion police might give you a failing grade for dressing for brunch, but not me."

Kassie slipped on the white oxford shirt he'd slung over a desk chair. "Is this better?"

"That brings me back," Chris said, unwrapping an English Breakfast tea bag for her. "Venice."

"That was just the first time. There were many other white shirt moments. Remember, Seattle. San Diego. What about Napa last year? What was the name of that B&B we stayed at?"

"Courtland Inn?"

"That's it. So romantic. What we did in that hot tub!" She grimaced.

"One of our best trips, don't you think? The weather, the wine—"

"The sex," she said, taking the last bite of the omelet and croissant Chris had ordered for her and licking her fingers. She passed on the bacon; Chris didn't.

"Little Miss One Track Mind. I was going to say that's the trip you decided you were ready to leave Mike."

"Hah, Mr. Know-It-All. I made my decision long before Napa. I just hadn't told you."

"Really. When?"

"Oh, about a year after we met. Mike burned me once too often. I'd had it. I didn't tell you. It was too soon. We weren't serious yet. I figured I'd give Mike one last chance."

"So, what happened." Chis poured himself another cup of coffee.

"It was Seattle."

"But . . . I met you in Seattle."

"Yes, but I'd asked Mike to join me there first," she said, fiddling with a silver napkin ring. "I had two clients to visit, so I planned an extended trip so I'd have a long weekend there. On the long flight out, I got the not-so-bright idea of inviting Mike to join me."

"You never told me this."

"That's because it didn't matter. He refused to come. I pleaded with him; can you believe? We hadn't had a vacation together in years. Remember he wasn't with me in Italy."

"How could I forget?" Chris raised his eyebrows appearing unsure of where this was going.

"It was about two in the morning, his time, when I called him. He was annoyed that I'd woken him up. Please, Mike, just fly out here. A long weekend together in the beautiful Pacific Northwest might do us good."

"And?"

"He declined. Work was crazy. The dishwasher broke. And it'd be stupid to fly clear cross country."

"Even for you?"

"Even for me."

"And then you called me? I remember now how surprised I was you were so close to San Francisco and hadn't given me a heads up. You said it was spur of the moment. Liar?"

"No, the trip was spur of the moment. So was my invitation to Mike." Kassie rose from the leather desk chair, walked to the window, and turned facing Chris. "But I offered *you* a similar deal, silly. And *you* took it."

"What does that make me? Consolation prize?" Chris sounded skeptical. "Or was it a test?"

"None of the above. Don't go there, Chris. It wasn't a test. Even if it was, you passed! And I decided to leave Mike after being with you in Seattle. You know when I knew?"

"Do tell."

Kassie went to Chris, sitting on the edge of the disheveled California king bed, and lifted his chin. "Remember you suggested we meet on the top of the Space Needle? When I got off the elevator, you came up to me, took my hand, and kissed it." Kassie mimicked what Chris had done.

"It was the Seattle version of *Sleepless in Seattle*. Except not the Empire State Building, the Space Needle. I went all the way to Seattle and found you. Get it?"

"You're hopeless . . . and sleepless."

"Whatever. I was devastated when we left each other at Sea-Tac. I blubbered all the way back to Boston. The only time I'd ever cried on a plane before was once on a trip from San Francisco to LA. I was reading *Bridges of Madison County*. The guy next to me thought I was nuts."

"That was me, goofball. I still think you're an incurable romantic."

"What's wrong with that? It's not a crime to be a romantic. And that's why I chose you. I could only be with someone who gets me. And that's you."

Kassie continued her story about how withdrawn Mike was when she returned from Seattle. They never talked about how he rejected her, just as they never talked about her trip to Italy.

"It's impossible for relationships to succeed when both parties employ conflict-avoidance techniques," Chris kind of lectured.

"You mean denial. Both of us, for years. And even after Seattle, I couldn't leave him. My mom, ya know. It's as if she got sick just so I wouldn't leave Mike."

"That's pretty cynical, don't you think?"

"Maybe so. But she's been gone a year now. I've mourned her long enough. It's time for me. It's time for me to move on."

"Speaking about moving on, I'd love to hang out, but I've got to meet the rental agent in Charlestown at two."

"Look who's being the adult in the room. I have things to do too, but one for the road wouldn't hurt." She slipped off her thong, knelt in front of him, and reached into his boxers.

Chris peeled his shirt off her shoulders, lifting her onto his lap. She threw back her head and moaned. He lowered her, as she took him back to the little inn in Napa.

Finally, they got dressed. Both agreed it would be best to leave the hotel room for a while if only to get it cleaned. Kassie needed to run home to check on Topher, go to Mike's office to pick up a few things, and then swing by the hospital for a short visit with him. The shorter the better. They'd meet back at the hotel later.

Admiring themselves in front of the full-length mirror hanging on the front of the bathroom door, they agreed they'd cleaned up pretty good—Chris in his gray Italian trousers and light blue oxford shirt, Kassie in her skinny jeans, white tank top, and black blazer. Looking dapper, Kassie and Chris grabbed their briefcases and walked out of the hotel together, beaming as though they had just negotiated the Paris Climate Accord. Well, if not quite that, something else was consummated. Kassie could feel it.

15

A Sleuth is Born

Another brilliant Saturday afternoon in Boston. Kassie was bummed she had to spend it running around for Mike rather than spending it running around town with Chris.

She figured the highway would be crowded, so she took the back roads home from the hotel. Maybe it would take longer, but it'd give her blood pressure time to recover so she could concentrate on Mike. Whether or not she liked it, she had to muster enough brain cells and energy to solve the problem with one man so she could be with another. So much for all she'd done to arrive at that weekend. Only thing that had gone according to plan was her reunion with Chris. Big sigh. Why was it she always felt thinner and taller after a romp with Chris? *Be still my heart.*

As usual, Topher greeted her with his alley cat mewl as she walked in the house. She hated leaving him alone all night. *Oh, shit.* Her face grew feverish, her stomach convulsed. She fished in her bag for her phone.

"Chris, oh thank God."

"Miss me already?"

"Yes, but. I forgot Topher."

"Thought you were heading home."

"I am. I'm here. I can't leave Topher with Mike when I move out. Oh my God, how did I forget him? He's *my* cat. Mike would never take care of him. Bastard. And once he finds out about you, who knows if he'll take it out on Topher."

"I guess you'll need to bring him with you to my place, our place."

"You think we can do that? Is it allowed?"

"Let me talk to the realtor. Probably cost something. Just chill. I'm good with pussies."

"Great. I'm panicking and you're joking."

Next up. Mike's goddamn book. Kassie looked in the living room. Not there. On the stairs. Not there. Where would Teresa put a book? *Oh, Hemingway, where art thou?*

Was that her phone? She'd left it in the kitchen. It wasn't Chris, not his ringtone.

"Hi, Annie."

"Where are you? How's it going? How'd Mike take the news?"

"Slow down. I'm home. Kind of a change in plans. At least a change in timing."

"Oh poor dear. Chris a no-show, huh? I'm so sorry. After all these years—"

"Annie, cool it. Chris is here. In Waltham. It's Mike. He's in the hospital."

"What the hell? Hospital? What hospital? He had a heart attack when you told him, didn't he? I knew it."

Kassie chuckled, raising her eyebrows. "No, not yet, anyway. I haven't told him."

"Okay, from the beginning. Don't leave out a single detail."

Kassie filled her in starting with taking Mike to Boston Clinic Thursday night, the short doctor, and most of all, Mike's chronic kidney disease, which he had never told her about.

"How did you not know? Shame on you, Bad Bad Kassie."

"Stop that. What, now I'm to blame? I've been a little preoccupied the last few years, you know, with my mom and all."

"And all, meaning Chris."

"Sure, Chris is part of it, but I have a life besides Chris, besides Mike. My career and stuff. Are you getting all moral on me, too?"

"Too?"

"Chris thinks it's ironic I'm angry at Mike for lying about his kidney thing when I've been lying to him about my Chris thing."

"He has a point."

"I don't have time for that now. I've gotta pick up some things for Mike and get to the hospital."

"Are we still on for dinner tomorrow? You still going to let me meet Mr. Wonderful?"

"Can't see why not? Mike's in the hospital until Monday. Let's make it early. How about Tryst's in Arlington at five? We'll need a reservation. It's Easter."

"Tryst's. How appropriate. I'll make the reservation."

Kassie went into the downstairs bathroom to pee. Bingo! There it was sitting on the back of the toilet bowl. Did Teresa leave the book there accidentally, or did she put it in there for Mr. Mike's convenience? Maybe Teresa knew more about Mike than Kassie did.

What else did Mike want? His phone. She found it on the antique desk in his den. It'd been idle since Thursday. She booted it; the battery displayed a sliver of red. Clearly on life-support. It hadn't been charged in what two, three days? She had to find his charger. Gracious. His desk needed some serious Container Store help, unlike his bureau. Kassie shuffled green and red folders around, lifted a stack of books, a mound of paper, but no sign of the charger.

There she was again, in uncharted territory. Though he had never told her to stay out of his desk, she'd considered it, like his bureau, Mike's domain. Until now, she'd never had a reason to go there. She assumed there was an unstated, mutual understanding, and Mike stayed out of her desk and bureau, as well. Nevertheless, to be on the safe side, Kassie refrained from storing photos, notes, itineraries— any incriminating evidence—in her home desk in case Mike became suspicious and nosy.

There were six drawers in the desk, three on each side. She sat in his overstuffed black leather chair so high off the floor her feet dangled, just like Lilly Tomlin's Edith Ann.

She started on the left. Each drawer screeched like fingernails on a chalkboard as Kassie slid it open. The wooden drawers must have warped. Nothing a little WD40 couldn't silence. Lots of papers, folders, pens, normal office supplies. No sign of the charger.

She moved to the right. Same deal on the noise and contents. Finally, she found the charger in the bottom drawer which was empty, except for a white envelope underneath the charger.

Figuring that it was remnants of a utility bill or some such thing, Kassie flipped it over. The return address read, Dr. Richard Peters, Urology Associates, Massachusetts Avenue, Arlington, MA. She looked inside. Empty. That's odd. So was the doctor's name. What parents would do that to their child? But of course he'd end up being a urologist. Maybe that was their grand plan all along.

Kassie returned the envelope where and how she'd found it, having no desire to spend any more time than necessary rifling through Mike's things. But she had to find his office keys. The Brooks Brothers bag she'd given him two years ago for his birthday at his request leaned against the side of the desk.

"To be the best, might as well have the best," he'd said. So she humored him.

Mike was all about image. Sometimes when a client visited his office, he'd have Jaylene, one of the account executives, bring in her mink coat and hang it in her cubicle in plain sight.

"It shouts success." Mike rationalized if one of his people could afford a mink, it reflected on him and his firm. He never considered the client might be a PETA activist. Nevertheless, Jaylene did what he asked. As did all of his employees.

Kassie picked through all four pockets of the four-hundred-dollar bag. Some gum, mints, tissue, and loose change. Ooh money. A fifty. She could use a fifty. She hadn't had time to go to the ATM. *Leave it.* She made a mental note to stop at the bank.

After piling the *Wall St. Journal* and a few folders on the chair, she found the burnt-orange carabiner with a bunch of keys in the bottom of the case. She took all the things he requested and dropped them on the kitchen counter. She would not be called useless again.

Nearby the sound of a truck started and stopped and started and stopped. The mail. She headed down the driveway, making another mental note to get the new Charlestown address so she'd be able to give the post office forwarding instructions.

"Hello, Mrs. Ricci. Double mail today with yesterday a holiday—"

"Hi, Tom. Thank you. Happy Easter!" Tom had been their mailman ever since they moved there. She never asked him to call her Ms. O'Callaghan, or even Kassie, though she should have. Soon it wouldn't matter.

On the way back to the house, she noticed something blue and white hanging on her front doorknob. A FedEx delivery notice addressed to her. It was too late in the day to get them to bring whatever it was back, and tomorrow was Sunday. No sender's name, just a zip code. She looked it up on her cellphone. Newburyport. Her mother's attorney? She shoved the slip into her purse to handle Monday.

What else? She checked the fridge for anything past its prime. Yogurt, cheese, overripe strawberries, and grapes, and then she took out the trash. She'd be back at the house Monday, in time to put the garbage and recycling bins out. Normally Mike's job. Under the circumstances, she expected she'd be doing it rather than establishing new household routines with Chris, which would've been her preference.

Kassie did a fly-by around the first floor, ensuring lights were off, the sliding doors to the back porch locked. The house looked shipshape. She shook her head in approval of Teresa's performance. A-plus as usual. She took good care of them. Unlike her daughter, Amelia, who filled in for her mother occasionally. Amelia paid little attention to details, displaying instead a slam-bam-thank-you-ma'am approach to house cleaning.

Kassie tossed Mike's phone and charger in her purse and grabbed his keys intending to toss them in as well, but stopped. His key ring seemed heavier than her carabiner. There were five individual large rings with keys and tags hanging off them. Car key. House key. Office keys. A bunch of membership tags from places he frequented, like CVS, Wegman's, Boston Library, Ace Hardware. And two small keys she couldn't identify.

Kassie raced out of the kitchen almost falling over Topher. "Move!" She stumbled up the stairs, her heart rate increasing with each step.

Without hesitation, Kassie opened the bottom drawer of Mike's bureau and put the metal strongbox on the bed. No time to have a conscience. She fumbled trying to locate the little keys among all the crap on his key ring. *Clunk*.

"Damn." She picked up the carabiner and flipped through the keys again. She swallowed so hard both ears popped. Her mouth void of saliva. Her hands shook as she inserted one of the keys in the lock. It wouldn't turn. She held her breath and tried the other. The key fit like the backing on a pierced earring, and it turned.

16

Key Note Address

This time Kassie took the money. She didn't know why, but she knew she couldn't leave it. As she put the money on the bed, Topher pounced to see what all the excitement was about. She shooed him onto the chaise lounge.

"Stay there, big guy." She coddled him. "Mommy's busy."

Stacked neatly with a thick yellow rubber band, it didn't seem to be a lot of money. She fanned it, like they do in the movies. All Benjamins. He'd graduated from fifties.

Kassie counted it once. Twice. And one more time to be sure. Easy math. *Why was Mike hiding fifty-two hundred dollars in his bureau?*

She joined Topher on the chaise, at least she tried. Leaning up against the back and fully outstretched, Topher occupied most of the long seat cushion. Kassie claimed an empty spot on the edge still holding the loot in one hand, slapping it onto the palm of the other.

She closed the box, locked it for who knows why as there was nothing left in it, and returned it to his bureau. She took the money and the keys and headed for the stairs. Wait a minute. Not so fast.

Two keys. One fit, one didn't. She searched his bureau again but found nothing that needed a key. No boxes or padlocks, no diaries. What a hoot if Mike kept a diary. She couldn't imagine it. If he did, it would most likely be in Italian taking for granted Kassie would never be able to translate it.

Kassie walked into his closet. She was greeted by a sea of khaki, navy, white, black, with a sprinkle of pastels that broke the monotony. Organized to a tee, Mike's pants and shirts were aligned like soldiers and arranged by color, season, and function. She'd always teased him it was Garanimals for adults. He'd reserved the closet floor for shoes she'd asked him to keep in the downstairs closet. If she weren't planning on leaving, she'd have Teresa move them there where they belonged. Now it didn't matter.

The upper shelf was home to his porn and pot, stored in an opaque plastic box with a tomato red top. She didn't have to open it. Mike had shown it to her years before, probably in a rare moment trying to seduce her. She'd declined to take part in either activity. Not her scene.

Back downstairs to Mike's den, she rummaged through his desk, swiped a new envelope to house the cash, and did a quick look-see in the closet. Nothing, nada. Maybe the garage.

Kassie stood with her hands on her hips staring in disbelief. What a mess. The state of his workbench mirrored the top of his desk. Probably because Teresa cleaned all the common areas and because Kassie was a neat freak about the house and her own possessions, she'd never noticed what a pig Mike was, or maybe had become, about some things anyway. Not quite obsessive-compulsive, but Kassie embodied one of her mother's favorite sayings, "A place for everything, and everything in its place." She picked up a hammer and a screwdriver. She put them inside the large gray toolbox, out of Mike's easy reach. He would never harm her, not physically anyway. Just the same.

The afternoon slipped away from her. It was almost four, and she still needed to get to Mike's office and the hospital. Before leaving the house, she counted to fifty-two while washing her hands. What a cluster.

For once Kassie applauded Mike for insisting they buy a home just ten minutes from his office.

"Commuting is a time-waster. And wasted time means wasted profits." Mike's words nagged her like a recurring nightmare. She could compile a book of Mike's favorite sayings as a parting gift and see if she could profit from the time she'd dedicated to their crumbled marriage.

She'd already decided that she would not let on that she'd found his hidden money. For now, it would be her secret. She had about forty-eight hours to figure how to tell him and find enough courage to demand he come clean.

What if it wasn't his? Could he be holding it for someone else? Maybe Bill. She knew Bill had had an affair, maybe more than one. Mike hadn't told her about Bill. Another secret he'd kept. She'd learned about it from his wife, Nancy, who had confided that she'd suspected Bill for a while. All the overnight trips to New York City. And then she saw a text from someone named Stella with heart emojis.

"Do you ever send texts with hearts to your male co-workers?" Nancy asked through her tears.

"Can't say that I do. The middle digit occasionally." Kassie tried to lighten the mood, while stifling the urge to reveal her own infidelity. No matter how juicy her story, telling Nancy about Chris wouldn't help her feel better, even though women loved to gossip, or so they say, whoever they were.

Instead she and Nancy spent over two weeks together having

coffee and lunch plotting how to get Bill back. The internet provided a treasure trove of explicit videos and advice, some of which Nancy adopted and put into quick action. Folks on the internet sure knew what they were talking about. Bill was back. Better than ever. Nancy couldn't thank Kassie enough. She owed her one.

Why then, if not to bail Bill out of a dilemma, would Mike squirrel away that much money instead of putting it in their joint accounts, or even a separate bank account? Maybe he was stealing from the company? *No reason to. He could draw whatever he needed.* Maybe Mike was saving money to take her on a long vacation? *Fat chance.*

As she unlocked the door to Mike's office building, Kassie racked her brain trying to remember the last time she'd been there. Before Chris, before her mother's death, for sure. It smelled stale with no air being circulated over the long weekend and the trash not yet emptied. She didn't plan to hang around long enough for it to matter. Her original mission was to get the folders Mike wanted and get to the hospital posthaste. The second key put a crimp in that plan.

First things first. *Nice digs, Mike.* Even though no one worked that day, Kassie ambled her way past the work areas of the firm's creatives and administrative staff as if her presence there might be disruptive. She could've mistaken the modernity of the office space for where she worked, except it seemed out of place in this cozy Victorian home in Cambridge, while her office was in a glass tower on Boylston Street in Boston proper.

She found the back stairway and made her way to Mike's office. When the business started, it occupied only three out of eight offices on the first floor. Within ten years, he'd bought the whole damn building, booted out the other tenants, and renovated it in his image. He claimed the entire second floor as his office suite and built out his digs—a small kitchen, a full bathroom with a shower, and two conference rooms.

Whoa. Mike's office was impeccable. From the doorway, Kassie surveyed the room, a stark contrast to the antique decor she remembered. The once charming and cozy office now resembled a Herman Miller showroom. With its smooth elegance, the furniture conveyed the success he'd tried to achieve with Jaylene's mink.

He'd traded his antique desk for a streamlined walnut one, with a matching black leather desk chair. A complementary leather lounge chair and ottoman had replaced the green Queen Anne chair Kassie had given him as a gift. *Where had that gone?* Opposite the desk, a glass coffee table separated two leather couches. The green striped drapes they'd picked out together were missing in favor of off-white vertical blinds. All that remained from the prior era were the original hardwood floors and two oriental rugs with rich red and camel-colored tones her mother gifted him when he started the business.

The folders he requested sat on the desk exactly where Mike said they'd be. Aligned on the right side and labeled New Business, Outstanding Invoices, Résumés. The three most important things to Mike—new clients, money, talent.

"Fresh blood is a good thing. Keeps the dream alive," Mike said when she'd encourage him to think about what would happen if something happened to him.

"What of the dream then?"

"You'll figure it out."

Kassie turned her attention to the matching walnut credenza behind Mike's desk. She recognized the deep-lilac and sea-green Murano glass paperweight they'd bought on their honeymoon in Venice. A matching one sat on her office desk. She fondled it. Its meaning had shattered over the years.

Five photos of varying sizes stared back at her. One of his parents and sister. Another of their wedding. *God, how young we were.* No recent photos of the two of them or of Kassie alone. But then again, she had none of him on her desk either.

A snapshot of Topher he'd asked her for. "Clients love to talk about pets. 'Oh, is that your cat?'" he said they'd say. Hard time imagining Mike accepting any ownership of Topher except for the sake of the business.

A five-by-seven of her mother. A professional headshot she'd taken celebrating the divorce of Kassie's stepfather and her decision to retake the O'Callaghan name. She displayed a similar one in her office. At least they had that much in common.

On the far end of the credenza, an eight-by-ten color picture she didn't recognize. She leaned in to look closer. A college photo, faded. Five preppy guys and gals. The guys all dressed the same. Tan pants, navy sweaters. The girls all had the same long, flipped hair and wore plaid skirts, knee socks, dark sweaters with white collars. The photo could pass for a private school advertisement.

She picked up the frame and traced Mike's image with that captivating smile. Who was the girl in a dark red, maybe maroon, sweater sitting on his lap? *I'll be damned.* She could've been Kassie's twin, or at least a relative. She'd read a study a while back that men tended to be attracted to similar women. If this gal defined Mike's type, did that make Kassie a copy? Had Kassie replaced his first love?

No time to psychoanalyze Mike. Time to look for something locked. The credenza wasn't. She flung open the two center cabinet doors. The one on the left was overstuffed with folders. The one on the right had black Nike running shoes that looked brand new sitting on top of a metal box, like the one in his bureau. *Booyah!*

She placed the box on his desk. Her phone rang.

"Have you been to the hospital yet?"

"No, soon. How's it going?"

"Good news on Topher. I'll fill you in later."

"Where are you?"

"Just driving around, getting lost in Boston."

She checked the clock on Mike's desk. Five-thirty already. "Don't make me send a search party out for you."

"I've got GPS. I'm good."

"I'll be the judge of that."

Kassie said *ciao* and turned her attention to the lockbox. Her pulse pumped through her ears. She found the two small keys on Mike's key ring. Which one would fit that box? This time she chose the right one.

Inside she found a plain white envelope addressed in black ink to Mike at the office. No return address. The postmark was clear. December of last year. Elephant Butte, New Mexico.

Elephant Butte? Must be a scam. A joke. But why hide it in a locked metal box. She turned the envelope over. It was unsealed.

In thin red marker the thank you note read, "Always, KR." Underneath, a heart with an arrow through it.

The Mercedes couldn't get her to the hospital fast enough.

17

Adventure Capital

Chris was happy to get out of the hotel even if it meant not being with Kassie for a spell. He could use a breath of non-hotel-conditioned air and time to regenerate brain and other essential cells.

"There are other things in life than sex, right? Negative on that," Chris said aloud, grinning as he merged onto the highway toward Charlestown to meet with the realtor he'd only talked with on the phone to lease the apartment.

She buzzed him into the building, leaned over the third-floor banister, and waved. She greeted him at the end of the long-carpeted hallway with an ear-to-ear smile. *Pleasant enough.*

"Don't want to scratch up these gorgeous cherry wood floors," she said as she slipped off her super high heels, making her about the same height as Kassie.

She took his arm and showed him around the furnished apartment, pointing out the snow-white cabinetry, the upscale silver-flecked black granite countertops, and the stainless-steel appliances.

"The crown molding is such a wonderful accent, wouldn't you agree,

Chris?" He grunted, not particularly into interior decorating. As long as the apartment had a kitchen, bathroom, and bedroom, he was happy.

Speaking of, the realtor ushered him into the bedroom and emphasized how "unusually huge" it was and then pressed down on the mattress of the king-sized bed. He nodded approval and asked about adding a cat to the short-term lease. No problem for an additional thirty bucks a month.

"Did you say you needed one parking space?"

"No, two. My girlfriend. It's her cat."

"So I guess a drink at The Warren Tavern is out of the question?" She inched so close to Chris her floral perfume struck a nerve below, and their eyes met.

"Maybe another time." He smiled as he tapped her arm and turned toward the door. She pouted like a five-year-old who didn't get to go on a playdate. He wouldn't have been surprised if she stomped her feet.

"You can move in Monday afternoon. The place will be ready then." She lifted his right hand and placed a key in his palm and directed him to the hardware store up the street where he could get another made for his lady friend.

"By any chance is it near the post office?" He pulled his hand away, putting the key and his hand in his pocket.

"Why yes, it is. And the tavern, too, if you change your mind." She winked.

Persistent little devil.

With keys made, he swung by the post office and picked up the small package he'd been expecting and kept the junk mail that had stacked up instead of throwing it away. There might something helpful to a newbie. He wondered if he'd get a call from Welcome Wagon as he did when he first moved to San Francisco.

When he'd lived there, Chris relied on public transportation. He considered doing the same in Boston but opted for renting wheels until he worked out the commute and Kassie's schedule. Perhaps the Saturday of a holiday weekend wasn't the best time to drive around Boston, but he had the afternoon to kill so why not? And he needed the practice. His friends had warned him being a tourist in Boston was one thing, being a resident quite another. Falling victim to Boston's legendary rotaries and one-way streets was not his idea of fun.

He zigzagged through the city's main streets and crawled through the back alleyways, avoiding jaywalkers and fathers pushing baby carriages; and he bucked the traffic around the Boston Common and Public Garden, up Newbury Street with a gazillion shoppers not looking where they're going, through the crossroads at Kenmore Square and past Fenway Park where the early afternoon game crowd had dispersed. Phew! He'd made it.

After he'd checked in with Kassie, he decided to drive by the office where he'd have an interview the following Wednesday. Turning the car around, he headed toward Cambridge via the Harvard Bridge. He'd keyed the address into his iPhone before leaving the hotel.

Chris clicked on *Ricci and Associates.*

18

Red, Red Whine

If asked, Kassie wouldn't be able to recall how she got from Mike's office to the hospital late Saturday afternoon except for one small detail she'd like to forget.

She wouldn't remember starting her car or fastening her seatbelt. She wouldn't remember honking at a moving van unloading a mattress. She wouldn't remember veering around not one but three cars that were double-parked. Nor did she see Chris sitting in his rented SUV checking the route to Ricci and Associates on his phone while stopped at the first intersection she'd crossed.

Kassie would recall seeing red. Her mother's carpet blanketing Mike's office. A sweater in a photo. The heart on a note from KR. The flashing lights of a police car in her rearview mirror.

She handed the cop her license and registration, waited while he checked her out, tapped her fingers on the steering wheel, and bit her tongue, all the time willing Bad Kassie to remain silent. She knew the drill.

"You blew through the stop sign back there."

"I'm so sorry, Officer McCarthy. On the way to Boston Clinic to see my husband."

"You're related to Daniel O'Callaghan?"

"Yes, sir. My uncle."

"Nice guy. Worked with him about ten years ago in Revere."

"He died since then."

"Oh, sorry. Just be careful around here young lady. Do you need an escort?"

Kassie turned down the offer and thanked the officer for letting her go without a ticket. Being Irish and having an uncle who was a cop had its advantages, especially in Boston. She promised to be good. Heaven only knew how long the luck of the Irish would safeguard her from future vehicle violations.

Officer McCarthy wouldn't have known Uncle Dan's influence, while he was living or after his death, had squashed multiple tickets for Kassie in and around and north of Boston. Usually for speeding. Running a stop sign was a first for her. After her father died, Uncle Dan tried to step in and fill the void. He taught her how to ride a bike, ski, and drive. Uncle Dan would not be pleased. *Sorry.* Her eyes veered toward the sky.

Her mother had accepted his help to raise Kassie at least for a while until she remarried. Kassie's stepfather, whose name she refused to utter after their divorce, tried to replace either Matthew or Daniel O'Callaghan. After a few years of physically abusing both Kassie and her mother, the man who remained nameless flew the coop just as Uncle Dan seemed ready to unleash his Irish temper on him.

Kassie had overheard Uncle Dan tell her mother, "What that man needs is a good swift kick in the ass." Kassie agreed and was confident that he would do it when the time was right.

The divorce was uncontested and Uncle Dan reclaimed his well-earned place as Kassie's role model and protector. When she was in high school, he'd just show up in their living room when she'd have a first date and hide behind her mother while giving Kassie the thumbs up or down.

He didn't seem to care much for Mike. "This marriage could be a heartache in the making, darlin'" he'd told her. Even so, Uncle Dan gave into the little girl he never had and walked her down the aisle.

Uncle Dan was broken-hearted when she'd lost the baby and crushed when she confessed he was right about the heartache thing.

"Hang in there, baby. Marriages are like the Red Sox. They have a way of turning around," he said, half-sympathizing, half-joking with her in 2004 after the team had won their first World Series in eighty-six years.

Kassie was delighted that Uncle Dan had lived long enough to see at least one more Red Sox world championship and to have shared the experience with him. She'd always have those memories and wished he was with her that day. Maybe he was.

Though shaken by her close encounter with Officer McCarthy, when she parked in the hospital garage, Kassie had the presence of mind to double check the money envelope was zipped inside her purse. Even though the garage was busier than the day before, the sounds of cars starting and breaks squealing combined with voices of people talking on their phones confirmed she was not alone. She needed to keep her head up and her bag close.

She also had the wherewithal to know how critical it would be for her to get hold of herself before facing Mike and not barge into his room, spewing all kinds of accusations she hadn't thought through yet. *Tea time.*

"What would I be accusing him of?" She mumbled as she sat at the same table in the hospital's café that she'd occupied the day before.

Saving money? Keeping an old photo on his desk? Renovating

his office without consulting her? Memorializing her mother with old carpets and her picture? Knowing Mike, he'd wriggle his way out with excuse after excuse. All plausible explanations. And then he'd make her feel like a fool . . . again. But what about New Mexico? What's that all about?

Her phone buzzed. A text from Chris.

What's your eta?

90 mins. @ hospital. Going to c M now.

OK. Dinner in?

And?

Movie?

And?

Whatever turns u on, KO.

Kassie turned off her phone, not wanting to take the chance Chris would text or call her while she was with Mike. She sat back, closed her eyes and willed Uncle Dan to give her strength now.

Remember the end game.

Uncle Dan had taught her whether in sports or in business or in life, the most important lesson was to keep the goal in mind.

Her end game was waiting for her at the hotel. The main obstacle was waiting for her four floors up.

"Where have you been all day?"

"Hello, to you too, Mike. How are you?"

He prattled on and on and on about being stuck in the hospital and expected to be riddled with bed sores by the time they released him. Suddenly he liked the waterbed. Being in the hospital provided at least one benefit.

"The cute nurses are taking good care of me. You could take some cues from them."

Kassie bit her lip and remembered the end game.

"My blood pressure seems to have stabilized. Look, no more wires."

"Was stopped for running a stop sign on my way here."

"And I'm peeing regularly."

"Uncle Dan warned me years ago."

"I actually slept well last night for once."

"So did I." Kassie bowed her head, trying not to smile.

She placed Mike's phone and charger, along with the Hemingway biography on the rolling tray table. Mike turned on the phone.

"No juice, Kassie. You didn't charge it? What good—"

"Am I?"

"No. The phone, it's dead."

She snatched it from him and plugged it in a wall socket.

"You didn't answer me. Where have you been? Did you go to my office like I asked? What did ya think?"

"About what?" She handed Mike the three folders he wanted.

"The office. I don't think you've been there since I renovated it, huh?"

Kassie expressed her honest surprise—the new furniture, the pictures. When had he done all that?

"Five years ago. You were off gallivanting in Italy doing who knows what. Your mother was a godsend. Don't know what I would've done without her."

"My mother? How's that?"

Mike chronicled how her mother had called him all boohooing and nervous about Kassie traveling to Italy solo. He said he'd reassured her that Kassie was a big girl who could take care of herself. Then he had an idea, a way to distract her, to occupy her while Kassie was away. Would she help him redecorate his office?

"I gave her a blank check. It was the ultimate quid pro quo. A win-win. She had a ball flitting from one store to another. Showing swatches to the staff. Even asking their opinions, which of course she ignored. So proud of herself. And everyone at the office loved the end result."

"She never told me. Why didn't she tell me? Why didn't you?"

"Don't know why she didn't tell you. Hate to let you in on a little secret, sweetheart. Your mother didn't tell you everything."

"What does that mean?" The thought of her mother conspiring with Mike made Kassie's blood boil. She could feel her heart pounding in her ears. Bad Kassie bubbled to the surface and erupted as she walked in a circle like a dog searching for a place to settle. There was no turning back.

"Who's KR, Mike?" She spewed, her cheeks reddened.

"KR? Um. *You,* when you think using my name is to your advantage." Mike pointed at her and threw his arms in the air.

"Don't be such a smart ass. Last I checked, I don't live in Elephant Butte, New Mexico." She threw the envelope at him. "I think we're done here. And I suspect you'd agree."

"What the hell?"

"I want a divorce."

"Divorce? Why? This is nothing." Mike gritted his teeth. "Don't be ridiculous. I can explain. I tell you *this* is nothing." Mike waved the envelope in the air.

"It's not nothing. It's not all."

"All or nothing? You're talking gibberish as usual. Give me one good reason we should split? Now." Mike pounded the rolling table that straddled his bed sending the small plastic water pitcher splashing to the floor.

"One reason? How about fifty-two hundred reasons?" Kassie blurted and made tracks out the door with a lump in her throat and water in her eyes.

Kassie texted Chris. *On my way. Get food & lots of wine. Red wine.*

19

Romper Rooms

As if searching for divine guidance, Mike looked to the ceiling and said in a voice louder than what was acceptable in a hospital, "What the hell? She's lost her mind. Drugs. It must be drugs."

"What must be drugs, Mr. Mike?"

Though startled by hearing a response, he easily recognized Teresa's accent but was surprised to see her daughter at the foot of his bed. He straightened out his sheets and blanket, covering all things private. There'd be no issue if it was just Amelia standing there, but he had no desire to flash Teresa. Bad enough for more than a decade she'd washed his soiled and sweaty underwear, changed his stinking sheets, and stowed any porn flicks he'd forgotten to put away.

"Oh, it's nothing, Teresa. Just Kassie fuming about nothing. So, what else is new?"

Mike fixed his eyes on Amelia and inhaled and exhaled with a smile he didn't realize he could muster that day. Good thing he'd pulled up the sheets and put his hands on his lap concealing any little thing that could arise.

It had been about a year since their last night together in Providence, still the sight of her nipples pointing through her white top sent blood to all the right body parts. Despite her mother standing there, Amelia's presence made him hard as a rock. Boy, it felt good. If only he, or she, could do something about it. People had sex in hospitals, right? Maybe her mother would get lost, and he and Amelia could get it on. Unlike Kassie, who'd never consider such a thing even in the best of times and who now had her knickers in a twitter about something that was none of her business, he reckoned Amelia could be game if the circumstance presented itself.

Spontaneity was not the only thing that set Amelia and Kassie apart. These two women were total opposites. In fact, Amelia was unlike any other woman in Mike's life. All the others were clones, physically and temperamentally. If asked, he'd admit he'd had a type during his single years. They were blond, petite, intelligent, and submissive. Not surprisingly he'd married his type. Mike was comfortable with that and pretty much remained faithful. Okay, he'd had one-night stands occasionally. Never anything to write home about.

Until Amelia came along. She'd redefined his comfort zone on the Friday she came to clean the house when Teresa was on vacation. Kassie was on vacation, too, in Italy, and Mike was working at home while his office was being renovated. He'd met her before, but her mother and Kassie were always around. Had he detected a vibe between them? He wasn't sure. Imagination or wishful thinking?

On that day, however, it was just the two of them alone in the house. How convenient. He greeted her when she arrived, all proper and friendly. A handshake. A smile. He soaked in her beauty as if meeting her for the first time. Her skinny jeans accented all the right places in front and behind. The black, V-neck, short-sleeved t-shirt revealed just enough cleavage to cause him to salivate. Her hair was tied up and her chocolate eyes twinkled as the morning sun peeked through the sheer, white curtains in the hallway. He imagined her lips would taste like merlot if he could just lick them even once. Did she dress like this to clean every house or was it on his behalf? Did she expect he'd be home alone—lonely and horny?

Amelia wasted no time getting to work cleaning. About an hour later, she appeared in his office doorway. "What should I do with these?" She smiled, waving three movies Mike had watched during his solo escapades the night before.

"Let me see. Bring them here." Mike knew full well what they were.

As Amelia walked toward him, she released the scarlet red ribbon and her hair, which was the darkest brown it could be without being black, fell down below her shoulders. He shut the computer and cellphone down. Then he got up.

Cleaning Mike's house took two or three hours longer than usual that day. It's said the first time is always the best. Especially when it's impromptu. Hot, fast, furious. Such was the case with Amelia and Mike. Clothes decorated his office. A bra on the closet doorknob, boxer shorts over a lampshade. Her black thong just missed Topher's head as he escaped to another part of the house. Minimal foreplay occurred or was needed.

The scene that day mimicked Goldilocks and the Three Bears. Before Amelia would clean a room, they'd test it out, give it a whirl. Then she'd clean it, giving them time to re-energize before advancing to christen the next room. Mike liked the game, especially because he was able to keep up with this alluring woman twenty-five years his junior.

After their romp on the kitchen counter, the words *birth control* were spoken. Didn't matter who uttered the words. Mike thought they'd said it simultaneously, just like their orgasms.

"Not to worry, my dear. Vasectomy. Long time ago."

"Not to worry, my darling. Pills. Every day."

With that potential barrier out of the way, Amelia swiped a

super-sized can of creamy Reddi-Wip from the refrigerator, took Mike's hand, placed it on her breast, and led him to the last room yet to be cleaned. Kassie's office.

"No. Not here" Mike was a risk-taker, but no fool. Instead he took her to the family room. He opened a drawer in a side table and pulled out a video.

"Now this is my favorite. You game?"

Amelia giggled. "I love that one. Put it in. Get ready, Papa Mike, for the last ride of the day."

As the movie played in the background, Mike settled in his favorite chair, which he subsequently nicknamed the Pleasure Chair. She climbed aboard. A few hours ago, she'd smelled like lavender. Now she smelled like sex, as did he.

She draped her silky, dark-brown hair over him.

She wrapped her long and slender body with her never-ending legs around him.

She offered him one breast and then the other.

Her moans were so loud, she drowned out the porn stars. Mike thought he'd died and gone to heaven as she rode him like a bucking bronco until he exploded once again.

As their blood pressure subsided, she smothered him with kisses. Forehead. Nose. Ears. Lips. Neck. Chest. Enough of that. Maybe this was her idea of cuddling. He had another.

He lifted her, laid her gently on the plush gray carpet, and spread her legs. She raised his chin and was greeted by a whipped cream smiley face.

Their affair had started with a bang, actually multiple bangs, that day and lasted on and off for about four years, coordinating their meet ups when Kassie traveled, which was easy to do. Neither Amelia nor Mike put any demands on the other. It was just sex, with enough caring thrown in over time to characterize some of their interactions as making love. It was so much fun while it lasted, and Amelia helped distract Mike from his kidney problems. Or maybe she kept him in denial. Whatever, it worked.

When they'd met in Providence a year ago, Amelia told him she'd met a guy she'd like to get to know better. That meant she'd need to cool it with him, at least until she knew whether there was a future with the new guy. They made love for the last time that night. No porn or whipped cream in sight.

Once in a while Mike would call her to see how things were going with her new beau, bemoaning how he was relegated to going solo in the Pleasure Chair. Amelia said her mother kept her apprised of the obvious rift between him and Kassie, and she was sorry about that. Not that they were keeping their options open to be with each other. Married to Kassie, Mike didn't have any. He'd never leave her. He and Amelia had fulfilled a need in each other for a certain period of time. Mike accepted that Amelia had moved on. He wasn't so sure he had.

And now as Amelia walked toward Mike sitting in his hospital bed, she untied the red ribbon in her hair and kissed him deeply just as she had five years ago. Mike took her left hand, put it in his lap, and covered it with both of his hands.

"Well, hello, Amelia. Teresa. How did you know I was here?" Mike's face flushed and his eyes widened.

"Miss Kassie told me yesterday. At the house. Lucky I arrived just as she was leaving with her suitcase. Otherwise maybe I wouldn't know you was here. And Amelia wouldn't know either."

"Her suitcase?"

"Yes, Mr. Mike. I was so shocked to hear you was sick. I called Amelia right away."

Amelia nodded in agreement, keeping her hand in place, though her fingers fiddled.

"*Her* suitcase. You sure? Oh, God," Mike murmured, squeezing Amelia's hand, and shifting his right leg under the covers.

"Yes. She had two. One was yours, over there." Teresa pointed to the duffel bag on the floor. "I'm sure the other one was hers. She said she was going to stay at a friend's house over the weekend. I asked if she wanted me to take care of the kitty cat. But she said no, she already asked a neighbor to do that. Is that okay?"

"Of course." Mike wondered what neighbor. That would be a first.

"Where was she going in such a hurry?" Amelia piped in.

"When? Yesterday?" Mike asked.

"Just now. We passed Kassie in the hallway. Almost bumped into her. But I don't think she seen us," Teresa said.

"I know I took a chance coming here. But I'm sure she didn't see us. She seemed to be talking to herself and rummaging through her purse. I wanted to see how you were. I gather you're not as bad as I thought." Amelia winked.

Mike raised his eyebrows and looked at Teresa.

"Would you mind?"

Alone at last. Mike accurately predicted Amelia's willingness to join him for a quick romp in the bathroom. Maybe she shared his fantasy because she wore a skirt which would make his getting in her pants easy peasy.

Once Amelia made sure her mother was seated outside Mike's room, she closed the door and met Mike in the bathroom. He was ready, and Amelia was rarin' to go. It didn't take long. It was like sausage, sweet and hot. And quiet. Mostly. Mike pinned Amelia against the stark white bathroom wall with one hand and covered her mouth with the other, stifling her moans.

"I've missed you," they said, fully synchronized.

Amelia kissed Mike's forehead. Nose. Ears. Lips. Neck. She kissed all of him. This time he didn't stop her.

Amelia left Mike's room and returned with her mother, who'd guarded the door. It wasn't the first time Teresa had covered for them.

"Good job, Mama, thanks."

"Well, that was quick," Teresa said. They shared a laugh.

"Seriously, Mike, what's going on with you?"

"I'm just here for observation for a few days. I should go home Monday."

"Will you let me know what's going on somehow?"

"Sure, I'm sorry I didn't call. I didn't have my phone. Kassie just dropped it off, and it was dead. It's over there charging. Would you hand it to me, please?"

A pretty young nurse came in to check Mike's vitals, breaking up the party. "Now, Mr. Ricci, I hope you're resting and aren't letting these ladies raise your blood pressure."

"We'd never do that." Amelia winked and bit her lower lip. "Anyway, we're outta here." She rubbed Mike's arm and shooed her mother out the door.

Indeed, Mike's blood pressure was up. How could it not be? In the space of two hours his wife told him she wanted a divorce, and he had sex in his hospital bathroom with an ex-lover.

What a freakin' afternoon. Mike decided it was time for him to gain some control of his life, such as it was, and as much as he could, sitting there limp and confused.

He started by calling Bill. No answer. Of course not. A long holiday weekend. *He's off doing something fun, while I'm getting bed sores, and wasting away in pajamas and eating lime Jell-O.*

"Hey, Bill, Mike here. Surprise. Surprise. I'm at Boston Clinic for the weekend. No worries. Just observation. I'm here until Monday. So I need you to help me out at the office. If you can, call me tomorrow."

He called Kassie. Voicemail. Waited five minutes. Voicemail. He slammed the phone face down on the bed and crossed his arms in a huff. Waited ten minutes. Voicemail.

"Hi, this is Kassie O. I missed your call, but you know what to do. Talk later."

"Really, Kassie? I'm stuck in this hellhole, and you won't answer my goddamn calls? The least you can do is put on your big-girl pants and let me explain. It's time to get real."

20

Escape Artist

Knock, knock. Knock, knock, knock. Once the secret knock of her sorority at Missouri, Kassie and Chris adopted it as theirs over the last five years. This time, no answer. Crap. She'd hoped Chris would be back at the hotel with food and drink. She lost her appetite on the ride from the hospital but craved a glass of wine to steady her nerves.

As she fumbled to find the keycard, her bag took a header, spewing most of its contents onto the green and red striped carpet in the almost-always-dark hallway.

"Fuck," she said as a man and woman approached.

"Are you okay?" the woman asked as they passed. "Do you need help?"

"No thanks. I got it. Sorry for the language." She groped through the mess, not really sorry, and rescued the envelope, grateful the money hadn't tumbled out.

Never known for smooth entrances, Kassie stumbled into the room, kicking items from her bag she hadn't shoved into it. She'd straighten it out later.

Thank God, he didn't see what a klutz I am.

The suite welcomed her without judgment, without a sound, not even the annoying clunk of the air conditioner shutting on and off. No Chris asleep in bed. No meowing kitty cat. Good. This sanctuary would give her time to get her shit together and assess all that occurred that day before Chris returned. Classical guitar music would help. She powered up her iPad. Found Pandora, her lifesaver.

Kassie stood at the large picture windows, taking deep cleansing breaths and stretching toward the ceiling. Boston's distant towering buildings sparkled amber, a reflection of the sun setting to the west. Oh, how she loved the city. She couldn't imagine ever moving away. After all, her family and career were there. Or had been there. Most of her relatives were gone, and once she divorced Mike, there wouldn't be much family left. And her career? She could take that anywhere, right? Or maybe she'd do something else with her life. She'd been so focused on getting out of her marriage, Kassie had dedicated little quality time to figuring out the rest of her life. Not yet anyway. First things first.

Divorce Mike. After years of practice, she'd finally said it to him. Not quite how, when, or even where she'd planned, but she'd done it. She'd left without giving him time to react. That wasn't the plan either. Why did she run? Scared, coward, or just relieved to have uttered the words? Probably all the above.

Kassie stepped out of the shower, wrapping the extra-large white towel around her. Despite the whirring of the fan, she could hear the TV and a "He's out! You mother." Baseball. Chris was back.

"Caught ya naked!" He popped his head into the bathroom.

"Save it for later, big guy. I need a drink."

"Now who's the spoil sport?" He opened the door displaying himself in all his glory.

Chris tripped over her clothes piled on the floor, falling into her arms. Her towel joined the pile. She could never say no to him for long.

They spent the evening before Easter in their hotel suite recounting their day over one of Kassie's favorite dinners—steak tips cooked medium rare, mashed potatoes, green beans and a simple garden salad. All of which Chris had arranged with the hotel staff. He confessed he'd originally ordered lobsters but changed the menu to accommodate her request for red wine.

"So, how's Mike?"

"Mike who? Just kidding. I've got a lot to tell you, but you go first. How'd things go in Charlestown?" Kassie let Chris describe his day, giving her time to figure out how to tell her story with minimal theatrics.

Over the first bottle of Chateau Ste. Michelle merlot, Chris described the apartment and the realtor who'd put a move on him.

"If it weren't for you, maybe I would've taken her up on it. She was hot. In fact, when she stepped out of her shoes, she reminded me of you," he said with a wink.

"If it weren't for me, you wouldn't have had the opportunity," she said with a little kick under the small stainless-steel room service cart.

Chris told her about the joy and challenges of exploring Boston, the traffic, the rotaries, but especially the Fenway Park drive by.

"Oh, and we're all set with Topher. Do you think Mike will ever put two and two together?"

"Who knows? I'm not sure I care if he does at this point."

"Why not?" He uncorked the second bottle of merlot and moved from the table to the couch.

"Yes, get comfortable, my dear, I'm not sure where to begin." She stood and tightened the belt around the plush hotel robe. Now was not seduction time.

Still standing and pacing around the suite's living room, Kassie started with the end.

"Well, let's see. I did it. I told him I wanted a divorce."

"You're shittin' me. How come you didn't tell me right away? You told him while he's in the hospital? A low blow, don't you think? How'd he take it? What did he say?"

"Not much. I didn't give him time to react. I left."

"Did you tell him why? About me?"

Kassie shot him a you've-got-to-be-kidding look. She found her bag and handed the envelope to him.

"Now you're paying me to be with you?" He looked confused.

"Don't be silly. I found this money in a box in his bureau." She explained how she came to find it. "I told him there were fifty-two hundred reasons I wanted a divorce."

"That's how much is in here? Wow!"

"I don't think he heard me because of Elephant Butte."

"Elephant Butte. New Mexico?"

"You know Elephant Butte?"

"I've heard of it. I'm not sure why. A client or somebody was on *Jeopardy* from there. What about it?"

Kassie told Chris how there were two keys, but only one box at home. She'd looked all over the house, the garage, and how she continued her search when she got to his office to pick up his files.

"You wouldn't believe his office. It's nothing like I remember."

"How's that?"

She explained that since they'd met in Venice, she'd adopted a practice of what she called "Mike-avoidance." Her goal was to stay away from him as much as possible, except at home where she had no choice. The less interaction the better.

"Then why do you continue to sleep with him?"

"The operative word is sleep. I've told you we haven't had sex in years, many years."

"Don't you think you were sending him mixed signals? From a man's perspective, if you're sleeping in the same bed with a woman, there's always the expectation of getting laid."

"Well, I'm sorry to have disappointed him, and you, too. That was not my expectation. Would you be happier if I had been screwing both of you these past five years? Gross. The thought of it creeps me out."

"Me, too. Go on. Back to the part about his office."

Kassie described her visit to his office. The renovation stunned her. It didn't reflect the Mike she once knew.

"And you know what?" She joined him on the couch.

"What?"

"I was right. It was my mother's doing."

"How? She's dead."

"True. But she was quite alive five years ago. Mike told me all about it this afternoon. He waited until today! My mother redecorated his office while I was in Venice with you."

"He said that? He knew we were in Venice together?"

"No, I mean, she redecorated at the *time* we were in Venice."

"So what's wrong with that?" He kissed her neck as he swept away her hair. "Sounds like your mom was a nice lady. If I had an office, I'd be thrilled to have someone help me out. Especially with redecorating. Not my wheelhouse."

"I know your wheelhouse." She snarled as she moved to the bedroom and gazed out the windows. She hadn't expected Chris to push back. "Just whose side are you on?"

Chris approached her, reaching around and unwrapping her. Kassie turned and brushed past him. She slung the robe on the bed and rummaged through her suitcase for clean clothes.

"I've gotta get outta here. It smells like a fraternity. I'm going for a walk."

"What? I'll come with you. Wait."

She didn't.

By the time the elevator doors opened to the lobby, Kassie had lost it. She couldn't hide the tears even if she'd been wearing sunglasses. A boisterous wedding party swarmed the lobby. A throng of guys who looked like penguins and gals all dolled up in pink, lilac, and yellow gowns sucked the air out her space. Of course, Easter weekend. How frigging original, Bad Kassie thought as she pushed through the human Easter eggs and out the revolving door to the parking lot.

Before stepping off the sidewalk, she looked both ways and scoped out the perimeter of the lot for the best path to walk laps. The long spring day had settled into a dark chilly night. She'd left the suite without her jacket, so she crossed her arms for warmth and walked with her head down, appearing as vulnerable as she felt.

The last thirty-six hours had not gone at all the way she'd planned. She and Chris should've been celebrating and spending time at Target buying brooms, dishwasher pods, and paper towels. And at Stop & Shop filling their basket with bread, butter, milk, eggs, and yogurt. All the essentials.

But that was not the case. Instead she had to defend herself to Chris of all people about whether she should have told Mike she wanted a divorce while he's laid up in the hospital. And why was he defending her mother's complicity with Mike? Long ago she'd resigned herself to the fact that she couldn't rely on Mike for emotional support and from time to time even doubted her mother's allegiance. Was Chris deserting her, too? She'd assumed he was a rock-solid fan.

After three laps around the lot filled with white and silver foreign SUVs, her shivering got the best of her. She headed back to the lobby.

"There you are," Chris said as he joined her at a table in the bar.

"How did you find me?" Kassie stared into a glass of white wine.

He held up his phone. "Remember you're on my *Find My Friends* app. Now that I'm here, why don't you put me on yours?"

"Now that you're here, we need to talk," she said her eyes meeting his, yet ignoring his suggestion. "I didn't finish—"

"Would you care for a drink?" A waiter asked Chris.

"Go ahead," she said annoyed. She could tell by the look on his face Chris wasn't sure if he should.

"Do you think this is wise?" he said out of the corner of his mouth. "Out in public? At a hotel no less."

"I don't think it matters anymore. There's no turning back. Anyway, I think Mike's involved with another woman. So the divorce could be simple, a *fait accompli*."

Chris gulped as he swallowed his Guinness.

"I tried to tell you before. I found another metal box at his office. There was an envelope inside with a note from some woman who lives in Elephant Butte."

"And what did he say about it?"

"I told you, I didn't stick around. I threw the envelope at him and walked out. There must be a connection between the money and the Elephant woman. Don't you think?"

"Don't ask me. Ask Mike."

Kassie caught the waiter's eye and mouthed, "The check."

"Let's get out of here." She rushed out of the bar with Chris on her heels.

He grabbed her left arm. "What the hell is going on, Kassie?"

"The money, Chris, where is it? In the room?"

She seethed, but kept Bad Kassie under wraps during the elevator ride they shared with a peach and a penguin who whispered and giggled until they stumbled getting off on the third floor. Kassie kept her control only slightly longer than the lovebirds.

"What's going on?" she exploded once they were alone in

their room. "You tell me. Seems you're taking Mike's side. About everything."

"I'm not. I'm trying to help," Chris insisted as he tried to put his arms around her. "Look at you. You're a tempest in a teapot. Pacing back and forth. And you keep running off. Calm down and tell me everything."

Kassie found the money and put the envelope in her bag.

"What are you going to do with it?"

"Not sure. Half of it's mine. And it's evidence."

She disappeared into the bathroom and emerged wearing nothing but a short black silk nightgown. She poured herself a glass of wine, and lowered herself onto the couch in a Lotus position.

"Now isn't that better, sexy lady? But you expect me to sit here and keep my hands off you?"

"Control yourself."

"Me?"

For the next hour they refrained from attacking one another, physically and verbally, as Kassie shared her whole day. The money, note, renovated office, the brush with the law. And the visit with Mike. He'd broken her.

"I thought I knew him. Concealing money and another woman?"

"Which is bothering you more?"

"It's not an either-or. Both. Marriage and financial infidelity. What else has he been hiding?"

"At the risk of stating the obvious and having you run out the door again, you've been lying to each other for years. But that's not why you're divorcing him, right?"

"Right, but I never lied to him about you. He never asked if I was having an affair with anyone, so technically I haven't lied. Deceived, yes, but not lied."

"Splitting hairs, aren't you?"

"I consider you one continuous five-year cover-up. And *I'm* ready to tell Mike the truth. Think about it, in less than forty-eight hours I've learned Mike lied about his health, money, a woman in New Mexico, and my mother. And if his stupid kidney thing hadn't flared up, I may not have known about any of this. I think if we're keeping score, Mike's won."

"We're not keeping score. But try to put yourself in Mike's position. If you were sitting alone in a hospital bed and your husband told you he wanted a divorce, would you feel like a winner?"

"There you go again. Why, are you defending him?"

"I'm not. Two sides, that's all," he said, shrugging his shoulders. "You tired?"

They continued the repartee for another hour in bed. Going in circles. Kassie expressing her anger at Mike and frustration with Chris. He tried to convince her he had her back while rubbing it.

"Tomorrow's Easter. I need to go to the cemetery. My parents."

"Alone?"

"No. You're part of the family now. I might as well introduce you."

"Any living relatives I should meet?"

"You'll meet Annie tomorrow," Kassie said, checking her phone for messages. "She's my best friend. Does that count?"

Kassie saw one message from Annie probably confirming dinner. And Mike had called three times and left one message. She played it aloud.

"Really, Kassie? I'm stuck in this hellhole, and you won't answer my goddamn calls? The least you can do is put on your big-girl pants and let me explain. It's time to get real."

She bolted upright. "Big-girl pants! Bastard. Who does he think he's talking to? I'm not a child."

She replayed the message. "Time to get real? I'll show him what real is. See what I've had to put up with?" She shook the phone in the air.

"Sounds like he wants to explain," Chris interrupted her tirade.

"There you go again." She laid down and rolled away from him. He pulled her close to spoon. She didn't push him away but didn't encourage him. His strong arms around her were all she wanted.

"Kassie," he whispered, "you know you should put the money back."

She didn't fulfill his expectations that night.

21

With a Doubt

Daylight poked through a skinny opening in the double set of drapes as Chris opened his eyes. Easter morning. Only one more night in the hotel. Tomorrow he and Kassie could move into the apartment in Charlestown. It would be their place, at least until September when they'd figure out what's next. He searched the other side of the bed. The sheets were as cold as a hot water bottle in the morning.

"Hey, Kassie, get in here," he called out, figuring she was in the living room reading. No answer. He stood up, naked and half wilted. The lights were off in both the living room and the bathroom. Her jacket was gone, so was her bag. He scratched his head.

Standing at the sink to wash his face, he noticed an orange Post-it note on the mirror. Only Kassie would have Post-it notes at her fingertips.

"Out. Be back 9ish. Go ahead and eat. KO."

"Happy Easter to you, too, Kassie." Where'd she go? The gym? Nope. Not with her sneakers under the desk.

It was only 7:30. Not ready to start the day, Chris slid back under the sheets and stared at the ceiling. He retrieved the small purple box with the silver ribbon he'd tucked under his pillow the night before, placed it on his chest, and gazed at it as though it were a crystal ball. Now what? His plan to give it to her when they woke up that morning had slipped away. It'd have to wait. Perhaps that night at dinner with Annie. Or would that be rude? Knowing Kassie, she'd prefer they were alone when he gave it to her. He put the box in the nightstand.

Chris rolled to the empty side of the bed and buried his nose in Kassie's pillow, indulging himself in the sweet smell of vanilla that lingered there. The hunger inside him grew. His morning wood returned right on cue. He wished she were there to handle it. Instead he did.

He checked the clock. There was time for him to go to the gym. The hotel didn't have an indoor pool, which would be his preference. He made a mental note to search online later for gyms with pools in either Cambridge or Charlestown. Convenience, cost, cleanliness would be the criteria he'd use to choose the right gym. He'd check with Kassie on what gym she used. Maybe they had a pool.

That day, running on the treadmill would have to be a good substitute for swimming laps. The gym was empty, as he liked. No stranger's sweat flying around stinking up the place. No need to make small talk with gym rats in tank tops and spandex. No television blaring talking heads he couldn't care less about.

A good time to plug into his workout playlist and think.

Indeed. Where was Kassie? If the last few days were any indication, what would the future be like? On the spur of the moment and without explanation, she bolted. She hightailed it after telling Mike she wanted a divorce, skipped out for a walk alone the night before, and snuck off that morning without waking him or kissing him goodbye.

He'd uprooted his life in San Francisco to be with her. He expected something more after five years.

Maybe she'd changed her mind about the divorce or even their moving in together. A lot had happened since he'd stepped off the redeye. He'd flown there thinking he was making a commitment of sorts to a strong, independent woman who was leaving a bad marriage. Now she's a woman with a sick husband who has his own baggage that seemed to be driving her to act crazy.

Elephant Butte. Where had he heard that name before? He shook his head clueless.

Should he go back to San Francisco? Give Kassie a chance to figure things out without him in her way.

"Don't be a wuss," he said out loud to no one. The freelance gig was a great opportunity that would boost his résumé. Even if it were only until September. No matter what happened with Kassie, whatever decisions she made, he could survive five months on the East Coast. San Francisco was always waiting.

On his way back to the room, he stopped at the Starbucks in the lobby.

"Whatcha gettin'?" He heard a soft voice, felt a firm hand on his butt, followed by an intimate mini pinch.

"The usual. You want something?" He turned to see Kassie with her blue eyes twinkling at him. Thoughts of leaving her vanished as quickly as a shooting star.

"No, thanks. I had tea at home."

"Home?"

"Yes. I did what you told me to."

The money, he nodded and smiled.

As they returned to their suite, Kassie hung out the Do Not Disturb sign. Hippety-hop.

22

As the Worm Turns

Mike's Easter started out like a basket of rotten eggs. Everything around him stunk. The room, the bed, the food, himself. A shower and shave were in order, especially if he might entertain any visitors that day. He didn't think he needed to ask permission anymore to feel human. There were no fluids being pumped through his veins and no monitors surveilling his vitals. Statistically he was cleared to come and go as he pleased as long as he stayed in the hospital.

With a fresh pair of pajamas and a comb through his salt-and-pepper hair, Mike donned his bathrobe, which still had that clean Downy smell, and was ready to make the rounds. Before starting his adventure, he peeked both ways out the door in case a cranky nurse was heading his way with different ideas. Why were nurses always ornery, even the hot ones? Maybe it came with the job. He bet there was a required course in nursing school: *How to be Nasty and Nice.* What if, he snickered, the course name was reversed? *How to be Nice and Nasty.* Once a marketer, always a marketer. They could lock him up and force him to take his foot off the pedal, but his mind was still in full throttle.

Mike lucked out. The coast was clear. Not a cranky nurse in sight.

Nearly noontime. His lunch would arrive soon. He didn't care to wait around. Nothing special for this Easter to be sure. There wouldn't be any lasagna. Not like his mother's. God rest her soul. She died ten years before, shortly after his father. Long before her death, she taught Kassie the secret of being a good wife. Cook Italian. Kassie tried, but it was never like his mother's. But isn't that always the way? He couldn't remember when Kassie last made lasagna, or whether he even enjoyed it when she did.

There wouldn't be any Chianti for him that day, either. Or beer for that matter. He wondered if there'd be any tomorrow, or the day after that. How'd he'd like a cannoli right now. Ba humbug. Wrong holiday.

Usually the lights in the hospital hallways were as bright as those during a night game at Fenway. They blinded as they bounced off the sterile not-quite-white walls and utilitarian-beige floor tiles. Today was different. The lights behaved like spotlights on an Easter parade. Purple, pink, blue, and yellow pastels greeted Mike on his promenade. Balloons, streamers, even a larger-than-life stuffed white rabbit with an oversized pink-and-green polka dot ribbon around its neck sat in a chair by the elevators to greet visitors and staff. A large wicker basket with a handle and a matching ribbon sat on a table next to him. Him? Mike wasn't sure if the rabbit was male or female. The only rabbit he could remember was Peter Rabbit. Oh, there was also Br'er Rabbit and Roger Rabbit. All of the male persuasion. The only female rabbits he could think of were Playboy Bunnies.

Hoping no one would notice, Mike peeked in the basket. Yum. Hershey's miniatures. He liked the Mr. Goodbars with the nuts. Mike considered swiping a few and then reconsidered, remembering why he was there in the first place and how desperately he wanted to go home.

He didn't want to do anything that would prevent him from leaving Monday. He shoved his hands in his pockets and shuffled along.

Soon enough, he walked by a nurses' station where three ladies were busy doing whatever nurses do when they're not poking and prodding some poor patient. At least he thought they were nurses. Why don't they wear those white caps anymore? With so many women becoming doctors these days, how can we tell who's who?

And what's with men becoming nurses? Yikes. Everything's upside down. Who was that guy he'd met when he checked in the other morning? Oh yeah. Tommy Thompson. Who names their kid like that? Or maybe it was an acquired nickname. It would be like someone calling him Ritchie Ricci. Ridiculous.

A female voice interrupted his internal dialogue. All he wanted to do was walk around. No chitchat. "The best conversations I have are with me, myself, and I," was a Mike-ism friends and family knew all too well. Most agreed with him, especially Kassie who'd suggested on more than one occasion he should keep his thoughts to himself. Humph. She should talk.

"It's about time, Mr. Ricci."

"Time for what? Hope you don't mean an enema?" Mike laughed, as did the nurses.

Ah-ha. He knew he still had it, sensing a newfound giddyap in his step.

"You're out of your room and walking around. It took you long enough. You need some exercise."

Exercise? As Amelia's visit the day before flashed across his mind, Mike gave a quick salute, and kept moving. No way he'd engage in a contest he knew he'd never win. After all, he was on their home turf.

Further down the hallway, he recognized a young, rather buxom gal who'd delivered his breakfast the past two days pushing a cart full of lunches, he presumed. Tall, strawberry blond, a fine behind to go along with her chest. Now we're talkin'.

"Excuse me, Celia, is it?" He tried not to stare at the name badge sitting on top of her left boob. "Short for Cecilia?"

"Oh, yes, Mr. Ricci. Can I be of assistance to you?"

"Just wandering around looking for something to do on this fine holiday."

"Have you explored the library? It's kind of like a teeny-tiny resource oasis, nothing like our sprawling, splendiferous Boston Public Library certainly, but intellectually stimulating all the same."

"You mean it awakens the theatre of our mind?"

"Yes, very good, Mr. Ricci. Or the chapel? It's like a miniature replica of a European cathedral and provides all of our patients and families with a spiritually rewarding haven."

"Now I'm guessing you mean a sanctuary." Mike smiled suppressing a laugh.

Dreading the prospect of continuing this word salad with this sweet young thing while he was in pajamas, Mike asked for directions to both.

"You must descend one level of this magnificently constructed concrete edifice to discover the joys of the mind and the awakening of the soul. It might be good for you."

"May I ask? Are you in college?"

"Why, yes, Mr. Ricci. How did you guess? I'm studying American Literature. I will be a famous writer one day."

"That explains it. Happy Easter, Celia. Oh, and mind those adverbs." Mike gave her a thumbs up and retraced his steps back to the elevator.

Well, Celia was right. The library was the size of his walk-in closet. Did that mean the library was unusually small, or his closet unusually big? Probably both. It had a window, though, which made it more inviting, and more intellectually stimulating, than his closet. Except his closet housed his pot and porn collection. Also stimulating.

The Sunday *Boston Globe* was scattered on the floor. He wasn't the only one bored that day. Whoever it was could've at least put the paper back together again. He rifled through the pile, found the sports section, and plopped down in a somewhat cozy brown leather chair near the window. Not quite his Pleasure Chair, but it'd do.

Pictures of the Red Sox game and stories about the Celtics chasing their tails as usual reminded him how out-of-touch he'd been in the last few days. When he wasn't trying to figure out how to handle Kassie and her paranoia, or living the fantasy called Amelia, he was reading the Hemingway bio. *The Globe* was a welcome diversion.

His eyes fixed on the picture of Fenway. Unfortunately, this hospital mess screwed up Kassie's plans to hobnob with her boss and show off her vast baseball knowledge to the new hires and interns.

No other woman he knew understood baseball or football like Kassie. There was a time early in their marriage when they'd take in at least one Red Sox game during every home stand. If they could, they'd sit behind home plate, and she'd call balls and strikes. She'd stop short of calling the umps every f-ing word in the book. Pissed off everyone who sat around them. For such a small fry, she had one loud mouth. She claimed she inherited it from Uncle Dan. Mike believed it.

It'd been years since they'd been to a game together. Once he recuperated from whatever this was, and she'd gotten past her divorce hogwash, he'd look into getting tickets for them. Yankees–Red Sox for sure. That would make her happy. At least for four, maybe five, hours.

Time to move on. As he got up, he felt a twinge in his back. A familiar, yet unwelcome pain. He shrugged it off as the result of lying in a hospital bed for days. Or maybe it was just the aftermath of his romp with Amelia. He preferred to think it was the latter, not the former. With that, his dick took notice. *Hold that thought*, adjusting himself, hoping no one saw.

Next stop. The chapel. That shouldn't take long. Hunger pangs shot from his gut to his brain. Maybe he should've taken one of those candies.

Celia was right again. The chapel looked like a mini-cathedral, dark, almost medieval, with four electric candles glowing, and two stained glass windows, allowing a slight ray of sunlight to form two paths across the hardwood floor. Probably designed with a nod toward the strong Catholic influence of all the Irish and Italian families in Boston.

He was surprised, but relieved, the chapel was empty so he could sit wherever he wanted. There were six rows of two pews that could seat three across in each. Thirty-six souls, he calculated. Mike sat his soul in the front row on the left side, closest to the altar.

Growing up Italian meant Catholic schools, first communion, confirmation, spending every single day of Holy Week in church. He was old enough to remember the masses being said in Latin. Not anymore. Another tradition upside down. He kind of liked the Latin. Since Italian was the language spoken at home, he'd developed an ear for foreign languages early in life. Becoming an Italian professor was not too much of a stretch for him. The path of least resistance.

Mike never became a regular churchgoer. Except when he was fifteen and went to Camp Harvest Moon where he lost his virginity.

"It might be good for you," his mother said, insisting every teenage boy in Boston should get out of the city and into the hills and forests of New Hampshire for two weeks. "It'll make a man out of you," he recalled her saying. It sure did.

Camp Harvest Moon was not one of those specialty camps that focused on one thing, like dramatic arts, music, or boating. He'd tried and failed at baseball in high school, so a baseball camp was out of the question. His only option was a run-of-the-mill, all-boys outdoor camp that just happened to have a Girl Scout camp across the lake.

He and three of his newfound buddies salivated at the thought of scouting the girls. You'd have thought the camps would've organized a picnic, or some kind of get-to-know-you event. But no. The girls were off-limits. Except for church services.

On the second day of camp, the counselors rounded up as many boys as would fit in their small yellow bus they'd bought second-hand from a school, whose name you could see sticking out behind the cheap plastic sign tacked onto the bus with gray duct tape. Didn't matter if they were Catholic, Methodist, Jewish—the campers would go to church whether they liked it or not. Mike went willingly. Anything to get out of climbing trees or tying knots.

From that day forward, Mike believed in miracles. Lo-and-behold, the Girl Scouts had been rounded up as well, whether they liked it or not, and sat holier than thou in their pea-green shirts, shorts, and sashes in the pews on the right side of the church, praying to be saved. And Mike and his buddies were ready and willing to accommodate. The boys and the girls somehow convinced their counselors to let them sit together during the daily church services for the rest of the camps' sessions and to have a joint campfire on the last night hosted by Camp Harvest Moon.

It didn't take long. On the third day of church, Mike met a girl that made his heart stop, or at least made him hard. Gillian. You never forget your first. He'd picked her out of the twenty-five prospects on that first day. She sat across the aisle from him, two pews up. Her long platinum-blond hair was a stark contrast to her dull uniform, and when she turned to look at him, her smile could make flashlights obsolete. She probably sensed his stare, he'd thought. Never shy, Mike returned her smile to secure the deal.

That started a ten-day summer romance. They sat next to each other and not-so-accidentally brushed their hormonal fingers along each other's outer thighs. On the last day of church when they passed the sign of peace, Mike kissed her on the lips with no one noticing. That night, they snuck away from the campfire and found religion.

When he returned from camp, he told his mother he placed a high value on church attendance. That didn't last long. He fell into the holiday habit of going to church twice a year, Easter and Christmas. Nevertheless, Mike knew how to pray.

He looked around the chapel. A young couple, teenagers, had come in and sat in the last pew on the opposite side—murmuring, giggling. Probably not there to pray.

But since he was there and it was Easter, he might as well pray. As he knelt and bowed his head, Mike felt that twinge in his back again. Good time as any to have a talk with God. Automatically, he recited The Lord's Prayer to himself. His brain tripped over "Lead us not into temptation," but he kept going until the end.

"Deliver us from evil. Amen," he said aloud but not loudly.

Next up was an old Catholic favorite. Mike looked at the statue of the Virgin sitting on the altar not more than ten feet from him.

"Grant me strength, dear Mary, to convince Kassie to give up her cockamamie ideas and help me face whatever the good doctor says tomorrow." Not confident on either front, Mike continued to ask for divine intervention. "Hail Mary . . ."

As he recited the ending, "Now and at the hour of our death. Amen," he was dumbstruck by the last words of each prayer. Evil and death. *Aren't there any happy endings?*

He raised his head and looked smack dab at Celia's bosom.

"I thought I'd find you here. You have a visitor."

23

Reality Bites

"Can you find your way back, Mr. Ricci? I'm heading over to the cafeteria. It's lunchtime, ya know."

Mike assured Celia he was good. And he was. She hadn't said who the visitor was, nor did he ask. He assumed it was Kassie. She must've had a change of heart. It's Easter after all. Maybe they could resurrect their marriage. He was game.

"Happy Easter," Mike greeted a family on the way to the elevator. The fellow carried a huge basket of fruit so big it blocked his sight, almost bumping into Mike. A little boy hung on tight to a yellow teddy bear. "Excuse me," Mike said, scooting around them and patting the boy on the head.

Mike collided with a short elderly woman wearing a full-length tweed coat with a pink chrysanthemum in her lapel. He almost knocked her and her walker over as she tried to maneuver into the elevator while balancing an overstuffed green Whole Foods tote bag slung over her shoulder.

"Do you need help?" Mike said as he rescued the tote bag before it crashed to the floor. His nose hairs tickled. The smell of garlic almost made him sneeze.

She snickered, taking him up on his offer as she shoved the walker toward him. "Where you going in your jammies, sonny? Escaping?"

"No, ma'am. On my own Easter parade, I guess. Have a nice day now, ya hear?" Mike said as he got off the first stop.

The super-sized bunny still held court near the elevator but looked a little haggard as he'd slumped to one side. His bow was untied and someone had put a blue Red Sox cap over one ear.

"Having a hard day, dude?" Mike petted the stuffed animal and shifted his attention to the wicker basket. Oh, goodie! It wasn't empty, yet. Mike snuck one miniature Mr. Goodbar and then dove in for a second. Instead he pulled out dark chocolate. Damn it. Not his favorite. He'd take it for Kassie. A peace offering.

"Ya know that guy loitering near the elevator?" Mike said to a nurse as he passed her station. "He needs a little TLC. I think he's seen better days."

"Sounds like you're in better spirits, Mr. Ricci. Walk seems to have done you some good. You have a visitor," she said her eyes pointing down the hall.

"I know." Mike beamed and quickened his shuffle.

"Hey, buddy, how ya doin'?" Bill stood up as Mike entered his room. "Thought you might like company."

"Oh, Bill, it's you."

"That's a fine howdy doody."

"Sorry. Thanks for coming. I thought you were Kassie. Don't stand up." Mike motioned Bill and dragged a metal chair from the head of his bed nearer to Bill, holding onto it to maintain his balance.

"I met one of the pretty young things that's been taking care of you. Nice to have eye candy while you're here. Celia, right?"

"Uh, huh. Pretty. Young. Cockeyed optimist."

"What?"

"Never mind. You had to have been there."

Mike pulled the two candies out of his pocket, gave the dark chocolate to Bill, and unwrapped his. "So how have you been? Did your sister arrive?"

"Yes, she did. Friday. Question is, how are you? What's going on?"

"It's just my kidney thing again. Acting up. I had an incident Thursday night. Ended up here for observation and more tests. Home tomorrow I hope."

Bill asked if it was the same issue he'd had a year ago.

Mike said yes, but omitted the vomiting. Or the swollen feet. Or how scared he was.

"I'm glad you stopped by. With the holiday and your sister here, I thought maybe you'd call."

"Nancy's up to her elbows in the kitchen. She kicked me out. We're not eating until five-ish. And I wanted to see firsthand how you were."

"I'll live. Just don't know how long."

"None of us do." They laughed.

Mike grabbed one of the folders Kassie had brought him the day before. Résumés.

"Obviously I won't be in the office tomorrow. It's possible I'll take the whole week off. Would you mind?"

"Hell, no. Go for it. I've got the office covered. You're gonna need to rest from resting for three days."

"We have a new contractor who's supposed to start this week. I was going to meet him Wednesday. Could you do it?"

"Sure thing. We'll need him to start right away if you're—"

"Oh, I'll be back. Just need a little more time. I need him whether I'm in the office or not. Remember, I signed those two big projects with Southshore Hospital."

"Hope he's got a quick learning curve."

"Here's an extra copy of his paperwork. Call him. Apologize for me. Tell him how sorry I am. I couldn't help it. Wasn't my plan."

"Christopher Gaines. Humph. Sounds like a movie star. From California, eh? There you go. I rest my case. Wonder why he wants to work out here?"

"He comes highly recommended. The agency said he took a sabbatical from his job out there until the end of the summer. Perhaps he has family here, personal affairs to attend to."

"Maybe he's a Red Sox fan." Bill chuckled.

"I think I screwed up Friday's game for Kassie."

"How's that?"

Mike explained how she was supposed to attend the game with her company, in their box. Instead she was at the hospital with him.

"Hey, Bill, can I be honest with you?"

Bill got up and sat on Mike's bed.

"Sure, aren't you always? We've been friends forever. What do the kids say nowadays, BFF? Don't know where they got that from, sounds like biff or barf to me."

Mike gazed at the floor. "Kassie wants a divorce."

"What? What did you say?"

"She wants a divorce."

"No, shit. Why? When did you find this out?"

"Yesterday."

"Yesterday? She asked you for a divorce while you're here. In the hospital? Unbelievable. What a bitch. Sorry."

Mike rubbed his forehead. "Whatever. She was pretty stewed when she left here last night. She thinks I'm having an affair."

"That's no reason for a divorce. Take it from me. Wait. Are you having an affair? Tell me you are."

"Well, I did, but not with whom she thinks I did. Maybe I still am."

"Mike, you're not making any sense. Maybe you need to get back in bed. Should I get the nurse?"

Mike told him how Kassie found a letter from his old college sweetheart and jumped to the conclusion he was having an affair.

"How does an old love letter equate to an affair?"

"Not so old a letter. From last December. That's not all. Kassie doesn't know we've been corresponding for years. Phone, email, texts, letters."

"That's still not an affair. Infatuation maybe. Hot memories perhaps, but not an affair. No reason to get a divorce," Bill ranted, pacing the length of the bed, turning around and ranting some more. "You know all I've done! Jesus! Nancy and I aren't getting a divorce. Hope it's not contagious."

"The thing is Karen, that's her name, Karen. She and I are just good friends. We have a lot in common. History. How am I going to explain that to Kassie? And, as sure as the sun rises in the morning, I can't tell her about Amelia." Mike shook his head. "She'll definitely divorce me if she finds out about her."

"Whoa! Who's Amelia and why haven't you told me about her before now? You sly fox!"

"She's our maid's daughter."

"What? You're robbing the cradle?"

"No. I wouldn't do that. She's thirtysomething, I think. Maybe forty. Not sure. Doesn't matter."

Rubbing his hands together and through his hair, Mike gave Bill the highlights of the Amelia story up to and including the romp the day before.

"You got laid here? In the hospital? Man, you are my hero." Bill bowed and performed a petite flourish with his hand.

They agreed he shouldn't tell Kassie about Amelia ever, ever, ever. In their opinion, wives had a hard enough time accepting their husbands fooling around. Let alone with a younger woman. Let alone the maid's daughter.

"When I heard I had a visitor, I expected Kassie. I want to explain things before tomorrow. Before we meet with the doctor."

"What do you think he'll say?"

"I don't know. Hopefully good news, but I'm bracing for the worst. I may need your help at the office for longer than this week."

"Whatever I can do. I'm here for you, Mike." Bill proceeded to pace up and down Mike's room. His arms behind his back. Mike sensed Bill had something to say. He was right.

Bill sat on the edge of the bed facing Mike who had moved to the armchair Bill had occupied.

"I wasn't going to tell you this," Bill said. "Didn't think I'd have to. But under the circumstances."

"Oh, gee, that's never a good opening."

"Well, no, I guess not. But I think you should know. I saw Kassie the other day. Friday. After I picked my sister up at Logan, I took her to the Westin. That's where she's staying. With the boys home, we have no extra room. And she wants her privacy and bathroom. You know how women are."

"Get on with it, Bill. You saw Kassie Friday. Where?"

"After Maureen checked in, we were having a drink in the little bar there at the Westin. You know the one, right off the lobby. We went there once with those folks from St. Louis, remember?"

"Yes, Bill, I remember. You got shit-faced and tried to pick up the bartender. Go on."

"I did? Anyway, as I was taking a swig of my beer, I look out into the lobby and who do I see? Kassie. There she was strolling in with her head in the air pulling her roller bag and carrying a couple of other bags, too."

"You sure it was her."

"Absolutely. She looked good, man."

"She always does. So then what happened?"

"She stopped at the front desk. The fellow handed her something, and she headed straight for the elevators."

"What did he hand her?" Mike tried to process what he was hearing.

"Well, I wasn't close enough to see. But a key I'd guess. Their interaction was quick. It didn't look like she was checking in. She didn't give him anything like a credit card or anything. She grabbed something and walked off to the elevator."

"Did she see you?"

"No."

"When did you say this was?"

"Friday."

"But she didn't tell me she wanted a divorce until yesterday. She found Karen's letter at the office *yesterday*. Saturday. So why was she checking into the Westin on Friday? With suitcases?"

"Remember when I told you about Stella? Maybe Kassie has a Stella. Or in your case, an Amelia."

"She's not a lesbian. That I know for sure."

"No, Mike. Don't be a jerk. Get your head out of the sand. Maybe she's been fooling around, too, just like you."

Bill sat in the metal chair next to him and neither spoke. Mike's right knee quivered. His forehead dampened.

"I'm sorry. I shouldn't have gone there. When you told me about your lady friends, I just thought there's no need for you to feel guilty. What's good for the gander is good for the goose."

"I think you've got that backwards." Mike grinned and took a deep breath.

"I know, just wanted to make you laugh."

"Well, you did. And I'm fine. I'll work things out with Kassie somehow. And I'll take care of my kidneys and be back at work before you know it."

"If there's anything I can do—"

"What's in the box?"

"Oh here. I swung over to Mike's Pastry in the North End. Thought you'd like some cannolis. I got the miniatures if that's okay?"

"It's okay, Bill. It's all okay. Now get the hell out of here. And let's not forget Mr. Gaines."

Mike had no appetite. Either for his lunch that waited on the rolling tray or for Bill's gift. Why would Kassie be at the Westin? He replayed what she said her weekend plans were supposed to be before he'd gotten sick.

According to her, she was supposed to go to the Red Sox game, and then they were going to have dinner that night. She'd planned to fly down to Washington, D.C., to meet with her clients at Georgetown. Okay, so she would've had her bags packed for that trip.

Wait a minute. Teresa mentioned she had seen Kassie with her suitcase when she went to clean on Friday. She'd told Teresa she was going to stay with a friend. But she didn't say where. Maybe her friend was visiting for the weekend, and Kassie kept her company at the Westin.

But why do that? We have plenty of room at our house. Maybe Bill was right.

He reached for the cannolis.

24

Defense Team

After a quick room service breakfast and a shared shower, Chris grabbed the Red Sox hat he'd bought in Venice, and they headed off to see Kassie's parents and uncle. Their graves, that is.

"We should take my car," Kassie said. "And I'll drive." She'd always shuddered at the prospect of driving with a guy next to her in the passenger seat. In her experience, most men behaved badly—barking directions, criticizing her speed or lack thereof. Chris was different. If he drove, she'd navigate, and vice versa. And they'd keep their opinions to themselves.

"Why your car?"

"You'll see."

The backseat of the Mercedes was no longer black leather, but rather a rainbow blanket. Violet, yellow, pink, and white tulips and hyacinths filled the space and the air.

"I swung by the florist on my way back from the house. I just love flowers."

"No shit."

"Thought we'd take the scenic route to Newburyport," Kassie said as she made her way over to Route 1A. "You'll want to see Revere Beach and Marblehead Light. They have great antique stores in Marblehead. If they're open, maybe we could pick up something for the apartment. Something that's ours."

Chris didn't take her up on the suggestion. By the time they'd driven through Salem and Kassie waxed poetic about the witch trials, he was sneezing like one of the dwarfs.

"The flowers?"

"Allergies," he said between sneezes.

"Hope you're not allergic to cats."

"Nope. Had a cat myself growing up. Her name was Kassie."

She reached across and clawed his arm.

"Let's find you a drug store."

Stopping for a lobster lunch in Rockport was a lifesaver. It got Chris out of the car and away from the flowers, and they found a family-owned local drugstore that had a good selection of antihistamines and tissues. In the time it took for them to eat and admire the often-filmed red fishing shack, the two antihistamines Chris downed with a glass of beer had kicked in. Once back in the car, Kassie pointed the car straight toward Newburyport.

As they pulled into the sprawling cemetery which was naturally busy on Easter, Kassie felt a pang of guilt.

"I haven't been here in a while."

"How come?"

"I guess I was too busy planning my great escape from Mike. Worried my mother would talk me out of it."

"A voice from the grave? You're kidding, right?"

"Do you think it was a coincidence I found out just yesterday she was in cahoots with Mike to decorate his office while I was off canoodling with you in Venice? Fluke? I think not."

"Canoodling? Is that what you Yankees call it?"

"Shush. Ya know, Chris, they say there are no coincidences in life."

"I believe in coincidences."

"Good for you. I believe in signs. Just like Uncle Dan was watching out for me yesterday, my mother's watching now and trying to communicate."

"You honestly believe that? Or did the drive through Salem cast a spell on you?"

"You laugh. Just wait."

Locating her family's tombstones took no time at all. Years before, the O'Callaghan's had purchased several contiguous plots of land near a young oak tree, which had grown into a massive oak tree that as of that spring had not yet bloomed. Under the barren tree rested a statue the O'Callaghan men had commissioned of a man with a shit-eating grin on his face, sitting upright on a bench, wearing a Red Sox hat, holding a can of beer in one hand and a fishing pole in the other. Despite the objections by the O'Callaghan women for obvious reasons, the statue remained as a guidepost for the living and the dead.

"I thought your mother remarried after your father died. Why is she buried here?" Chris helped unload the flowerpots.

Kassie explained her mother insisted she be buried next to the love of her life. Kassie's father.

She arranged the plants around the several tombstones, having a friendly word or two with each grave's occupant until she got to her mother's. She looked toward Chris in silent appeal.

"I'm just gonna take a walk around. Won't be far. Give me a high sign when you're ready to go."

Kassie knelt down in front of Patricia O'Callaghan's headstone, pulling her jacket around her as a slight breeze swept by her and rustled through the grass.

"Hey, Mom. How ya doing? I'm okay. Hangin' in there. Finally told Mike I want a divorce. Imagine *that*. I heard you two had a little arrangement. How come you never told me? You thought I'd be angry? Well, you're right."

As she spoke to her mother, Kassie tidied up the ground around the tombstone littered with twigs, dead leaves, and even cigarette butts that had accumulated over the harsh New England coast winter.

"I wish you could tell me why you stood up for Mike time and time again when you knew how freakin' unhappy I was. Were there other secrets you kept from me? Well, here's one I kept from you. There's a man in my life. His name is Chris, and he's here with me now."

A sudden gust of wind knocked over the pot of tulips she'd placed next to the tombstone. "I gather you know that already."

Resigned to the fact she'd never understand the strange bond between her mother and Mike, Kassie stood, clapped her hands to shake off the dirt, and ended her visit with a silent prayer for her family, for herself, and for Chris.

She was about to return to the car, but stopped and gazed at the crystal blue sky. She prayed aloud for Mike, "Oh, please God, let him be well and leave the hospital tomorrow. It's time for us both to move on to happier lives before it's too late. . . and we end up here."

Kassie saw Chris walking back and tilted her head toward the car. As she made her way past other departed souls, she reached into her bag to get her car key.

"Ouch." Kassie sucked on the paper cut caused by the Fed Ex receipt from her mother's attorney. *Freaky.*

Back at the car, Chris wrapped his arms around Kassie, squeezed tight, and kissed her forehead. She gave Chris the package of antiseptic wipes and told him to remove the plant residue on his hands.

"Don't touch your eyes," she said as they settled in for the ride back.

"Yes, doc. Hey, that's an idea. How about we play doctor when we get back to the hotel? I'll let you examine me. All over."

Kassie reached over and massaged between his thighs. "Like that?"

"Uh, huh. But two hands on the wheel, young lady," he said, returning the gesture.

I was wrong. They're all the same.

Chris reclined his seat and pulled the brim of his hat over his eyes. By the time they'd reached I-95, he was out like a rock. All he needed was a can of beer and a fishing pole.

They had two hours to kill before meeting Annie for dinner in Arlington. It would be sort of a coming out party for them. The first time socializing with friends in public, especially in the Boston area. Under different circumstances, Kassie would have been nervous about whether Annie would approve of Chris. But with so much shit swirling around her and so much to tell Annie, she had no energy to spare.

"We need to clean up this mess and start packing," Chris suggested, looking around the suite. "We've gotta get out of here in the morning."

Clothes were draped on every chair, shoes were scattered and mismatched, and the number of electronic devices and their chargers made the room look like an FBI sting operation. Kassie had labeled all of her chargers with green tags so not only did she know which were hers, but she also knew which devices they belonged to.

"Aren't you excited, Kassie! We're moving into *our* apartment tomorrow."

"Right. You pack. I need to call Mike." Kassie walked into the bedroom and closed the door.

"Alrighty then. Have it your way."

Before calling Mike, Kassie sat on the bed gathering her thoughts. *If you fail to plan, you plan to fail* was a saying she'd once heard and adopted it as her personal mantra throughout much of her career. She was determined not to screw this up any more than it already was. And she would not let Mike take her down a path on the phone that would best be taken in person.

Here goes nothing.

"It's about time," she heard Mike say.

"How are you doing today? Better I hope."

"We need to talk. Are you on your way here?"

"No. Tomorrow. Do you know what time you'll be released?"

"Mid-morning."

"Then I'll be there nine-ish. We can talk then."

"What's this horse shit about a divorce, Kassie? You're acting crazy."

Don't take the bait. She didn't respond. She hoped the silence would speak for itself.

"Where have you been all day?" Mike changed the subject.

"Newburyport."

"What, you buying a plot for me?"

"Don't be an ass, Mike. You're not dying."

"You don't know that."

"Goodbye, Mike."

Kassie collapsed on the bed with one arm crossed over her eyes holding back the tears. She could hardly recognize the person she'd become. Once upon a time Bad Kassie was a joke. Lately, a bad joke. Was she as callous as she must've sounded to Mike? Is that why Chris defended him?

Remember the end game. Divorce and freedom. Mike could make her life miserable if she antagonized him. No way could she let that happen. She picked up her phone.

"Hi, Mike. Sorry I cut you off."

"What's up?"

"I'm not crazy. I want to know about the woman in New Mexico."

"I'll explain tomorrow. It was a long time ago."

"The envelope was postmarked last December. Four months is not that long ago. And the money. What about the money?"

"What money?"

"The fifty-two hundred dollars that's in your bureau."

"What the hell?"

Mike ended the call.

When Kassie returned to Chris, the living room no longer looked like a bomb hit it. He'd made great progress packing his things and had moved on to hers. Her shoes were aligned and the clothes she'd slung around the room were folded in a pile on the couch.

"Did you hear that?"

"What?" Chris whipped out his earphones.

"Mike asked me if I was buying a cemetery plot for him today. What a jackass."

"I'm sure he was kidding."

"There you go again. Please don't," she said. "If you keep defending him, I'll have to start calling you Little Mike."

25

What's in a Name?

The Easter dinner crowd with sugar-hyped kids and screaming babies had waned such that the neighborhood restaurant became recognizable again as a venue for mostly mature adults seeking a good meal and friendly conversation.

Annie was already seated when Kassie and Chris arrived.

"There she is," Kassie told the hostess as she matter-of-factly grabbed Chris's hand and hustled to meet her best friend. Double-cheek kisses all around as Kassie introduced Annie to Chris, Chris to Annie, and they took their seats at a round table in the middle of the room.

"Not very cozy, huh?" Annie said. "Sorry. I know you'd prefer a corner. It's the best I could get. Easter, ya know."

"We'll manage, I guess." Kassie shrugged. "I see you already got the wine list."

Though eager to bring Annie up to speed on the events of the weekend, she restrained herself. After they'd ordered a bottle of pinot grigio to accompany scallops for her and Annie, and a Guinness for

Chris who opted for steak tips, she let loose and hijacked the conversation and the evening. At least she tried.

"I'd like to make a toast. To friendships." Kassie lifted her wineglass to Annie. "To the future." She winked at Chris. "And to freedom." She patted herself on the chest.

"To friendships, the future, and freedom," they said, lifting their glasses in unison.

"And speaking of freedom." Kassie tapped the table. "I have news. I told Mike I wanted a divorce. Aren't you proud of me, Annie?"

"Wait a minute." Annie looked first at Chris, then Kassie. "Should I be? I thought Mike was in the hospital."

"He is," Chris said, shaking his head.

"You asked him for a divorce anyway? Kassie, come on. You're better than that. What did he say?"

"Not much. She didn't stick around to find out."

"Did you tell him why?" Annie looked at Kassie first, then Chris.

"She gave him fifty-two hundred reasons."

Kassie's head swung back and forth as though she were witnessing a tennis match.

"All right, you two. Quit ganging up on me." She raised both hands signaling she was giving up. "It's bad enough when you're attacking me one-on-one. Two-on-one is just not fair. And not right. I know what I'm doing."

Annie raised her eyebrows. Chris touched Kassie's shoulder, removing a blond hair off her black cashmere sweater.

"I'm not the cold-hearted bitch you're both making me out to be," she whispered. "Am I?"

"That depends. I'm just surprised you didn't wait until he was out of the hospital. What did Chris mean by fifty-two hundred reasons? You only need one. He's a cantankerous bully, a selfish bastard." Annie giggled. "I guess that's two. I could go on."

"Well, we always knew that," Kassie said. "But this weekend I discovered I didn't know him as well as I thought I did. He's also a lying bastard."

"Once a bastard, always a bastard, I always say. What's he lied about now?"

"I think he's got a woman on the side."

Annie about choked on her wine. "That's hard to believe, but if true, what a whoop that would be. Why do you think he's screwin' around?"

Kassie waited until the waiter opened another bottle of wine, and then she brought Annie up to speed.

"Do you think the money and the woman are connected?" Annie said. "Mike doesn't travel that much, right? Maybe he flies her here when you two are off doing your thing. Maybe he suspects—"

"No way he knows about Chris." Kassie shook her head and twirled her glass of wine.

"Don't be so sure. You should be ready for anything when you see him tomorrow," Chris said as excused himself to go to the restroom.

"He's gorgeous, Kassie. Those Bradley Cooper blue eyes. And he adores you."

"Not Daniel Craig?" Kassie split the remaining wine between them. "Let's change the subject."

"So, tell me, Chris what are your plans?" Annie asked when he returned.

"Simple, I guess. Move into the apartment in Charlestown tomorrow. I'm sure Kassie's told you about that." Chris signaled the waiter for the check.

"Yes, she did. Did you get a job?"

"What are you his mother?" Kassie chirped at Annie.

"That's okay. I've got a freelance gig lined up, I think. I have a final interview this week to secure it. I'm excited. It's a great opportunity for me."

"Where?" Annie asked.

"In Cambridge. Near here, I guess. Ricci and Associates. You know it?"

They couldn't get back to the hotel fast enough. Kassie was soaked. She'd sprayed her wine across the table and knocked over not just one but all three glasses of water. Annie and Chris were spared the waterworks. Kassie took the brunt of the deluge. Two waiters rushed to her rescue with cloth napkins and offered to move them to another table. No need. They were leaving anyway.

Kassie laughed so hard she was a human cliché. Her tears melted her black mascara, forming unflattering raccoon eyes. She headed straight for the bathroom, peeled off her wet clothes, and buried her face in a hot washcloth.

"Glad you think this is funny," Chris said. "That's my big opportunity going down the tubes. What am I supposed to do now? Bow out?"

"No way. He doesn't know about you and me. And doesn't have to know." Kassie waved the washcloth at him.

"He will after you move in with me tomorrow."

Kassie wrapped a robe around her and sat on the bed.

"Or have you changed your mind, Kassie *Ricci*." Chris crossed his arms and leaned against the bedroom door jamb.

"Oh God." She buried her head in her hands.

"Why didn't you tell me your real name?"

"O'Callaghan is my real name. I never took his. You never asked what my married name was. Even after this morning at the cemetery."

"My brain was in a fog this morning. It never occurred to me—"

"Why didn't you tell me you were going to work for Mike's company?"

"I didn't know. Obviously. Guess we should've talked about it."

"You guess? Why didn't we?"

"You were too busy practicing your divorce speech, and I was too busy closing things down in San Francisco. You knew I was working through an agency. Beyond that, it just never came up."

"My bad."

"Our bad."

Kassie approached Chris and laced her fingers in his belt loops. "What do we do now?" Chris shook his head.

She untied her robe.

The long night didn't provide Kassie with any answers as she tossed and turned. Chris slept as if he'd been drugged. Sex often knocked him out.

She checked the clock. It was just after five. She'd told Mike she'd be at the hospital around nine. Only four hours to figure this out with Chris, pack up the car, swing by the house, and drive to the hospital during rush hour only to confront Mike. Sheer madness.

Time for her to take control of whatever she could. No more slip-ups. Working backwards in her mind, she decided she needed to leave by eight, be in the shower by seven, wake Chris up by six. That meant she had less than an hour to come up with a plan that would allow Chris to work at Mike's company during the divorce. Impossible mission.

If she moved out of the house and in with Chris, Mike would find out who she was living with. And then he'd fire Chris, blackball him from jobs in the area, maybe even ruin his career forever. God, maybe he'd destroy her career, too, forcing them to flee the area to parts unknown. Horror show.

Why do life's problems always seem their worst in the dead of night?

She went to the bathroom and turned on the light. She sat on the john with one elbow on her knee and fist under her chin. Looking at herself in the mirror, she chuckled. The Thinker. How appropriate.

And that's what she was for the next half hour.

"Wake up, Chris." She rubbed his back with more oomph than she normally would. "We need to talk."

"Oh, God, no. Talk? About what?"

"I need to be out of here in two hours. We've got some figurin' to do."

"Did you say figurin' or fuckin'?" He rolled over and buried his face between her thighs.

"Stop it. We've got to make some decisions. Here. Now."

"Okay, boss." Chris sat up, propping two pillows behind him.

Ignoring his sparring, Kassie began, "Here's what we know to be true."

"Number one, you're here and moving into an apartment in Charlestown today. Number two, you have an opportunity to work at Mike's firm until September."

Chris nodded his agreement. "Go on."

"Number three, I've told Mike I want a divorce. Mike will fight me about the divorce, but I'll go through with it anyway."

"We don't know that for sure."

"Which? That he'll fight me or that I'll go through with it?"

"Both."

"I do know for sure. I know me. And I know him. Well, at least I thought I did until this weekend," she said more to herself than to Chris. "Number four, I was planning on moving in with you today."

"Planning?"

Kassie ignored his question. She was on a roll.

"So what are our alternatives? I think there are two," she said, answering her own question and pacing as Chris stretched out leaning on one arm, a sheet covering his naked body.

Kassie presented the options as though she were standing in

front of prospective clients making a sales presentation. Something she'd perfected.

"First, if I move in with you, you can't work for Mike, so you'd have to stop the process now and find another job."

"May be harder than you make it sound."

"Or, if I don't move in with you until the divorce, Mike wouldn't have to know about us at all. And you could still work for him, which would get us to September, anyway. What's that, about four months?" Kassie counted on her fingers like a kindergartener and then continued.

"Divorces take at least that much time, right?"

"I wouldn't know."

"If only the legal process of getting married took more than an hour, maybe people would have second thoughts and not go through with it in the first place."

"That's pretty cynical, don't you think? And you're rambling. Cute, but rambling." Chris rolled on his back, putting a pillow over his head.

"I'm not cute. I'm totally focused. You should be, too. This is important. What time is it? I've got to get going soon. Are you listening?"

"Yes, ma'am." Chris got up and walked into the living room with a towel wrapped around his middle.

"I could either get a short-term apartment, or maybe live with Annie. She's got room. And we could still see each other like we've done for years, just not live together. We'd at least be in the same town. How does that sound?"

"Which? Not working for Mike and living together. Or working for Mike and sneaking around. Those are my choices?"

"I think so, unless you have anything better to offer."

"Sounds like you'd prefer we wait to move in together until after the divorce."

"Financially it would make sense. For you to be working. And it would mean our relationship wouldn't play a prominent and public role in the divorce."

"So, what you're saying is that it's not a question of *if* we're together, but a matter of *when*?"

Kassie nodded and bit her lip not thrilled with having to delay their plans and scared Chris would call an audible and take the next plane back to San Francisco.

Chris took a purple box with a silver ribbon out of the nightstand and handed it to her. He kissed her forehead. "Until then."

26

Shaken and Stirred

They danced . . . around each other. It seemed neither Kassie nor Mike wanted to pick up the conversation where it had left off the night before when he'd hung up on her. Instead they danced, that is, around the elephant, or more so, the elephants in the room as they clung to their talismans.

Mike twirled his gold wedding ring, which Kassie recognized as his go-to anxiety and avoidance technique. She'd seen this act before. And he hummed, no song in particular. That was new. He just hummed. Most likely to annoy her.

Kassie settled into a chair at the foot of Mike's hospital bed, staring at the floor, tapping her right foot and fiddling with her new gondola necklace. Something meaningful to hang onto. To give her strength. Keep her focused.

When Chris had handed her the purple box with a silver bow, she'd gasped. What the heck was this? She'd quickly assessed and was relieved that it was larger than a ring box, but she was a little disappointed that it wasn't a light blue Tiffany box. The best things came in those, she knew, as she'd bought Tiffany gifts for friends and family, clients and colleagues over the years, and their excitement on receiving her gifts was often more about the packaging than its contents. Branding at its finest. Marketing 101.

Kassie didn't know where the purple box with the silver bow had come from, and she didn't much care since it was from Chris, which made it extra, extra special. They had rarely exchanged gifts, tangible gifts anyway. It was one less thing Kassie would have had to explain away. One less cover up. "We have each other which is gift enough," she'd told Chris on more than one occasion that could've warranted a present exchange. He'd reluctantly agreed.

But that morning Chris broke their unwritten pact and surprised her with a lovely necklace, a gondola with five diamonds embedded. "One for each year we've been together." He'd beamed. "I hope you'll wear it and think of me. Especially if we're not living together for a while."

As he unclasped the Moissanite solitaire necklace she'd bought for herself on eBay and replaced it with the one he'd had made especially for her, Kassie reminded him it was just a matter of time. More than anything, they had to focus on the end game. Focus. Focus. Focus. That had to be their new mantra.

Kassie figured getting Mike released from the hospital and home was now the first step toward getting the divorce, the ultimate end game.

"I see you're packed," Kassie interrupted the standoff with Mike. She had never bought into the theory that whoever spoke first loses. Sometimes offense trumps defense.

"Ready to go as soon as the doctor signs me out." Mike handed her the folders she'd brought him from his office. "Do me a favor, put these in the bag for me?"

The top one was labeled *Résumés*. She turned her back to Mike and opened it. There it was, incontrovertible evidence, right on top with a big red star, Christopher Gaines. A note scribbled in the left column read *Bill, Interview Wed.*

Kassie closed her eyes and gulped. What a nightmare. As usual, Mike didn't notice a crack in her composure. Why would he? He was rarely in tune with her emotions.

"I'm assuming you'll drive me home."

"By all means. Why wouldn't I?"

"What you said the other night about divorce and—"

"Let's get you home, and then we'll figure out what's next. How does that sound?" Kassie fixed her eyes on his, not wanting him to think she'd changed her mind overnight. Would he think she had cooled down? Maybe she hadn't been clear enough.

"I still believe with all my heart," she said, placing her right fist between her breasts. "We both know it's time to move on. It's over, Mike. We've been at sixes and sevens far too long."

"Maybe you're right," Mike said almost to himself, looking out the window and away from her resolute eyes, and then added, "But if it's about that letter and money, it shouldn't be."

Here we go. If mentioning divorce was the first elephant in the room, here came the second and third. Were there even more hiding in plain sight?

"Since you brought it up, why don't you tell me about the letter and the money. I want to hear all about it." Kassie repositioned herself in the chair. Might as well get comfortable. It was going to be a whopper.

It took Mike only a few minutes to tell Kassie a story she could hardly believe she was hearing. In fact, she hardly heard it.

According to Mike, the KR in the note in the envelope she'd found in his office stood for Karen Ricci. But that wasn't her real last name. It was a joke between them ever since she was his college sweetheart. Well, one of his sweethearts. The only one he'd gotten pregnant, thank God. That is, as far as he knew. He hadn't married her though he wanted to.

Her parents had made sure that didn't happen. They'd whisked her away from college and from him much to the lovebird's dismay. During the courtship, Karen had fantasized if they'd gotten married, she would've been able to take his last name. Anything to spite her parents whom she'd had a love/hate relationship with throughout her teenage years. The name thing was just a game they'd played.

"A game? A game that lasted how many years, Mike?" Kassie demanded. "Is she the girl on your lap in the picture on your credenza?"

"Oh, you saw that."

"Are you having an affair?"

"With Karen? No way. That was over a long time ago. Before I met you."

"Then why . . ." Kassie suddenly grasped the source of the intense, rumbling pain in her stomach and the throbbing in her right temple. "Wait, you got her pregnant. You got her PREGNANT?" Kassie yelled.

"I did," Mike said almost in a whisper. "Shush, Kassie, remember where you are."

"You've got to be kidding. I will not shush. Tell me there was no baby. She lost it or had an abortion. Please tell me there was no baby, Mike." She pleaded.

"I can't tell you that. I wanted her to have an abortion, but she didn't. She, and her parents, gave the baby up for adoption. She told me it was a boy. I never saw him. Neither did she."

Kassie wanted to run out of the hospital room, down the corridor, the stairs, outside, and never return. But she stayed, just like she'd stayed in the marriage. And instead, she opted for the bathroom. First things first. She had to pee real bad, and she had to think. As she washed her hands, she peered into the mirror and saw shock looking back at her. How could she process what Mike had just told her with her heart pounding through her chest? *Move over, Mike, I'm the one having a heart attack.*

She splashed cold water on her face, not caring if her makeup melted. *Pull it together. Focus.* Drawing on lessons she learned ten years ago while on an Outward Bound adventure with her team, she sized up the situation. First, Mike was, or still is, somebody's father. Second, there's a boy, no he must be a grown man by now, out in the world somewhere who's Mike's son. A man who doesn't know who his father is. Lastly, he's a frigging liar. About Karen. A child. The money.

When Kassie came out of the bathroom, Mike was sitting on the edge of the bed as though he was about to get up.

"Stay right where you are, Mike. We're not done yet. You still haven't explained why this Karen wrote you back in December. What was she thanking you for? And why do you have a shitload of cash locked in a box in your bureau?"

"Come sit next to me, and I'll tell you."

"No. I'm just fine here." She returned to her chair at the foot of the bed. A safe, sturdy place. At least if she fainted, she wouldn't have far to fall.

Mike explained that around the time he and Kassie had gotten married, Karen had married Barry Copperman, a nice Jewish boy, much to her parents' liking. Nevertheless, he and Karen stayed in touch. Once a year, around Thanksgiving they'd talk on the phone just for old time's sake. Then with the internet and email, they began communicating often. After all, they were friends.

"Friends with benefits?"

"No, Kassie. Sometimes all we need is our friends, especially when bad things happen."

"I'm not friends with my college sweetheart."

"Wasn't I your one and only?"

"That's beside the point. Go on. The money?"

"Yes, the money. Well, Barry died about eight years ago. Suddenly. A freak skiing accident. Broke his neck. It was horrible. Karen was waiting for him at the bottom of the run. He never showed until ski patrol brought him down on a stretcher in a full body bag. She was devastated. You can understand that."

"What does that have to do with you?"

"Since his death was so sudden, they weren't prepared financially. Karen had a hard time making ends meet. She did all the right things. She sold their house and moved to a condo, she got rid of his car. When Barry was alive, she only worked part time. So she got a full-time job. It still wasn't enough."

"So you've been bankrolling her? Without my knowledge. Behind my back."

"Kind of, but you don't have to make it sound so illicit. So shady. It was my moral imperative."

"Oh, no. You, too? Why is everyone getting so moral on me?" Kassie mumbled shaking her head.

"What?"

She didn't repeat it.

"It was the right thing to do, Kassie. I deserted her once. I couldn't do it again. After all, she was the mother of my child."

"A child you gave up. Didn't want to have."

"I did, we did. Her parents didn't. We were young. I wasn't working yet. Full time anyway."

Mike's words cut deep. The realization she didn't know this man was a major wake up call. So was the fact that she was sitting in a hospital room waiting for the doctor to show up to release him. *Focus. This matters.*

"My husband, the philanthropist."

"Better than a philanderer," Mike said with a crooked smile.

"How much, Mike? How generous have you been with our money?"

"We've done well, Kassie. We could afford it, you know that."

"How much?"

"Just a thousand a month."

"For eight years. That's around a hundred grand, if my math's correct."

"I never thought about it like that."

A long pause.

"Do you think I should get out of these damn pajamas and into some street clothes?"

"I don't know, Mike. I don't know what to think anymore. You're not the person I thought you were," Kassie said, now standing arms crossed in front of him face-to-face.

"Nice necklace. New?"

27

Food for Thought

Neither Mike nor Kassie uttered a single word on the twenty-minute ride from Boston Clinic to their home. Even when Kassie rolled through two stop signs, Mike stayed silent.

Once inside their garage, Mike said, "Boy, I'm glad to be home." As he opened the door to the kitchen, Topher sashayed over and purred up against Mike's leg. He leaned over and gave him a quick tummy rub.

"Looks like he's glad, too." Kassie tossed his duffel bag in the laundry room just off the kitchen to handle later.

"What about you, Kassie? Are you glad?"

"Of course. I'm happy you're out of the hospital. You scared the shit out of me the other night."

"Where do we go from here?"

"One thing at a time, Mike. We'll talk later. Tonight. Why don't we start with a cup of coffee? How does that sound? Let's sit and look at the nutrition and diet plan Dr. Singleton gave you."

Kassie plugged in the Keurig and made Mike his flavor of choice,

Italian Roast, in his favorite extra-large white mug with a Nantucket logo stamped in black. Before adding milk, she took a sniff of the just expired half gallon that had sat idle in the refrigerator for four days.

"Can you have milk?"

"I don't think so. Black's okay."

She poured the milk down the drain. Even if it were still fresh, she'd have disposed of it on principle. Since childhood, Kassie refused to eat or drink whatever lived at the bottom of food containers, like milk cartons or cereal boxes. And the bottom of a bowl of cereal and milk with its dregs was a definite gag-trigger.

"Good, we don't have any milk that's fresh anyway. I'll need to run to the store soon. The cupboard's pretty bare."

"Maybe I could go with you."

She heard what he said, but his words rang hollow. Throughout their marriage, Mike had never shopped for groceries, with or without her. Even when she traveled for a week at a time, he wouldn't go to the store. He'd order takeout and whatever Kassie had stocked up on before she left. She knew his indulgences and made sure the pantry was chock full of pretzels, chocolate chip cookies, and ice cream. Beer was considered a staple she bought by the caseload. Last thing she needed if she was off somewhere with Chris was for Mike to call and complain about not having enough food in the house.

"We'll see how you're feeling when I'm ready to go. It might be a while."

No way she'd let him accompany her to the store. That would not happen. She had phone calls to make. To Chris. To her lawyer. In the previous twelve hours, her plans had become fucked up beyond all recognition.

"FUBAR," she said under her breath.

"What did you say?"

"Nothing," she said, bringing her attention back to the task at hand. "We need to figure out what you can eat, and I need to make a

list." Kassie fist bumped the air and grabbed a pre-printed pink notepad that read SHOP out of the small desk drawer. She had a notepad
for all contingencies—to-do, ideas, tasks, notes, memos. She'd even
had one printed, Topher. It was yellow, just like him.

She pulled a chair around from the end of the oak table so she
could sit next to Mike and admire the flowers blooming outside the
bay window. The sun that poured its rays across the kitchen in the
morning had already shifted to its afternoon position on the backside
of the house.

Mike with his Italian Roast and she with her English Breakfast
tea sat as they did in the car ride home. In silence. Not a sound except
for the tick-tock of the teapot clock on the wall, a five-year anniversary gift from her mother. While Kassie prepared their drinks, Mike
had placed a light-green folder with his name printed in bold, extra-
large black type in all caps on Kassie's place mat. They looked at it,
and then at one another.

Kassie breathed in searching for more than a pound of courage
and centered the folder between them. "We have to do this, you know.
It's critical. We'll go through it together."

Mike opened the folder. Again his name, along with the words
"Stage Four Chronic Kidney Disease," stared back at him imprinted
in smaller letters than on the folder. But to Kassie those five words
appeared immense, grotesquely ominous as though they were plas-
tered on a billboard with flashing yellow lights: *Game changer. Your
future is at risk. Proceed with caution.*

There were several documents in the folder. The first contained
the diagnosis with all the supporting test results and definitions.
They'd heard it all earlier in real time from Dr. Singleton. No need
to review it then. There would be plenty of time for that. Hopefully.
She was certain Mike would examine it line by line and Google every
word he didn't know. After he did it once, he'd do it again. She'd do
the same thing when he was otherwise occupied.

Next was the script, the doctor called it, ordering follow-up blood tests to be done in three months.

"That's May, June, July. July," Kassie said, using her fingers to count the months. She took the wall calendar down with a picture of The David accompanying the month of April, flipping it to July. "How about the middle of July? A week after the fourth. That should be about right."

"I'll need to check my office calendar. Isn't the annual company picnic around that time?"

Kassie put her elbow on the table, her fist to her mouth, and gnawed her thumbnail. She stared out the window at the green bush that would blossom into pink azaleas in a week or two.

"I said, I'll need to check my calendar. Kassie, did you hear me?"

"Yes, company picnic. How many should we plan for?"

"What are you talking about? It's too soon to think about that. Go ahead, put the tests on the calendar." Mike jabbed the eleventh square on the calendar one, two, three times. "We can always change it if we have to."

"I think we had about forty people last year, with spouses, significant others, and children. Maybe more this year with interns and freelancers?"

"Yes. Maybe. Who cares? Are you trying to distract me from *this*?" Mike asked, upending the folder, its contents tumbling to the floor. "If so, it ain't working." He stormed out of the room.

Mike's abrupt exit did not faze Kassie. She'd seen him in denial before, most often when she'd try to get him to talk about the downward trajectory of their marriage. He'd appear to be engaged in a meaningful conversation, but as soon as it got a little too hot for him, he'd change the subject, or more often than not, he'd go watch television or smoke a cigarette.

Distract wasn't quite the word Kassie would use to describe her line of questioning about the company picnic. Probe was more like it.

She wanted to see if he'd react. Was hiring Chris on his mind at all? Apparently not. Why would it be? He was just a new guy from San Francisco. A talent that would fill a need. Not the man who fulfilled her needs. She touched the necklace.

Focus. Focus. She picked up the papers and re-ordered them as Mike returned.

"Sorry, Mike. I can only imagine how difficult this is. Let's keep going. Here's the referral to the nutritionist."

He looked at it, shaking his head. "Humph. Not just any nutritionist. A renal one."

"Dr. Singleton explained that you must be on a strict diet designed especially for you. To watch for diabetes and control your blood pressure. It's a good thing there are folks who specialize in this. Don't you think?"

"I guess. But shouldn't this suffice?" Mike held up the last group of pages that said, Nutrition. Its sub-head read, Important information to minimize CKD symptoms.

Four days ago, CKD was a meaningless acronym to Kassie. Now she knew what it meant—chronic kidney disease. The operative word was chronic. And now that he'd progressed into Stage Four, it wasn't going away anytime soon. Not in the near future at any rate.

Kassie pulled out the staple in the corner of the document, chipping her nail polish. She spread four sheets of paper out on the table so they could share the experience. No way was she going to take full responsibility for his diet. Mike would have to embrace this new way of life with or without her, or he could face dialysis or a kidney transplant according to the doctor. She was determined to do whatever she could to prevent that from happening or at least delay it as long as possible. But Mike needed to be all in on this as well.

"Look at this," Kassie griped. "It always frosts my ass. They always tell you what not to eat. Look, limit cheese, nuts, ice cream, milk, yogurt, tomatoes, bananas, chocolate."

"Oops. I guess I ate my last Mr. Goodbar yesterday."

"I wish they'd tell us what you could eat. It would make my life so much easier."

"Your life?"

"Oh, here we go. You'll need to get enough protein. But not too much. They want you to balance between lower protein foods and higher ones. Red meat, poultry, fish and eggs in moderation and for balance—bread, fruit, veggies, and pasta and rice. Three cheers for pasta and rice. But without the tomato sauce, I guess. Maybe a stir fry would work for tonight. Yes?"

Kassie moved into list-making mode. "Mike, read me the list of veggies they recommend. Look, here."

He gave in and recited the list. "Red bell peppers, cabbage, yuck. Don't think you're gonna feed me cabbage."

"I wouldn't dare. Go on."

"Cauliflower. Oh great, better get used to me farting a lot."

"More than you already do? I doubt it." They shared a brief chuckle, the first in a long while.

"Oh, garlic and onions. I'll be able to keep the vampires away."

Mike switched to the list of fruits. Berries, cherries, and red grapes. "Seems like the diet is heavy on antioxidants. Did you write down, red grapes, not just grapes? Oh, and make sure they're seedless."

"Mike, I know, I've been buying seedless grapes; what, forever?"

"Do you think I can have alcohol? I will not be able live on water and coffee alone. I'd rather die."

"Don't say that, Mike. Don't ever say that. Dying is not an alternative. Flip the page. What you can drink is on the other side."

"I think I'm hungry. All this talk about food."

Kassie surveyed the contents of the side-by-side stainless steel refrigerator. "How about an omelet? We've got eggs and vegetables. And toast. That should hold you until dinner. Go relax. It's after one. There should be a ballgame on. I'll call you when it's ready."

With Mike out of sight and earshot, Kassie turned on her phone. She had received six calls, but only four messages. One from the office, two from Nancy. Chris had called three times, but left only one message. The only one she listened to.

"Hey, Babe. Hope all is going well today. Unpacking and going to find the nearest grocery store. Got a call from a guy named, Bill, from Mike's office. He said Mike's taking the week off. But you probably know that already. Anyway, we had a great chat. Seems like a nice guy. Sounds like they're busy and could use my help. We're meeting—"

Wednesday, Kassie mouthed what she already knew and clicked off the phone. She closed her eyes, shook her head. This can't be happening. She shifted her focus to feeding Mike.

"This is good. Real good," Mike muttered between bites. "I can't remember the last time we had lunch together here at home, on a weekday no less."

"What are your plans for the week? Are you going into the office tomorrow?" Kassie played ignorant.

"I haven't taken any time off yet this year. I think I'll take the week off. Bill's in town. He told me yesterday he'd cover with the team and clients."

"You talked to Bill yesterday?"

"He came to see me. How about that? On Easter. With his sister visiting no less. Gather Nancy was whipping up quite a spread. The house was full with the kids home for the long weekend. He said his sister had to stay at the Westin. Do you know what he did?"

"No, what did he do?" Kassie said, picking up the empty plates and depositing them in the sink so her back was to Mike. She closed her eyes.

"He brought me cannolis from Mike's Pastry. Don't worry. I didn't eat them."

"I'm not worried about your eating a cannoli." She put one her hand over the necklace and held onto the side of the sink with the other. She needed to listen to Nancy's messages soon. What did Bill know? Had he seen her at the Westin? Was Mike playing her? Impossible. If he knew or suspected something, he'd confront her. Wouldn't he?

"I gave them to the nurses on the evening shift. They were thrilled. I guess I showed them I wasn't such a sonofabitch after all."

It was late afternoon before Kassie could manage to escape the house. Mike had retired to his chair again, and over the cracks of the bat in the background, his snoring reverberated all the way up the stairs into the master bedroom. He'd conked out. If he were even half as exhausted as she was, she couldn't blame him for taking a nap. But she had to get a move on. She had places to go, calls to make, adding Nancy to the list. First she had to unpack the suitcases she'd dropped off at the house earlier that morning before Mike caught sight of them.

On her way out the door to do her errands, she checked on Mike still snoring to beat the band.

"Hey, Mike," she whispered, touching his arm, not wanting to startle him.

"What?" His body jumped as he opened one eye and then the other. Kassie looked down into the beautiful eyes of a man whose life had just been turned upside down, not by her, but by his own doing. Could he have mitigated the progression of this disease if he had just been honest with her about his diagnosis years before? But then she had to accept there was much Mike had hidden from her over the years. Much more than what she held back from him, she rationalized.

"I'll be back. Going to Stop & Shop, CVS, and the cleaners."

He released the chair's footrest and started to get up. She placed her hand on his arm again, but this time more firmly, to stop him.

"No, you stay here and rest. We'll talk tonight."

She grabbed her purse, dry cleaning, her list, and her phone. She threw everything in the car and got the hell out of there as fast as she could.

Kassie pulled into the busy shopping center and parked in an area along the far corner of the lot where few shoppers parked. She didn't mind the walk and from there she could make the calls on her list without the distraction of shoppers, carts, and cars coming and going.

She'd decided she'd go into the office on Tuesday, so she texted her assistant that news. Staying home with Mike all week was not an option. She'd itch and bitch. It wouldn't be pretty.

Her first call was to her lawyer. She had to stop her from serving Mike divorce papers the next day. No answer. She left a message: "Hey, it's Kassie O'Callaghan. Don't do it tomorrow. I'll explain later. Gotta go."

She knew Chris was waiting to hear from her. Was it only seven or eight hours since they'd left each other in the hotel parking lot? It seemed like a lifetime. It was a lifetime, their lifetime, and the pit in her stomach made her feel that their future was on the verge of destruction. Somehow she'd have to save it, if she could.

Her phone rang. It was Nancy trying to reach her for the third time. Charming? Or alarming?

28

Cleaning Crewed

"Now we're even."

"We're what?" Kassie felt as if Nancy had reached through the cybersphere and punched her in the gut.

"Remember when I was having trouble with Bill and you helped me get him back, I said I owed you one? Well, now we're even," Nancy said with what Kassie interpreted as a not-so-nice smugness in her voice.

"I guess." Kassie ended the call. She'd heard the words that came out of Nancy's mouth, but her mind blanked and stomach swirled at the same time. She opened the window on the passenger side a smidge to let fresh air dilute the lingering stench of antiseptic she attributed to Mike's occupancy in the car that morning.

"He knows," Kassie blared as soon as Chris answered her call without either of them saying hello.

"Who knows, and what does he know?"

Kassie blathered through her conversation with Nancy, first having to explain to Chris that Nancy was Bill's wife. "The Bill at the office. You know, the guy you'll meet Wednesday."

"Oh, that Bill."

"Nancy told me that Bill knows, and he broke the news to Mike, so Mike knows." Kassie sniffled, sucking up tears that converged with her runny nose. She rummaged through her purse for a tissue. On their way home from the hospital that morning, Mike had tossed the box she kept in the passenger seat onto the floor in the back.

"Wait a minute. Calm down. Tell me exactly."

Kassie opened the driver's side window about four inches so she could breathe in some fresher air, then she continued.

She said Nancy explained that Bill told her when he'd picked up his sister at the Westin on Friday, they stopped and had a drink at the bar, and while they were there, he saw Kassie walk into the lobby, go to the front desk, pick up something, and walk over to the elevator.

"Dragging my roller bag!"

"That's it?"

"There's more." She paused, squinting her eyes, distracted by background noise coming from his side of the conversation. All she could detect were murmurs, some high pitched, some low. *Birds? Must be birds.*

"When Bill visited Mike at the hospital yesterday, he brought him cannolis."

"Damnation. Sounds like we're in mighty big trouble, girl. Guilty by cannolis."

"Shut up. This is NOT funny. It's serious, Chris."

"You're right. Go on."

Was he mollycoddling her?

"That's not all Bill gave him. Nancy, oh, she's such a busy body, I think she enjoyed our little chat. She was just itching for me to tell her what I was doing there."

"Who cares what she thinks, Kassie. What else did she *say*?"

"She *said* Bill told her that Mike told him that on Saturday I asked for a divorce. That's a stupid saying. I didn't ask him for a divorce, I told him I wanted a divorce. I think that's what I said. Anyway, I don't need his permission." Her tears subsided, her nose still required wiping.

"Focus, KO, focus. What else did Bill give him?"

"A seed. He planted a seed in Mike's brain that I may be having an affair. It takes one to know one. Bill's had multiple affairs. He's always on the hunt. It wouldn't be a giant leap for Mike to connect Bill's idea with the divorce, since his best friend set that scenario in motion."

"Whoa! Down girl. You're the one taking the giant leap. What did Mike say? You saw him today, right? The doctor released him?"

"Oh my God, Chris, I've got so much to tell you. But I need to figure this out before I can go back home and face Mike."

"Where are you?"

She told him and switched gears to answer his questions. It wasn't what Mike said, but what he didn't say that tied Kassie up in knots. When he told her about Bill's visit, he omitted the part about Bill seeing Kassie in the hotel lobby. In other words, Mike didn't let on that he knew she was at the Westin. What game was he playing?

Kassie listened as Chris launched into a rehash of the situation from where he sat wherever that was. What was that tinkling she heard among the murmurs?

"Fact. All Bill knew was that you walked into the Westin with a suitcase *alone.*

"Fact. He didn't know whether you were staying there with someone or *alone.*

"Fact. He didn't know how long you stayed, or if you stayed overnight.

"Fact. Based on Nancy's recount, he didn't see us together, right?"

"Right."

"So if we assess just the facts, ma'am, I'd say Mike didn't ask you about it because he suspects there's no there-there. Or maybe he doesn't want to rock the boat any more than it already is. Maybe he's scared."

"Mike, scared? What a concept."

"Listen, Kassie, you're the world champ of cover-ups. If he asks what you were doing there, you'll think of something. You've done it before, you'll do it again. No thanks, I'm good."

"What? Who are you thanking? Where are you anyway?"

"Warren Tavern. Nice place. Have you been here?"

Many times, she told him, pouting at the thought of his having a good time without her. Even in its infancy, this new arrangement was not playing out the way she'd envisioned. Come to think of it, nothing was.

"Did Nancy ask you why you were at the hotel?" Chris turned the conversation back to the situation at hand, unaware of Kassie's long face.

"She asked me who the lucky guy was. I told her I didn't know what she was talking about. I'm sure she hoped I'd share some deep dark secret with her. Which it is, of course. But I wouldn't budge. Wild horses, and all. You know, if three people know a secret, it's not a secret anymore unless two of them are dead."

"Uh-oh. Would I be the one who would die in this scenario?"

"You're not dying, Chris. Mike is."

There she said it. It took all day, but the reality of Mike's diagnosis finally emerged from her lips. She'd never be able to get it back.

"What?"

"Not today or tomorrow, but some time . . ."

"Aren't we all?"

"But we don't know how. Now Mike knows his fate, though he could die of something other than chronic kidney disease."

"I'm confused. You knew about the kidney thing on Friday, but you didn't pronounce him dead then? Why now?"

"It's Stage Four, Chris. Not Stage Three like he thought, we thought. Heading for either dialysis or transplant. Most likely dialysis. No family around to give him a kidney." *Who would want to?* Bad Kassie wanted to say but swallowed the thought.

Chris questioned whether that diagnosis was really a death sentence. With modern medicine, don't people live longer today?

"Ten, twelve, fifteen years. Depends," she mumbled scratching her head.

"What are you saying? Depends on what?"

"His commitment to whatever treatment his doctor prescribes. Like a better diet and not smoking."

"Sounds reasonable."

"One thing I'm certain of. I'm one hundred percent committed to making sure Mike does whatever he needs to do, on his own, without me. I'm not staying married to a man who deserted a pregnant woman, gave the baby up for adoption, and then concealed it from me before and during our marriage."

"On second thought, make it a double."

Enough was enough. Kassie heard all she needed to realize this exchange was doomed if it continued with her sitting in a car and Chris in a bar. Kassie noticed the time. She'd already been away from the house for an hour and had done nothing but talk on the phone. And even with that, she'd accomplished nothing. Who knew if Mike was still knocked out in his chair or if he was up and about conspiring how he'd confront her about the Westin.

"Hey, I've gotta get groceries and get back." Kassie excused herself from the conversation. "Think you'll be at the apartment tomorrow afternoon?"

He said he'd arrange his day so he'd be there.

"Good. My meetings are done at noon. I can fill you in on everything then. We won't solve anything tonight."

"You sure you're okay? You sound like a ticking time bomb."

"Welcome to my world." Kassie shut off her phone, gathered

the dry cleaning, and retrieved three canvas grocery totes from the trunk.

Kassie strolled around Stop & Shop in a trance as though she were a Stepford Wife, stopping along each aisle selecting the usual weekly items.

What a freaky day. Why did organic bananas cost thirty cents more?

She stared at the grapes display. Green with seeds. Red with seeds. Finally, red seedless. *Did they really care if she sampled them? And why do they put three pounds in heavy plastic bags when I only want two pounds? What's with the holes?*

Next stop vegetables for the stir fry. Onions, peppers, zucchini, broccoli. *What else could he eat?* She searched her purse for the list she'd made, removing her wallet, phone, brush, lip gloss, notebook, Post-it notes, an expired Barnes & Noble coupon. Nothing. *Damn it.* It must've fallen out in the car when she hunted for a tissue. No way she was going out to the car to get it.

She closed her eyes and visualized herself sitting at the kitchen table making the list. What color ink? What was on the first page, the back page? *You can do this. You don't want Mike calling you useless again. Not today. Never again.*

Convinced she had succeeded without the list, she got in the checkout line, always busy in the evening. A woman with a navy-blue shirt bearing the store's logo suggested she move to the self-checkout line. It'd be faster. Though she hurried to get off the call with Chris, in all honesty, she wasn't in a rush to get home. Anyway, she preferred interfacing with a real live person rather than a scanner. Job security for them, friendly personal interaction for her, which she relished on Mike's cranky days.

Kassie didn't realize soon enough that she should've listened to the woman in the navy-blue shirt, who was after all only doing her job, and chosen the scanner aisle. While she waited and waited for two shoppers ahead of her to unload their overflowing baskets and pack their groceries in plastic bags, she bent over and pressed her head on the cold bar of the metal shopping cart, seeking relief from a day that started as a bad dream and evolved into a raging nightmare. Even talking to Chris didn't help. In fact, it may have had the opposite effect.

Lapsing into a habit she'd adopted from her tai chi practice, she stood on one leg for about a minute and then the other. Balance work like that not only strengthened leg muscles, but was supposed to instill calm and focus. She wasn't feeling the groove that evening, although it did help pass the idle time while her mind was on overdrive.

While Nancy's call set her off in a tizzy, she knew that was a minor part of her anxiety. Searching for the source of what was distressing her most, she relived the day starting at the hospital. As was her ilk, she sorted the problems into three buckets—Karen, Mike, Chris.

Karen was at the nexus of what was ailing Kassie. Her influence on Mike after all these years had to stem from the common bond of their son. Was that why Mike refused to adopt when she couldn't get pregnant? Why wasn't he honest with her? Did he think she couldn't empathize with what must've been a difficult decision for both of them?

What to do about Mike? She'd meant it when she told Chris she'd do everything she could to ensure Mike would get the medical care he needed so he could live without her. Yesterday, the chance their marriage could be saved was slim to none. Now, the chance was even less, if that was possible.

Who was Christopher Gaines anyway? Since he'd arrived on Friday she'd begun to question if she'd made a mistake having him come out there. Could she survive his constantly defending Mike, let alone his working for him? A worst-case scenario she could've never predicted no matter how clairvoyant she was.

Kassie felt pressure within her ears as her cheeks warmed and a bitter bile seeped into her throat. She clung to the cart handle as she vaguely heard the checkout clerk say, "Next?" She hadn't noticed the woman ahead of her had finished checking out. The conveyor belt moved grocery-less. She saw the clerk's lips moving, but it was as though she'd pushed a mute button. She lost it.

The red insulated canvas tote used for freezer items captured Kassie's lunch. The woman in the blue shirt and the checkout clerk caught her as she collapsed onto the scuffed yellow linoleum. A fellow with a bucket and a mop showed up out of nowhere.

So did a voice from above. "Oh my God, Kassie, are you all right?" Like the angel she was, Annie appeared, pushing her way to her side.

She sat helpless on the floor and let Annie take charge of the checkout process. About fifteen minutes later, after sitting near the service desk sipping a ginger ale, Annie wiped her face with a wet cloth. Kassie groaned at the haunting smell of antiseptic.

"How embarrassing was that?"

"It's okay. No one cares. They were thrilled you missed the tabloids and candy display."

"You're my hero, Annie."

"If you're looking for a hero, thank your red tote bag."

"Oh, no. My favorite." They laughed.

Annie asked what she thought caused her collapse. Was she sick? Something she ate?

"Three words. Mike, Chris, Karen."

"I can understand how Mike could make you heave. But not Chris. He's too yummy. Oops wrong word, sorry, Kassie. But who the hell is Karen?"

With the back of her hands, Kassie wiped her watery eyes still recovering from the ordeal. "Are we're done here? Did you get what you needed? Walk me out to my car and I'll fill you in."

What would normally take about three minutes to walk to Kassie's car took fifteen, though not nearly enough time. Kassie gave Annie the condensed version of the day. Every twenty paces, they'd stop, huddled together in the parking lot lanes among the white and silver SUVs and foreign sedans. Kassie threw her hands in the air. Annie covered her mouth with hers. Kassie rocked from side to side. Annie steadied her.

"Come stay with me," Annie said, as she finished loading Kassie's groceries and slammed the trunk. "You know you're always welcome."

"Funny isn't it? I have three places I could live, and none feel like home."

29

Match Point

As soon as Kassie walked out the door to go shopping, Mike whirled into action. He located the clicker that had slid between his butt and the chair's cushion and muted the television. But he waited until he'd heard the heavy steel garage door clang shut and the kitchen door rattle before he turned it off and flipped the lever of his Pleasure Chair forward.

Taking two stairs at a time, he made it to the bedroom without realizing he'd huffed and puffed his way there. He had money on his mind. Fifty-two hundred dollars to be exact. She better not have taken it.

What a fool he was to think she wouldn't have found the box. He'd kept her out of his bureau forever. But this was his fault. He'd gotten sick and, almost like he'd dropped breadcrumbs, had led her right to it. There wasn't anything he could've done to prevent her from finding it. He needed clothes at the hospital after all.

Except the box was locked. She couldn't get into it without the key. But he's the one who placed the key right into her palm when he told her to go to his office. How ingenious of her to notice two lockbox keys on his carabiner and then go hunting for the other one. Whoever said women aren't smart didn't know Kassie.

Still gasping for breath like a train trudging up a hill, Mike retrieved the box from his bureau and set it next to him on the bed.

Though he'd seen this movie before, Topher was as curious as any cat would be. He'd skulked up the stairs in Mike's wake, leapt onto the bed, rocked back and forth as it sloshed, and stuck his white button nose between Mike and the lock on the box.

"Move over Beethoven." Mike shooed him away.

Topher swatted Mike's arm and released his distinctive alley cat mewl as if to say, "That's not my name."

Mike tried to open the box, but the key wouldn't work. No problem. He knew the other one would.

"Ah-hah! That's how she figured out there was another box somewhere." Mike pursed his lips and smiled though he wasn't happy.

"She's not as smart as I thought after all." Mike shot a glance at Topher, who had curled up against Kassie's pillow, resting his head on his crossed paws. "Listen you, don't tell her I said that."

Mike closed his eyes and turned the key. He held his breath expecting it to be empty.

"Thank you, Lord." The money was still there.

Mike picked up the stack to count it when a green Post-it note with red tulips stuck on the bottom of the box caught his eye. He recognized Kassie's calling card and perfect penmanship, courtesy of St. Mary's elementary school. He read the message.

"What you do speaks so loudly that I cannot hear what you say. *Ralph Waldo Emerson*"

"What the fuck are you doing with $5,200? *Kassie O'Callaghan*"

He read the note again. He'd heard the first quote before. Echoes of her mother. She was always quoting somebody. How crafty of Kassie to involve her mother in her snooping. But it wouldn't work.

Her influence on them was limited, if negligible, given she was six feet under.

Patricia had taken to her grave the one secret that would destroy his marriage. Karen and the money, or failing to tell her about his kidneys, were mere transgressions. Hell, Karen and the kid happened before he'd met Kassie. They weren't even violations of their marriage vows. He was even confident she'd make allowances for Amelia, since she hadn't touched him in years. She'd probably be thrilled that he was getting it from somewhere. He certainly was.

But if Kassie learned about his vasectomy, it would be curtains for him. The only other person, besides the doctor, who knew his original sin was Patricia. And if he hadn't bumped into her in the elevator as he left the urologist's office carrying a pamphlet about care after a vasectomy, even she wouldn't have known. Fortunately, he'd been able to persuade her that it was in her daughter's best interest not to know. He'd sweet-talked her into believing that one day he'd be willing to adopt. It would all be good. He promised to keep Kassie happy.

Mike took the money, left the note in the box, locked it, and returned it to the drawer as if untouched. Next stop, a hot shower.

His last had been in the hospital the day before. A lot had gone down since then. Dr. Singleton's Stage Four diagnosis was not as great a surprise to him as it was to Kassie. He'd googled the symptoms and knew they were getting worse.

He could tell by the look on her face when Dr. Singleton gave them the news that she was shocked.

"This can't be," she'd kept repeating, shaking her head. She wrapped her arms around herself and walked in circles, as if she was trapped in one of Boston's rotaries, before Dr. Singleton convinced her to sit down.

"It was not supposed to happen this way. Please, tell me it isn't true." She seemed to beg the doctor to change his diagnosis.

The good doctor took great pains to assure them that it was too soon to decide whether dialysis or transplantation was the best alternative for Mike. His near-term treatment would include medication and nutrition. They'd monitor him and lay out plans for both courses of action so they'd be prepared when and if either became necessary.

"Mike is not going to die tomorrow, Kassie."

"You mean I don't have to call my priest or my lawyer?" Mike tried to make light of the situation.

He'd done his research and had resigned himself that dialysis would be his treatment of choice, if not necessity. Chances of his getting a kidney from the national donor list were slim to none, and he had no viable relatives who'd be able to give him a kidney. Even if he did, who'd be willing to donate one of their kidneys to him?

Kassie's reaction in the hospital and in the hours since his release disappointed Mike. He expected more moral support from her even if she was angry at him. All she wanted to talk about when they'd gotten home was food. He knew from how she'd handled her mother's illness there'd be a point she'd snap out of denial. Whenever that time arrived, he needed to be ready to handle whatever her frame of mind.

He wasn't totally an insensitive bastard. He'd concede that he laid some heavy shit on her that morning. Besides his CKD, Kassie had to reckon with his revelations about the baby, Karen, and how he'd been "bankrolling" her for eight years, to use Kassie's words.

"It's like I have my own trifecta. The mother, son, and holy money." He laughed as he washed his hair. "She'll get over it."

He wondered what upset Kassie more. Karen and the baby were from a by-gone era in his life, with no impact on their marriage. What's done was done. Most likely she was pissed about the money. It's not like he'd given away "their" money. For years, they'd compartmentalized their finances. There was his money, her money, and their money. What he'd given Karen wasn't child support or alimony, but it was a payoff all the same, even if Karen didn't see it that way. To tell the truth, it helped relieve the deep-seated guilt he'd carried for forty years.

"I should've been man enough to stand up to her parents. I deserted her and that child. Forgive me," Mike confessed to no one who mattered but the shower tiles and Topher who'd stretched out on the fluffy green area rug in the adjoining dressing room.

All this kidney stuff could be a good distraction for Kassie. He'd make sure she went with him to the nutritionist. He'd assign her the responsibility of planning and preparing his meals. Right up her alley. That'll take her mind off all this talk of divorce. He plotted as he toweled himself dry.

"Right, big guy?" Mike snapped the towel toward Topher. "No one's getting a divorce in this house if I have anything to do with it."

He checked his watch. Time to take control. He dressed, grabbed his keys, and drove to the office. It was after five. By the time he'd get there, everyone would be gone for the day. Job One was to make sure there was no more incriminating evidence around for inquiring minds to find and muck up the works.

The hot shower and drive to the office invigorated and transformed him. He felt pumped like Hulk Hogan, unchained from both the confines of the hospital and the house that was the source of the latest conflict with Kassie. He knew he'd made a grave mistake by leaving the money in his bureau in the first place.

Nevertheless, he rationalized the process of telling Kassie all about Karen lifted a heavy burden. No more crosses to bear in that regard. From that day forward with all of that secrecy off his back, he'd be able to concentrate on preserving his marriage and his life. In retrospect, Mike reckoned the events of the day weren't as tumultuous as they appeared, and even her escapade to the Westin wasn't worth obsessing about. He was convinced Kassie would see the error of her ways in due time.

And Mike was right. About one thing. Not one car was in the parking lot when he pulled into his reserved spot.

"When the cat's away, the mice will play," he sang.

When he opened the heavy oak front door, a smell of sweet success greeted him like he'd never noticed before. It wasn't an actual odor. It was what the upscale office furniture, the state-of-the-art electronics, the environmental lighting, all represented to him. And the employees, too. *Don't forget the employees.* He'd hand-picked them over the years and had created a firm of exceptionally talented loyalists. He loved them and his company that day more than ever.

Mike strutted around the first floor like a peacock, scanning the work stations for that day's output. He found a pad of yellow sticky notes on one of the desks and left his mark on several.

Great work. M. He wrote and stuck it to an Apple monitor.

Love what you've done here. Try it with a little more green. M. He suggested to a designer.

He stopped by the Xerox machine, took one piece of paper out of an opened pack, and turned on the light in Bill's office.

Hey, Bill. Couldn't stay away from the place. Just stopped by to pick up something. I was released today. Obviously. I'll fill you in on the details later in the week. Let me know about that Gaines guy. Hope he can start immediately. If by some chance he's considering other opportunities, make him an offer he can't refuse. I need him. Take care, M.

Mike re-read the note, crossed off *I* and replaced it to read, *We need him.* The grandfather clock in the main office area struck six o'clock.

Can't dillydally too long. He chastised himself and moseyed upstairs to his office.

Once there, he sprang into action, getting a file key out of the credenza. He unlocked a black file cabinet hidden inside a closet and slid open the bottom drawer. He pulled out two men's shoeboxes and set them on the coffee table between the leather couches his mother-in-law had picked out for him.

In the second to the bottom drawer, he retrieved an unlabeled, green Pendaflex folder, and dropped it on the desk next to the shoeboxes.

Retrieving his keys from his pocket, he removed the lockbox from the credenza, the one that had housed the note from Karen. He put that on the coffee table, too.

He put five thousand dollars in the lockbox, keeping two hundred for himself since he hadn't had a chance to go to the bank and who knew if he might need cash while he was "on vacation" the rest of the week.

It's my money after all.

He latched the box and locked it inside the credenza. He slid the keys off his carabiner and hid them in a secret compartment within a large raven totem his sister had brought him back from a trip to Alaska.

"Take care of my destiny, you ugly bastard."

Back on the couch, Mike flipped through the green file folder.

"Ah, there you are. Dr. Richard Peters. The dick doctor."

He took the two shoeboxes and the letter downstairs to the production room.

"Let the shredding begin."

Before leaving the office, he sat at his desk trying to figure out if he needed to bring any work home with him. The college photo caught his eye, seeing only Karen.

"I really loved you, ya know? Where would I be now if we had worked out?" He slid the photo into a drawer in the credenza in case Kassie showed up at the office unannounced. No need to aggravate her any more than she already was.

As he got up and turned to leave, he felt goosebumps crawl from his toes to his neck. He rubbed his left arm, trying to warm up. The picture of his mother-in-law stared back at him.

"You like quotes and proverbs so much? Here's an Italian one for ya. *E facile par paura al tore dalla finestra.* It is easy to threaten a bull from a window."

He contemplated turning her frame face down, but thought better.

"Don't fuck with me, Patricia O'Callaghan. There's nothing you can say to hurt me now."

30.

Patty Cake, Patty Cake, O'Callaghan

From the day she came into the world, Patricia O'Callaghan grasped the power of timing.

On a Tuesday in March 1940 during a pounding snowstorm in Boston that shut down all the major thoroughfares let alone the minor ones, Patricia Ryan arrived three weeks early, roaring into the world like the month she was born.

Growing up, she'd heard stories about her roots. Her parents, Louise and Dennis Ryan descended from hardcore and resilient Irish immigrants who had landed in America in the mid-1800s, dreaming of a better life, or at least having food on the table. To them, trudging through snow up to their whatchamacallits to flag down a brave truck driver who'd be willing to shepherd Louise in active labor to the hospital was no more than a minor inconvenience.

The onset of the war, however, was a different story. Dennis was drafted a month before Patricia's first birthday. A year later, he arrived at an allied ammunitions depot in the outskirts of London the day before it was destroyed by German warplanes. There were no survivors.

One Friday morning soon after her husband died, Louise gussied up in a new Kelly-green, knee-length, cotton shirtwaist dress with white ruffles around the V-neck collar, donned her favorite hat and gloves, and marched herself into the Gillette plant in South Boston. She'd heard, with so many boys going to war, the company was hiring women, *imagine that*, for the assembly line that produced razors for both military and civilian use. She started work there the following Monday, the only day she'd show up for work dressed as if she was going to early morning mass. After that, she wore her faded house dresses and with her first paycheck invested in a pair of sturdy black-and-white saddle shoes to replace her Sunday best.

A few years after the war ended, with her role as a single mother fortified and a demonstrated employment record, Louise landed a new job at a General Electric plant north of Boston, so they could flee the congestion of an ever-expanding Hub to the safety and tranquility of the suburbs.

Despite Patricia's protestations, her mother persisted. "Now, you listen to me, lassie, I will not let my only child frequent those sinful pinball parlors or loiter on Boston's street corners with lads who have only one thing on their mind. Don't you even think about it. It's time to move on. It'll be good, you'll see."

And it was a good move for her mother and for Patricia. They settled into a two-bedroom, third-floor walk-up convenient to schools, shopping, and the area's growing mass transit system. They thrived and were happy, even though Louise came home late each evening exhausted having worked twelve-hour shifts, while earning half of what the men did who'd returned from the war.

That inequality did not go unnoticed by Patricia.

After spending one summer vacation day working on the GE

assembly line when she was sixteen, Patricia made a life-changing announcement. "That was the worst day of my whole entire life! It was so hot, my armpits went on strike! Can't believe you put up with that. Not me! I am going to college."

"College? No one in our family been to college. Why should you be the first?"

"Because I have to do my own growing, no matter how tall my grandfather was."

"Who are you quoting now? Your friend, Emily Dickinson?" Her mother laughed.

"Nope. Abraham Lincoln. Don't change the subject, Mum. All I know is, you've done all you could for me. For that I'll be eternally grateful. But I want more than the likes of an assembly line. It's my time."

Since few of the major universities in the Boston area had opened their doors to women by the late 1950s, Patricia applied and was accepted to Simmons College, the esteemed women's school, earning a full ride. She studied one of the most popular majors of the times, Home Economics. Of course.

During the summer before her senior year at Simmons, she met the man of her dreams at Wonderland Ballroom in Revere. Matthew O'Callaghan, a young Boston cop, boogied his way into her heart and into her pants. Much to her mother's chagrin, they eloped a week after she graduated. Kassandra O'Callaghan arrived six months later.

To those looking in, the O'Callaghans lived a life in the clover. Matthew being the head of the household and sole provider and Patricia being the stereotypical stay-at-home mom. She never had to utilize the sheepskin she'd framed and hung in the hallway of the three-bedroom white cape with black shutters Matthew had bought as a gift for their first anniversary. They would have made *Leave It to Beaver* proud.

Ten years later he died.

Two years after Matthew passed, Patricia dusted off her dancing shoes and ventured back to the seductive drumbeat of Wonderland Ballroom, searching for the same magic she'd found with Matthew. This time a tall, handsome fellow with a cunning smile swept her off her feet and refused to take no for an answer when he got down on one knee just two months after they'd met. This time her mother would express no opinion of the marriage, because like Matthew, she was dead. Louise had lost her battle with pneumonia a year and a half before he'd died. And whereas Patricia and handsome dude number two got married hastily, this time it wasn't a romantic elopement, rather it was no more than an unceremonious ceremony by the local justice of the peace.

It didn't take long for the honeymoon to be over, because there wasn't one. And the new guy made no effort to create a new, loving home for them. Instead, he shuttled his belongings, which fit in the trunk of his '57 Chevy, into the love nest that once belonged to Matthew O'Callaghan.

Had Patricia given even a little bit more time for this relationship to bloom, she would've discovered what apparently his friends and family already knew. This guy was an unabashed alcoholic. A drunk. And not a happy drunk.

He was a drunk of the worst kind—nasty, mean, violently abusive. On more than one occasion, Patricia called the cops when he'd threaten bodily harm, only to be told there was nothing they could do until he actually harmed them in some way. And the times he did carry through on his threats, they carted him away in the paddy wagon. Patricia failed to file charges when he'd beg her forgiveness and vow to straighten himself out. Promises made, promises never kept.

When she couldn't take supporting this worthless excuse for a husband any longer, Patricia pleaded with Matthew's brother, Dan, to intervene on her and her daughter's behalf. Always there to help PattyCake, his nickname for her, Dan attempted to appeal to the guy's better angels and introduced him to AA. But as Dan expected, the good-for-nothing so-and-so attended one or two meetings and then chose instead to straddle a barstool day in and day out.

At about the time Dan was plotting the best way to throw him out on his keister, Patricia found the courage to file for divorce. She was devastated. Divorce meant she'd have the bizarre distinction of not only being the first member of her family to graduate from college, but also the first to get divorced. She was proud of the first accomplishment, ashamed of the second.

"I'm a complete failure." She buried her head in Dan's chest.

"Poppycock, PattyCake," he said, trying to get a laugh out of her.

"Easy for you to say. I failed in my taste in men, and I failed to keep together what God joined together. I put it asunder," she whimpered as her tears slowed.

"Now you're getting plain silly." He pushed her out to arm's length, looked her straight in the eye and said, "He didn't deserve you. He wasn't half the man Matthew was."

She agreed and didn't hesitate when the judge asked during the divorce hearing what last name she wanted, after all by now she had three.

"O'Callaghan, your honor," she said, thereby erasing any and all trace of her blundered second marriage.

From that time forward, Patricia focused on education and motherhood. She dedicated herself to teaching home economics at the junior high school, a position she took the September after Matthew's death. And she recommitted herself to the challenge of raising Kassie, who'd grown into a feisty teenager during the few years Patricia had been sidetracked keeping her second marriage together. No more Lindy contests for Patricia or Saturday night romps looking for possible suitors at Wonderland. All those good times were behind her. Though she'd learned a lesson the hard way, she believed the internal strength she'd built would serve her well later in life when she'd need it most.

For some, a diagnosis of a terminal illness could be as devastating as the illness itself. Some would adopt what Patricia called the "Oh, woe is me" attitude. Others, like Patricia, considered death a *fait accompli*. Like paying taxes, dying is life's only other certainty.

She was content to be alone in the pulmonologist's office when she learned her fate. If Kassie had been around, Patricia knew she'd have insisted on going to the appointment with her. But as luck would have it, Kassie was out of the country in Italy and, like her mother, alone.

When Patricia returned home that fateful day, to the same house Matthew had bought her decades before, the phone was ringing off the wall as if there was a fire somewhere.

"Where the hell have you been? I've been trying to reach you all morning. Why's your cellphone turned off?"

Patricia clutched the base of her throat. "Oh my God, Mike, what's happened? Is she all right?"

"Kassie? She's fine. I guess. Wouldn't know."

"That's a fine attitude. You're talking about my daughter and your wife. Remember that. Have a little respect."

"I do. But I'm not thinking about her right now. For heaven's sake, she just left yesterday. She's not been gone long enough to miss her."

"Well, I do. I miss her every day. Even when she's home. You should've gone with her, Mike. She wanted you to, you know. It would've been good for your marriage."

"Listen, Patricia. I didn't call to get a lecture. What's got into you anyway? I've got a job for you, if you're interested. Right up your alley. It'll keep you busy while Kassie's gallivanting through museums and churches. I promise, you won't miss her a bit."

And that's how redecorating Mike's office became an assignment Patricia wished she'd never accepted. He was right about one thing, though. It did distract her from worrying 24/7 about Kassie, but it also allowed her to focus on something other than her Stage Four lung cancer and the five-year prognosis she'd received from her doctor.

Mike was never her favorite person. She tolerated him, witnessing his true colors early as they planned the wedding. He was a selfish sonofabitch, first demanding a small wedding and then insisting they honeymoon in Italy rather than Ireland, which was one of Kassie's dreams since she was a little girl. Patricia bit her tongue and swallowed her opinions to keep the peace and not be dubbed an interfering mother-in-law.

She nearly broke her own promise, though, the day she emptied the contents of Mike's office credenza in anticipation of his new furniture being delivered. When she replaced the top of a shoebox that had toppled to the floor, she discovered it chock full of letters postmarked Elephant Butte, New Mexico. There must have been fifty letters in there, all unsealed.

Her ears grew so fiery that her eyes watered in an attempt to cool them down. She knew she'd jumped in her white Honda Civic, but she'd never remember the actual drive to Mike's house. However, she would recall pulling into the driveway and having to stop to let a woman pass she didn't recognize.

Patricia ignored the doorbell and pounded the front door.

"Did you forget something?" Mike greeted Patricia with a big smile that quickly turned upside down.

"Who was that?" she asked, tilting her head toward the direction of the dark-haired stranger.

"Cleaning lady. Why, what's up?"

"You tell me." Patricia shoved one of Karen's letters at Mike's chest, knocking him back a step, and pushed her way past him into the family room. "More secrets, Mike?"

"It's none of your business," Mike said, placing an issue of *Fortune* magazine over a DVD sleeve on the coffee table and then checking his fly. She didn't think he noticed she'd noticed. But she did.

"Kassie is my business. First the vasectomy, now a secret lover in New Mexico. I won't let you keep lying to her."

"Why not? You've been lying to her about her father's death forever."

"How do you know about Matthew?"

"I have my ways."

"You wouldn't dare, Mike. Have you no moral compass?"

"Sit down, Patricia, let's make a deal."

An hour later she gave in to her better self and agreed to leave Mike alone with his lies. After all, she'd learned from her favorite poet, Emily Dickinson, "Saying nothing . . . sometimes says the Most."

Her time would come.

31

Lie Detector

The orange sun setting to the west comforted Kassie as she pulled into her driveway after the embarrassing event at Stop & Shop. Mike's SUV was missing in action. She unloaded her trunk. As usual, Mike wasn't around to lend a hand. That day was no different.

Before putting the groceries away, she stripped, imagining the stench of vomit lingered on her clothes, brushed her teeth, and rinsed twice. It would take more than mouthwash to eradicate the bitter taste of the day. She tossed the toothbrush in the trash.

Mike showed up as she finished unpacking the groceries, leaving the stir-fry ingredients on the counter.

"Where d'you go?" Kassie asked.

"Just to the office. Dropped off those files you brought to the hospital. Bill needs them. You just get home? What took you so long?"

"Ran into Annie. We talked for a while. I brought her up to speed about you."

"What she say?"

"An uncle of hers has the same thing. He's on dialysis. Doing well," Kassie lied.

"She just said that to make you feel better."

"What are friends for?"

"When's dinner?"

Mike retreated to the family room, leaving Kassie alone to do what they both knew she did best. Take care of him. Once she chopped the vegetables and sliced the chicken, she put away the Cuisinart, and tackled Mike's laundry. She unzipped his duffel bag. His excuse for going to the office stunk as much as his clothes.

Kassie's hands trembled as if she'd been tasered, redefining the stir in stir-fry. Could her day get any worse? Either Mike didn't go to the office, or he lied about why he went there. And seeing the résumé folder on top of all the others when she opened his bag reinforced the implausibility of the Mike and Chris relationship. Sheer madness.

"Supper's ready," she shouted, clinging to a cabinet near the stove.

Despite her empty stomach, she wasn't hungry, and even if she were, there would be no way she could bring herself to share the dinner table with him that night.

"Aren't you gonna eat?"

"Nope."

"Thought we were gonna talk."

"Nope."

Kassie brewed a super-sized cup of green tea with lemon, opened a new box of chocolate almond biscotti, and disappeared to the sanctuary of her office. She gave Mike thirty minutes to eat in peace before she returned to the kitchen not empty-handed.

"You forgot these," she said, slamming the three folders on top of the magazine he'd been reading.

"What the—?" Mike jerked in his seat.

"Another lie, Mike? How many does that make today?"

Kassie didn't stick around for his answer. She marched up the stairs, the sounds of her cursing and footfalls in fierce competition. Storming into her walk-in closet, she pulled out one of her navy-blue pant suits and a long-sleeved white oxford shirt. Still cursing, she hauled them to the closet of the larger of the two spare bedrooms. She returned to select appropriate lingerie, earrings, and her "survival" ring, a one-carat, square garnet in a silver setting she'd bought a year after she met Chris. Similar to the new gondola necklace around her neck, she'd wear the ring when she needed an extra dose of courage, like during her mother's funeral or now as her marriage dissolved to dust.

Kassie threw her cosmetics, moisturizer, and a new purple toothbrush in an oval basket she'd found in her closet and retrieved one of her favorite knee-length cotton short-sleeved nightgowns from her bureau. Some people resorted to comfort food during times of stress. Kassie relied on tangibles to ease her tension. Last but not least, she grabbed the teddy bear and the afghan from the back of the chaise lounge.

Tears again filled her eyes as she balanced herself against the sink in the spare bedroom's bathroom. That would be the first night she wouldn't sleep in the same bed with Mike when they were under the same roof. Ever. In retrospect, no matter how much it shook her core, she conceded that she should've moved out of their bedroom a long time ago.

She rubbed her stomach. Hunger pains replaced the ache in her heart and reminded her of the incident at the grocery store. *Oh gross.* She ran her tongue around her teeth, praying no strange-tasting particles would make their presence known. But man could not live on tea and biscotti alone. Well, at least she couldn't. The thought of chicken stir-fry conjured up yet another queasy sensation. Toast could help.

As Kassie descended the stairs in more control of her stomach and her feet than before, she recognized the chummy banter of the NESN announcers emanating from the family room. Red Sox. Figures. Apparently Mike shrugged off the kitchen encounter as a Bad Kassie moment that would fizzle overnight, or he simply chose, as was his natural custom, avoidance over confrontation.

She picked up where she'd left off, moving Mike's laundry from the washer to the dryer and starting a new load more out of habit than generosity. Not surprisingly, when she refilled the Keurig reservoir at the kitchen sink, she saw he'd maintained his habit, too, of leaving his dishes in the sink for her to wash.

"How will he ever survive on his own? Do I care?" Kassie said to Topher who nuzzled his cold white nose against her leg begging for a treat.

With the baseball game providing Kassie a safety umbrella from the threat of a verbal attack from Mike, she plugged in her earphones, accessed a meditation app, and sought solace through her tea and cinnamon toast at the kitchen table.

About ten minutes later Mike interrupted her peace and quiet. "If you must know, I went to the office just to anchor myself to something positive in my life. The past few days have been hell."

Kassie unplugged, raised her shoulders erect but chose not to respond. Let him talk. Would he ask about the Westin?

"I waited until everyone was gone for the day. That way, I wouldn't have to explain why I was in the hospital or what's next."

She sipped her tea, tapping her fingers in sequence from pinky to index on the place mat.

"Their livelihood depends on me."

"Their livelihood? I depended on you, too, you know," Kassie muttered in a soft voice, clinging to her Starbucks mug as though it were liquid courage.

She let it go, stood, and walked toward him. "You let me down, big time, Michael." She glared up at him, her tone crescendoed as she said his name.

"Is it Michael now? Listen, Kassandra, I know you're upset. We can work things out. I'm sure of it."

"How can you be so sure? I'm not sure of anything. At every turn I discover a new lie, a new deceit. You've taken me for a fool. Our marriage was a fraud. We, you and me—" she wagged her finger at him, tapped her chest, threw her hands in the air "—we were a sham from the moment you left Missouri. You came back here under the guise of building a happy marriage. You knew how much I wanted a baby, and you had one all along hiding in the shadows." Sobs replaced her recent meditative state.

"Is that what this is all about? The baby?"

"Did it ever occur to you that you never had to give up that little baby boy? We could've brought him into our home. Given him every opportunity."

"That would've never happened. Karen already had him and given him up for adoption before I met you."

"There must've been something we could've done to find him and get him back. You're his biological father. You had rights."

"You're not thinking straight, Kassie, the events of today have messed with your mind. Go upstairs and lay down. You've clearly lost it." He turned away from her.

He might as well have slapped her across the face. His words triggered the return of her self-control as she wiped her tear-drenched face for the umpteenth time that day. Kassie snapped out of it. She was back.

"Don't patronize me, Michael. Look at me. I meant what I said Saturday. Your kidneys notwithstanding."

Before he could respond, she took his advice and hustled up the stairs to her new bedroom.

32

Child Support

Rise and shine for Kassie came an hour earlier than usual that Tuesday. She got up, showered, dressed, took care of Topher's needs, and backed down the driveway before Mike emerged from what was then his-and-his-alone bedroom.

Kassie thrived on routine, so going into the office that morning was a good thing, especially following the hellish weekend she'd just endured. Nevertheless, she found it hard to concentrate, let alone lead her 9 a.m. staff meeting. The final row the night before, when Mike discovered she'd chosen not to sleep in their bed with him, ended with a broken mirror and a sleepless night for her, and more than likely for Mike, as well.

In stark contrast, Kassie anticipated seeing Chris with the same heart-pumping and tingling she experienced over the last five years whenever she'd rendezvous with him. She knew they had serious issues to talk about, after all she'd only scratched the surface with him on the call the evening before, but her desire for him was always resolute and often distracting. From her perspective, she and Chris had aced her five-year relationship test with flying colors. Though they weren't married, she theorized her philosophy should still apply. She was the judge and jury after all.

As usual, her assistant had saved her butt. A five-topic agenda was already projected on the plasma screen mounted on the wall in the glass paneled conference room when Kassie walked into the meeting with a venti tea double-cupped with a brown corrugated sleeve in hand. Also compliments of her assistant.

She assumed her normal position in the middle of the long glass conference table and opened her light purple Moleskine notebook to a blank page. With her purple ballpoint pen, she scribbled the date and the words, "*duct tape*," and underlined it twice, reminding her to stifle Bad Kassie if needed. This subtle personal warning had saved her on more than one occasion from opening her mouth and inserting her foot.

Kassie's team of five account executives, three project managers, and her assistant were already seated, buzzing about her husband's ordeal and sharing tales about their personal experiences, both wholesome and gruesome, at Boston Clinic. After a respectful five minutes of you-know-what-happened-to-me stories, Kassie curtailed the conversation on the basis of too much information. She assured them Mike would survive to see another day, year, or even decades.

"Where should we begin?" she said.

Four hours later when she arrived at the apartment in Charlestown, she asked the same question.

"First things first," Chris said, "Come with me." And so she did.

"What's this?" Kassie propped two bed pillows behind her so she could sit upright. Unlike the little purple box Chris had given her the day before, the box Chris slid onto the bed was huge, white, with a large lilac-and-rose-pink bow on top.

"You're making a habit out of gift-giving. Didn't we agree not to do that?"

"All bets are off now that I'm in town. If you're not here 24/7, I want to shower you with love and affection—"

"You're not gonna start singing to me now?"

"If that'd make you happy."

Kassie jumped out of the bed and slid her naked body into the plush white robe with the Westin logo embroidered on it.

"Thank you, Chris. I just love it. Now when I come over, I'll have something comfy to climb into."

"And out of," he said as he lifted her and laid her on the bed, untying the robe, and burying his head in her chest.

"Later. We have to talk."

Chris put on a San Francisco Giants t-shirt and gym shorts, and they moved to the living room where Kassie reasoned she'd be able to keep Chris at arm's length, at least for thirty minutes. Who was she kidding? That was about as much time she could restrain herself from going for round two.

Kassie checked out the open floor plan of the apartment for the first time. The red-brick outer walls provided a sharp contrast to the whiteness of the place, especially the kitchen. Not bad for a short-term rental.

"Did you buy the plant, or was it a gift from the realtor?" Kassie touched the clay pot of the deep purple orchid that decorated a table in front of the big picture window overlooking Boston Harbor. Their place must be lovely at night. Their place? Was it their apartment, or was it Chris's? She wasn't sure how to refer to it yet. Give it time; everything will work out.

"What do you think?" Chris said.

Not wanting to know, Kassie curled up on the tan couch with large, fluffy throw pillows that was part and parcel of the furnished apartment. Her new robe covered her legs and private parts when she tucked it under her thighs. That was not the time to give Chris any incentive to make a move on her. Though she knew from experience, it didn't take much to turn him on.

"Take a seat," she said, patting the couch cushion, "You'll want to sit down for this."

"You trust me this close?"

"I trust you close, I trust you far away, I trust you any way, I trust you every day."

"Okay, Dr. Seuss." He settled in on the far end of the couch and massaged her feet. Kassie didn't object.

"What did I tell you yesterday? Maybe I'll start at the end of the day and then go back to the beginning."

"Whatever works." Chris crawled his hand up her leg exploring under the robe. She slapped it away, not giggling.

"I slept in the spare bedroom last night."

"Well, now, it's about time. That is a good start."

From there Kassie gave a blow-by-blow account of the day before, trying not to forget any critical detail. She told him that the KR in the note she'd found at Mike's office belonged to Karen Ricci, one of his college sweethearts, but that wasn't her real name. It was a game they played.

"I kind of like my maiden name." She tilted her head, her eyes studying the ceiling.

"I kind of got that message the other night." He lifted her foot and sucked on her pinky toe. She pulled her foot away, still not laughing.

Kassie explained that Karen had infuriated her parents by getting pregnant by Mike, a Catholic no less. If she hadn't mentioned it, Karen was Jewish; not that it mattered. Anyway, her parents intervened and separated them. In the end, Karen gave their baby boy up for adoption despite Mike's objection.

"So he's been paying child support all these years?"

"No, but that's a good guess. Kind of close, almost like paying alimony to someone you never married. Maybe I've invented a new concept."

"Don't get any ideas." Chris raised his eyebrows. "You thirsty?"

While polishing off a sixteen-ounce bottle of water in three gulps, Kassie recounted the sad story of Karen's husband's sudden death and how Mike had been helping to support her out of some kind of moral imperative.

"So she married at some point?" He sat on the couch again, putting his feet up on the coffee table.

"It was a win-win. To her parents' delight she married a Jewish fellow after all her shenanigans with Mike, and she got rid of her maiden name. She's Connor now. No, that's not right. Cooper, Cooperman. No, Copperman, I think."

Kassie buried her face in her hands. "I had a hard time grasping what Mike was telling me. I wanted to scream. I felt my insides would burst through my skin. But I was at the hospital, I had to control my hysteria or they'd check me into the psych ward. The words pregnancy, baby, money were blowing my mind."

Sunlight streaming through the window reflected tears welling from her eyes. "Did I ever tell you how much I wanted a child?"

"I think you mentioned it on more than one occasion. I'm so sorry that didn't happen for you, Kassie. But maybe just think, if it had, your whole life would've been different, and we would've never met."

Chris leaned toward her, lifted her chin, and kissed her salty lips.

Kassie nudged him backward. "I've got to pee. Don't move." Kassie excused herself needing to gather her thoughts and composure. Not having Chris in her life was unthinkable, unacceptable, a notion she would never entertain.

When she returned to the living room, Chris owned the couch having stretched his long legs its full length. She motioned him to move his legs so she could reclaim her rightful position at the other end of the couch.

"He noticed my necklace." Kassie touched the gondola.

"So?"

"So, nothing. Just sayin'. I'm not taking off something you've given me," Kassie said, making a pouty, yet flirty, face as if she was a teenager.

"What about this robe?" He reached for the belt.

"Incorrigible." She tightened it and shoved away his hand. "Let's see, where was I?"

Kassie took him through Dr. Singleton's news about the progression of Mike's CKD.

"Stage Four. That's rough. How did he take it?"

"How does Mike take anything? I think he's in denial, though it's hard to tell. He's mad as hell that he must make some life changes if he wants to delay the possibility of dialysis or transplant down the road."

"It'd be great if he could get a transplant, don't you think?"

"I know no one willing to give up a kidney, do you?"

"Maybe Karen. She gave up her baby," Chris said.

Kassie whacked him hard across his chest with one of the throw pillows. "That's some wise-assed thing to say. Now you're being just plain mean. You've been hanging out with me way too long, me thinks."

Chris picked up the pillow and slung it back at her. "So, you want to play?"

Half an hour later, Kassie and Chris spooned under the bed covers. He kissed her shoulders as she reached behind and rubbed his hip. He rolled her toward him and pulled her close.

"You didn't tell me why you're not sleeping with your husband anymore."

"Don't call him that. Anyhow, I was afraid I'd call him Chris."

"You lie."

"Not me, Mike. He lied again. After I puked at the grocery store."

"Excuse me. What?" Chris pushed her shoulders back ever so slightly.

Kassie filled him in on the gory details, including how Annie appeared out of nowhere, directed the face-and-life-saving operation, and invited her to stay with her if the situation became untenable at home.

"What are friends for?" Chris said. Kassie thought he sounded either disheartened or jealous.

"That's what I said. To Mike. Just before I discovered he lied about why he'd gone to the office while I was grocery shopping."

Chris sat up and slid her alongside him, wrapping the sheet around them both. She sensed a hint of green apples floating around them and was comforted by the warm and cozy influence his cologne had on her.

She told him about how she'd found the folders in Mike's duffel bag within minutes after he'd told her he'd brought them to the office for Bill.

"The one with your paperwork was on top. Creeped me out. When I confronted him, he gave me an excuse about needing to go to the office to feel better."

"That's probably true. Isn't it conceivable he's not in as much denial as you think he is, and he's afraid about his diagnosis and what it would mean for the future of his business?"

"You're doing it again. Defending him. Why?" She sat upright.

"It's a guy thing. Put yourself in his shoes. And, Kassie, he doesn't seem as bad as you make him sound."

"You've got to be kidding me. Where is this coming from?"

"Just listen a minute, Kassie, to what you've told me. First, he gave up a baby when he realized he wasn't ready to be a father. Then, he stayed in touch with the mother of that child and, whether out of guilt or just plain caring and kindness, he came to her aid when she needed it most. Finally, on the day he learns he's seriously ill, he goes and spends a few minutes at his office. The firm is his legacy, Kassie. You can't fault him for that, or for not telling you why he went there. He may not know himself. His business may not be the same as comfort food, but to a man, it's a pretty close equivalent."

"You're a better person than me." She rested her head on his shoulder, sorting through Chris's argument.

"Not really. I know you've tolerated his crap for years and the love you had for him has vanished, but there has to have been something good about Mike, and probably still is, or you wouldn't have fallen in love with him in the first place, let alone married him."

"You missed your calling. You'd make a good defense attorney. But I'm not buying it. Not for one cotton picking second." Kassie cut him off, slid out of the bed and into her robe. "You can defend him all you want, Chris, but my intuition tells me he's hiding something, and it's in his office, which is why he just up and went there without telling me earlier in the day he wanted to go there. In fact, he said he wanted to go to the grocery store with me. All this kumbaya about his dedication to his employees is bullshit. And all his lies? This has gone on way too long to paint him as Mr. Nice Guy."

Chris pulled on his shorts and shirt and followed her into the living room. "What? You think there's more money, letters, what? Maybe he's having an affair with the cleaning lady who comes by on Monday nights?" His eyes widened and his voice rumbled.

"Please calm down, Chris. I doubt that, but I can feel it, in my bones," she whispered. "There's something in his office he doesn't want me to find. And that's where you come in. I have an idea." She poked him in the shoulder, hard enough to make him take a step back.

"What? Wait a minute."

"Haven't you always wanted to be a spy? Aren't you writing a spy thriller? Consider it research."

Chris grabbed her by the arms and plunked her down in the paisley side chair that complemented the couch. "Sit right there," he commanded.

Kassie's jaw dropped. Even Bad Kassie was tongue-tied. She'd never seen Chris so upset. He'd never raised his voice to her. Visions of her mother and stepfather flashed through the crevices of her mind. Her eyes blinked rapidly; her pulse quickened.

"Don't even think about it, Kassie." Chris paced the length of the living and dining room area, ran his fingers through his hair, turned around and stood hovering over her. He bent down with his hands on the arms of the chair and looked her straight in the eye.

"On that I draw the line. I'll do many things for you, including waiting for you until you get your divorce, but spying on your husband is not one of them. Trust me, it would not end well for any of us."

"Sorry, Charlie. It was just an idea. Didn't really mean it." Her lower lip quivered as she tried to hold back another round of tears.

"My name's not Charlie. I'm sorry for yelling." He scooped her out of the chair and laid her on the couch.

Why is make-up sex so carnal and piping hot? They'd started on the couch, christened the rest of the apartment, including the living room floor, the kitchen counter, and ended up cooling down in the shower.

Standing behind her, Chris whispered, "What is this really all about, Kassie?"

"The baby, Chris. There was a baby. There is a boy, a man. Mike is a father. I'm not a mother. It isn't fair."

"I get that. Does he?"

"If he'd only told me when we were getting married, maybe we could've found the child. I would've adopted him in a heartbeat."

"Imagine it. Can't you see Bad Kassie as the wicked stepmother?"

"You're not funny." She turned and slapped his chest. "I'd have been a good mother. I'd have given him everything I had. Every part of me would've been his."

"How old do you figure that boy would be now?"

"Early forties, I'd guess."

33

Hot Mike

Mike made a mental note to oil the garage door hinges. Despite lying in bed at the opposite end of the house, the clinging and clanging of the garage door prevented Kassie from sneaking out of the house that morning, if that was her goal.

He looked for the clock that had occupied the nightstand for many years on what had been her side of the bed. It was missing. She must've taken it to the spare bedroom. The candle was gone, too. Good riddance. It smelled like crap. In fact, the only thing left on the table was the shell lamp. He was surprised she hadn't taken that too, except that was a symbol of good times they had on the Cape. Did she purposely leave it to remind him or to shun the memories?

He searched for his phone and groaned. It was too early to get out of bed when he had no place to go, no place to be, and no one cared one way or the other.

As he tossed and turned, punching the pillow to fluff it to the ideal shape, Mike wondered if he'd ever share the waterbed, or any bed, again with his wife. Analyzing the situation, he figured on the one hand, she'd come to her senses as she had every other time they'd argued. But on the other hand, he couldn't forget Kassie had said the day before that divorce was still on the table. Would his illness change her mind?

He got up to pee, grateful it was easier than it had been before he went to the hospital. The new meds must be working.

Ding dong. Ding dong. Mike rushed from the family room, opened the front door and there she was, in all her splendidness. Amelia.

"Come on in," he said, brushing her cheek with a light kiss once she was in the hallway out of the neighbors' prying eyes.

"I'm so glad you called, Mike. This must mean you're feeling better. I was so worried about you."

"There's nothing to worry about, and I have the day off." He winked. "And I'm home alone." His eyes pointed toward the stairs, and he followed close behind her. He could hardly wait.

"No pleasure chair today?" She teased. "How about the bathroom? We've got that one down pat."

Mike pulled her close and kissed her deep as if he was searching for something. He unbuttoned her clingy, black, silk shirt and, while one hand unzipped her pants, the other unclasped her push-up bra, proud that he hadn't lost his touch. She slipped out of her jeans, tossing them across the room onto the chaise lounge, jolting Topher out of one of the ten naps he'd enjoy that day. He made haste and fled the scene with his tail held high.

"Looks like you need a maid," Amelia said as she wriggled into the waterbed, trying to straighten out the sheets and comforter.

"Sorry, Kassie usually makes the bed." Mike cleared his throat as if something was stuck. "I was still in it when she left for work this morning."

Making the bed would be something he'd be forced to do as long as Kassie alienated him and slept down the hall.

"But you're right, I do need a maid. Time for you to grab my broomstick, young lady, and get to work."

While Amelia took a quick shower, Mike explored the linen closet in the hallway and found an oversized plush white towel and waited for her to open the shower door so he could swaddle her in it.

"Thank you, sir." She smiled and cocked her head to one side. "What's gotten into you? Catering to me here and under the covers."

Standing in front of the double sink, Mike unwrapped a tooth-brush for her. The towel around her provided no barrier to his wandering fingers or tongue. He felt a natural throb under his jockey shorts though he doubted he had the wherewithal for a repeat performance. He was satisfied that he'd been satisfied and that he could satisfy, one way or another.

"God, you smell good, like French toast." Turning her toward him and leaning her against the sink, he got down on his knees and flung the towel to the floor.

"I kind of like this side of you." Amelia moaned, running her fingers through his salt-and-pepper hair.

Mike stripped the bed and found clean sheets in the linen closet. What a concept, a treasure trove of household items in one central location. Were all husbands oblivious to this phenomenon, or just him? He couldn't remember the last time he'd been in that linen closet, or any linen closet.

As Mike humored himself with the prospects of his new discovery and confronted the almost impossible task of putting clean sheets on a rocking waterbed, Amelia dressed and freshened up, again, in the master bathroom.

"Something's missing," she shouted.

"What, you lose a tooth?"

"Where's her stuff? I'm assuming that was Kassie's shower gel, but where's her moisturizer?" Amelia stood in the doorway with her palms up, as Mike fought with the bottom sheet turning it in one direction and then the other.

"Don't laugh at me. Give me a hand with this. You've done this more times than me."

Amelia laughed. "So answer my question, Michael Stewart."

"You. Are. Not. Funny. Grab the corner of that sheet, and I'll fill you in."

After they made the bed, Mike led her down the hall and opened a door.

"This is where her stuff is. Some of it anyway. She slept here last night. She announced a few days ago, while I was in the hospital I might add, she wants a divorce."

"That bitch," Amelia blurted as they made their way downstairs to the kitchen. "Why? What have you ever done to her?"

"Want some coffee?" Mike asked as he tossed the sheets and Amelia's towel into the laundry room. He'd take care of that later, after he figured out how to use the new front-loading washer they'd bought the year before.

The Keurig was the one appliance Mike had mastered out of necessity. There was one in his office. He filled their mugs, sat across from Amelia, and confessed.

"Present company excluded, Kassie learned things about me this past weekend that upset her. In her eyes, I'm not the man she thought she'd married."

"Impossible," Amelia said.

"Oh, it's possible." Mike patted her hand.

He gave her his version of the college-sweetheart-unintended-baby story, placing his hand on his heart when he told her how devastated he was when they gave up his son. His chest inflated when he moved onto how generous he'd been to Karen after her husband died in a tragic accident on a ski slope. He was so young. She was so ill-prepared. What else could he have done but help her out?

"That's so sad. How could Kassie not see that?"

Not so coincidentally, he neglected to provide the circumstances under which Kassie had found out about his life before her or why she'd be willing to give up their long-tenured marriage.

Staring out the bay window, Mike ended by telling her the kidney problem that had sent him to the hospital was worse than he'd expected. So when they learned he might need dialysis or a transplant, Kassie flipped out.

Amelia oohed and cooed. "If she's that concerned about you as you say, she can't possibly want a divorce, can she?"

"You're a doll, Amelia, I think you may be biased." He reached across the table and tweaked her breast. "I think Kassie's focused more on the fact that I never told her that my kidneys were in trouble to begin with, than that they are. According to her, I'm a deceitful son-of-a-gun."

"She'll change her mind. She may be a bitch, but she's a bitch with a heart, right? She's always been kind to my mother. She wouldn't let you go through this health thingamajig on your own. Would she?"

"That's what I'm counting on. If I don't squeeze her, if I don't question her comings and goings, I'm hoping she'll come to her senses and stop all this divorce hullabaloo. I need her now." He looked at his wedding ring and rotated it back and forth.

"And I need to go."

Mike escorted her to the front door, stopping in the hallway where they'd started two hours earlier. He thanked her for coming, held her close, caressed her back, as if seeking her comfort and reassurance. She leaned up and kissed him with an emotion he didn't expect. He knew it wasn't love; he hoped it wasn't pity. Neither he nor

Amelia suggested another get together, but then again it wasn't their custom to do so.

As she walked to her car in the driveway, Amelia turned back and gave him a flirty wave and wide smile. She hadn't noticed the black sedan parked next to her or the man in the gray pinstripe suit who'd stepped out of it and was about to pass her. But Mike had.

He held the door open to greet the fellow.

"Michael Ricci?"

Five minutes later, Mike heard his phone ring. He shook his head in disbelief as he raced around the first floor, finding it in the family room.

"Hey, Bill."

"How you doin'?"

"I've been better. What's up?"

"Not sure what's going on, but I just got back to the office from a meeting and heard that some suit came in asking for you. I'm sorry about this, but they told him you were at home."

"I know. He just left. I've been served."

34

Up in Smoke

All seemed quiet on the home front when Kassie walked in the house Tuesday evening. *Cling-clang.* Her keys landed with a bang in the pewter bowl on the table in the entryway from the garage. Last thing she wanted to do was surprise Mike, as she had on more than one occasion, if he was porn watching in the family room.

The kitchen appeared sterile, lifeless, as the spring sun had shifted to the opposite side of the house. She flipped on the overhead light. Topher meandered in to greet her, mewing and swinging his tail in abandon. At least she could count on his unconditional love.

Something felt eerie, out of place. As her eyes adjusted to the light, she saw two mugs on the kitchen table. Did Mike have company? She picked up the empty cups and put them in the sink. She opened the trash bin. Sure enough. Two K-cups. One was Italian Roast, Mike's usual, the other was decaf hazelnut.

Still no sign of Mike. With Topher at her heels meowing to beat the band, she wandered around the first floor and slipped up the stairs. His bedroom was ajar, so she peeked inside. Nothing going on in there at the moment.

Back downstairs, she stood in the family room stretching, pulling her hands behind her head. *Where the hell is he?* His car was in the garage, so he had to be home. Or did he go somewhere with his coffee mate? Not likely. Mike preferred to drive.

She scanned the family room searching for some clue. Nothing. *Squeaaaak. Squeaaaak.* Ah. The back-porch swing.

Kassie opened the French doors and stepped into the not-so-fresh air. The acrid smell of skunk spray combined with a smoky haze billowing away from the porch onto the lawn gave Mike away.

"There you are. I've been looking all over the house."

"Really? That would surprise me more than a little, Kassandra Ricci. That is your legal name, isn't it? Rolls off your tongue easier than Kassandra O'Callaghan, wouldn't you say?"

Kassie waved her hand in front of her face as if she was shooing a fly and squinted her eyes trying to solve Mike's puzzling remark. Giving up, she changed the subject.

"Was someone here today?"

"Nobody that'd interest you. Then again, someone stopped by and left me a present. But then, you already knew that." Mike shook a legal-sized white envelope toward her.

Kassie grabbed the envelope and read the return address.

"Oh my God, Mike. No. This was not supposed to happen. Not today anyway. I called and left a message . . ."

Kassie realized her fatal error. She never followed up to make sure her lawyer got the message or asked her to confirm she'd received it. She shook her head in disgust. Careless and stupid. What was she thinking? Images of Dr. Singleton, Annie, and a cracked mirror flashed through her mind.

"Move over." She nudged Mike and sat next to him. "Anything left in that joint?"

They finished the first and agreed the occasion warranted another. As Mike ran upstairs to his closet to dip into his stash, Kassie grabbed worn-out jackets from the hall closet and an old University of Missouri black and gold blanket that had seen better days.

Mike handed the joint to Kassie for safekeeping while he wrapped the blanket around them, tucking it in around the edges.

"Cozy, isn't it?" he said. "Now tell me, lassie, what's this all about."

After she apologized up one side and down the other for catching him off guard, Kassie fessed up and admitted her original plan was to serve him divorce papers that day. But then Good Friday happened, and she had second thoughts about the timing. She'd called and left a message for her attorney Monday evening, but apparently she didn't get it.

"Tomorrow. I'll call her tomorrow and give her a piece of my mind."

"So, you'll stop the process, Kassie? Call it all off?"

She inhaled deeply. It'd been years since she smoked, she exhaled, coughed and said, "No, Mike, you and I know we were finished before Friday. Before I found your hidden boxes and learned about your love child. You've admitted it yourself. What I regret is the timing and its effect on you, not the cause behind it. The cat's out of the bag, horse out of the barn. Whatever cliché you want to ascribe. I'm going through with it."

"I was afraid of that."

They watched the bats flicker above the tree line and heard the crickets chirp the first sign of spring, as the swing rocked back and forth. They told remember-the-time stories and laughed so hard they wiped each other's tears, as the swing rocked back and forth. They expressed a shared sadness and accepted mutual responsibility for letting their marriage, once happy, spiral into a crevasse that neither believed could be rescued, as the swing rocked back and forth.

Mike rubbed her thigh. Kassie put her head on his shoulder.

"Where to now?"

"I'm starving." He jumped off his seat. "How about French toast?"

Kassie chose not to raise the issue of the mugs in the sink, and Mike seemed to ignore them as well when he loaded them in the dishwasher. She got out the ingredients for the French toast; he bumped into her as he opened the cabinets to discover an abundance of dishes, glassware, and pots and pans.

"I never realized we had so many intriguing kitchen things. Look at this glass bowl. It's amazing." He held it up to the light. A rainbow bounced off the wall. "Wow! That's cool."

"We bought it a long time ago at that quaint little shop on the Cape, in Dennisport, I think."

"Oh, yeah. Was that before or after we made love on the beach?"

"Which time?"

While Mike heated the griddle, Kassie whipped up the egg-and-milk mixture. He approached her from behind and held her hand as she stirred.

"Would you . . . um . . . get me the vanilla?" She swallowed hard.

"And where would I find that?" He pinched her rear as she directed him to the nearby spice cabinet.

Ten minutes later, as she carried dinner to the table, she paused, noticing Mike had positioned the chairs and placemats side-by-side.

"Hope you don't mind?"

"French toast was a great idea. How come?"

"I've been craving it all afternoon. Maybe it's the vanilla." Mike leaned into her space. "Say ah . . ." He fed her a piece off his plate.

"Don't know if it's on your diet, but we'll figure it out." Kassie tried to maintain boundaries.

"When's that appointment with the nutritionist? The anal one," Mike said.

"Renal, not anal." They laughed. "Thursday morning. Good

timing. We'll be able to plan your menu and shop before you go back to work Monday."

"You still going to come with me?"

"Yes, Mike. I'm divorcing you, not deserting you. I'll help you through this, however I can."

When they finished eating, as Kassie brought the dishes to the sink, Mike rinsed them and put them in the dishwasher. Bad Kassie was about to suggest he stack the plates in a different way, her way, when she corked her comments. She'd rearrange them in the morning.

"Well, this was some evening," she said, leaning against a cabinet next to the sink with a dish towel in her hand. "Now, I have to get ready for work. I'm gonna head upstairs, if you don't mind."

Mike lowered his head and shook it.

A short while later after transferring a couple of suits, shirts, and lingerie from the master bedroom to hers, Kassie slipped into a short, red, silk nightgown. While brushing her teeth, she looked at her dilated eyes in the mirror, not surprised she still felt a buzz. Despite all that had gone down that night, she felt relieved and in a happy place. Divorce, on. Yes! She pumped her fist.

When she returned to the bedroom, Mike stood in the doorway with one arm leaning on the door jamb, reminding her of John Travolta without the disco music. She must've forgotten to close the door. But then why would she have closed it, this was her house, too.

"Hello, beautiful lady in red." His hand slipped as he stumbled into the room.

Kassie caught her profile in the mirror above the bureau. One strap on her nightgown had slipped down her arm past her breast. She started to lift it back in place.

"Let me help you with that."

"Now *this* is when I'd like to have a cigarette," Mike said as he caressed Kassie starting above her knee and moving to her waist.

"You know you need to stop that." She rolled toward him. He kissed the tip of her nose.

"This was great. You were great. This bed is *great*. Who knew? Maybe if we'd gotten rid of the waterbed—"

"Don't start with the what ifs. It'll drive you, and me, crazy. This changes nothing, Mike. I've heard it's not unusual for couples going through a divorce to become lovers again. True, I had forgotten—"

"Forgotten what? How good we were together? Are we lovers again?"

"Just for one night."

"You mean I can stay?"

"Yes, but next time I'm on top."

Yet there was no next time. They both crashed. Kassie slept better than she had in days. But morning came too soon without the need of an alarm clock. She opened one eye as Topher pounced on the bed and then lifted the other eye as he licked her face with his sandpaper tongue. He stretched out almost like a child between them and rolled on his back.

"Topher. Oh, Topher." Kassie whispered as she rubbed his tummy, musing more about his namesake than him. *What have I done?*

The reality of the events of the night before slept undisturbed on the other side of Topher and was strewn around the room. Mike's jockey shorts were stacked inside his slacks, like nesting dolls. She cringed remembering how she'd unzipped his pants and exposed him in one swift motion. His shirt hung on the bathroom door handle. Had she done that? Mike more likely. Wiggling her toes, they curled around something silky. She reached under the sheets and fished out her nightgown. *What did I do?*

With all their clothing accounted for, Kassie hopped in the shower, amping up the hot water as high as her skin could tolerate. Thinking about the entirety of the day before, she debated whether a cold shower would've been more in order.

In that moment, she balanced herself against the tiles and declared a no-sex day. Not with her husband. Not with her lover. *But it's Wednesday, hump day,* she argued. *You are Bad Kassie, so for you today must be abstinence-Wednesday,* she chastised. "Or maybe I'll become a nun. That would solve everything." *Except my sex drive.*

Kassie let loose an audible sigh of relief when she returned to the bedroom and found Topher alone in the bed. A strong coffee smell drifted its way upstairs. Damn. She hoped Mike had retreated to his bedroom, instead she'd have to face him before she left for work.

Delaying the inevitable, she shooed Topher off the bed and pulled the comforter over the rumpled sheets and fluffed the pillows. She'd change the sheets later.

Before heading downstairs, she saw her reflection in the mirror. "Just five words," she said in a voice only Topher could hear. "Remember the end game." She counted them on her fingers. "Oh . . . and focus."

Was that bacon she smelled? She hoped not, certain that salt-cured meats were an absolute no-no for Mike.

"Do you have time for breakfast?"

"I don't think bacon is on any approved list for you."

"I know that. It's for you, not me."

Kassie's right leg quivered, and her left eyelid twitched. What was happening? Last night he helped her cook, tried to clean the kitchen, invited himself into her bed when she had no wits about her, and now he made her breakfast.

"This all smells . . . um . . . too good."

"Here, sit." Mike pulled out the chair for her where a glass of cranberry juice greeted her.

In short order, he delivered two eggs over easy, with bacon, and whole wheat toast on her good, rose-patterned china handed down from her grandmother. A steeping cup of English Breakfast tea arrived in his favorite Nantucket mug. When she picked up her fork, she realized it was her best flatware, used only on holidays and special occasions.

"This is lovely, Mike, but you didn't have to do all this," she said as she placed the white cloth napkin on her lap.

"Yes, I did. I'm grateful to you. For last night. I wasn't sure I could do it twice."

Twice? She only remembered once. Kassie took a bite, unsure if she'd be able to swallow.

"I've been thinking," he said, putting his plate of eggs and toast on the placemat opposite her.

"It was a mistake, Mike. All of it a mistake," she interrupted as her eyes met his. "Well, most of it." She lifted her tea, looking away.

"I know."

"I didn't mean for you to receive the divorce papers yesterday, right after you found out you have Stage Four CKD for God's sake. What would you take me for if I'd done that?"

"I know."

"And sleeping with you. That should've never happened. It was great if I remember. My mind's a fuzz ball." She waved her hands as if to clear the air.

"Mine isn't."

"But I should've said no. It's not fair to you. False hopes, and all that."

"I know. But—"

"But what?"

"I've been thinking. There's no reason to rush into divorce, right? You're not planning on moving out of the house this minute, are you?"

"To be honest, Mike, your kidneys screwed up my plans royally."

"Now see, that's one thing I can thank them for."

Kassie nodded and tried to eat but put down her fork.

"Listen, I've heard some couples continue to live together as they're going through a divorce if their home can accommodate them separately." She looked around the kitchen. "We could share common areas, and even a meal or two together," she said, picking up her fork and waving it across her plate.

"I'd be open to that."

"But our bedrooms are off-limits, you hear?"

"I could live with that." As Mike winked at her, Kassie was unaware he also crossed his fingers under the table. "What about the family room?"

35

P.S. I Love You

Glory be, thank God it's Monday. Kassie handed Mike his travel mug and hustled him out the door.

"You look good, Mike. A week's vacation did wonders."

"Like old times." He grinned and leaned toward her as if to kiss her goodbye.

"Have a great day," she said, stepping back out of his reach.

"You, too."

After closing the door, she leaned her back up against it. *Impossible.* Within the hour, Mike and Chris would meet face-to-face, and only Chris would be the wiser. There'd be no reason for him to spill the beans or for Mike to suspect anything.

Confident their secret was safe, Kassie clicked on the local NBC affiliate for coverage of the Boston marathon. With her office on the race route, she had the day off. She'd have time to relax and catch up on things she'd put off over the last insane ten days. Like yoga, which would help manage her high anxiety. And grocery shopping somewhere other than the Stop & Shop where she'd lost her cookies.

Were employees there still buzzing about her? If she wore a hat and sunglasses, maybe no one would recognize her.

Or perhaps she'd send flowers with a note: *I'm sorry I stunk up your store, but my life was in the toilet. Hope the fragrance of these flowers helps eliminate the stench and the memories. Sincerely, Bad Kassie O'Callaghan.* She laughed. It'd been a week since the ordeal, and she figured the statute of limitations for an effective apology had more than likely passed. Proper etiquette was never her strong suit, living up to her nickname.

When she returned home after her errands and a quick half chicken Caesar salad at Panera Bread, she cruised from room to room opening windows. Topher was on her heels.

She poured an oversized glass of pinot grigio, took the letter she'd picked up from her mother's attorney, and sank into the chaise lounge that still resided in the master bedroom, now Mike's bedroom.

Finally. Peace and quiet. Time to reflect on a week that had gone terribly wrong from the get-go.

Sipping her wine, she scanned the master bedroom. Had she'd left anything behind she'd want to grab before Mike locked her out of there as he did his life. Under the circumstances, she supposed Mike would have a right to be pissed if he caught her lounging in what was now his territory, even though it was her chair. They'd agreed the master bedroom was his safe space, but that was only after she slept with him.

That wasn't the case last Monday night after he'd been released from Boston Clinic. Mike freaked when she'd decided to sleep in the spare room.

"My day wasn't bad enough? You pull this shit?" Mike scowled and slammed the bedroom door so hard the full-length mirror hanging on it shattered.

Since then she'd transferred the entire contents of her bureau and walk-in closet to three bureaus and two closets in the spare bedrooms. She claimed the larger one, with the thirty-two-inch Samsung television on the wall and adjacent full-sized bathroom, as her main refuge and designated the smaller one for overflow.

"You have so much shit, Kassie," Mike railed at her each day while she moved her gear and purged. But he didn't stand in her way. For that she was grateful.

She justified the whole process of reorganizing her wardrobe and accessories as both cathartic and philanthropic.

"I filled three super-sized plastic bags with my fat suits," Kassie bragged to Chris on the phone the night before. "You know the ones you can't imagine ever having a use for again?"

"The suits or the bags?"

"The bags." She giggled.

"Seriously, KO, it's been, what, six days?" Chris fussed. "I miss you."

After the night she'd slept with Mike, she'd convinced Chris it would be wise for them to take a breather for a week or two, using the fact that he was starting to work with Mike as an excuse. They both needed to keep their druthers about them.

"Chill. Remember they say patience is a virtue," Kassie said, twirling her hair around her index finger.

"I don't feel very virtuous. I think I left it in San Francisco."

"Listen, love of my life," she said, trying to pick up his spirits, "I purged with a purpose. You'd be proud of me. And relieved. Less room I'll take up in the apartment," she whispered in case the walls had ears. She'd left Mike downstairs watching *60 Minutes*.

Each night in the week that followed the Easter weekend fiasco, Kassie crawled into a bed she hadn't expected to be in, let alone, alone. She'd made a promise to herself and to Chris—there was nothing that would stop the divorce from proceeding. Mike's illness added gates she'd need to hurdle, but she was committed and up to the challenge. *Roar!*

As she sat there resting her head on the back of the chaise, she closed her eyes and felt Topher's twenty-pound, toasty frame curl around the inside bend of her right leg. She adjusted her body, crossing her ankles, giving him as much room as he needed. She stroked his thick yellow-orange coat. His purring filled the room.

Despite the serene surroundings, Kassie's stomach churned knowing that morning her lover had met her husband. At that very moment Chris and Mike could be sitting across from each other at the conference table solving the problems of the world. Would they form the bond co-workers do? Would she end up as the odd man out?

She reached for the multi-colored afghan her mother had made for her when she was in first grade. *Damn it.* She'd moved it to her new bedroom. Topher climbed onto her lap as she emptied the glass of wine.

I should've brought the bottle.

Kassie had carried her mother's letter around in her purse for three days waiting for the right time, or the right mindset, to read it.

"It must be a doozy," she'd said to her mother's attorney. "She didn't want you to give it to me until she was dead a whole year? You think there's a winning lottery ticket inside? Is there an expiration date for collecting a big payout?" She shook the letter willing its contents to shift around. No such luck.

But she'd postponed the inevitable long enough, and her glass was empty. No more excuses.

"Here goes nothing, Topher," she said as she unfolded the letter handwritten in perfect script on ecru vellum with what looked like black fountain pen.

My dearest Kassandra,
        If you're reading this letter, it means I'm dancing with your

father in the Wonderland Ballroom also known as heaven. I hope you'll forgive me for what I have to tell you. I believe as gentle as the wind that blows across my grave, the truths that were buried with me, when shared, will set you free.

I hope you won't mind my taking a page from your play-book, providing a list of the wrongs I've done, all of which I was too weak in mind and spirit to confess to you face-to-face.

I know as your mother, I violated your trust, but I cross my heart and pray in time you will forgive me these transgressions:

For dying a slow death, which robbed you of time to live the life you so deserved. You were there for me day after day even though I sensed you would've rather been somewhere else. At least you could've told me his name.

For abandoning you, and not recognizing your inner pain as a child and an adult, because I was too consumed with relieving my own. If only we were given a second chance at forgiveness. Could this letter serve as such? That'll be up to you, my sweet.

For being selfish, and not teaching you to put your needs first, at least sometimes. You were always like your father, a good, nurturing person.

For marrying what's his name and bringing him into our home. I will never forgive myself for exposing you to the physical and emotional harm you witnessed and endured. On my knees I beg you not to allow those memories, or nightmares, to define who you are now or who you will become. That was my cross to bear that I've taken to my grave. Don't let it be yours.

For making a wretched deal with Mike. I believed in my heart if I stayed silent about his lies, he'd keep quiet about mine. The place and time for ending that silence is here and now.

Kassie put the letter face down on Topher's back, clamping her lips together, her teeth almost biting through her gums. Her heart pumped as if she was climbing a steep hill with a fifty-pound back-pack. If Topher noticed, he didn't budge; neither did she. She read on.

When you went to Italy all alone, Mike asked me to redec-orate his office. You can understand, can't you, I was grateful for the opportunity to take my mind off my disease? While cleaning out his old credenza, I found a box full of letters from New Mexico which, as any good mother would do, I read. So I confronted him. He gave me his word he wasn't having a long-distance affair. Their connection was a child they'd had, out of wedlock, and given up for adoption long before he'd married you. He claimed he supported her for a few years after her husband's death, for which she was thankful. Hence the letters.

Even though Mike believed it was the right thing for him to do, he never wanted you to find out about any of it. He referred to the box of letters as his Pandora's box. If opened, all his lies would tumble out and crush your marriage. Knowing Mike, and you, as I did, I agreed. To guarantee my silence, Mike threatened to tell you what I never wanted you to know.

Kassie slammed the letter on the arm of the chaise, chasing Topher off and onto the waterbed. "You knew! All along! You knew! You kept all of it hidden. Karen, the kid, the money. To protect your-self? Bitch!" she screamed. She paged through the rest of the letter. "And there's more?" She shook her head, her eyes filling, her hands trembling. She read on.

Which brings me to my biggest sin. I lied to you about how your father died. How could I explain suicide to a ten-year-old? We, that's Uncle Dan and I, believed a sudden heart attack would be easier for you to understand and accept. There was no need for you to know your father's schizophrenic mind convinced him he had a cancer that he never had, so he ended his life before he could become a burden on ours. Nonsensical, I know, but mental illness is elusive, and death in any form rarely makes sense, especially when it happens to those we love most. And because of my undying love for your father, I forgave him long ago, for leaving me and for leaving you, to survive on our own.

I'm begging you to forgive, as well.

Kassie reached for tissues on the small wooden table near the chair, almost knocking over the table, the wine glass, and the box of tissues. She didn't take just one, but a handful. If that was her mother's big reveal, it arrived forty years too late.

Who does she want me to forgive? My father or her?

She didn't need to forgive her father. She'd done that on her own a long time ago. Though a mere child when he died, her sixth sense propelled her to walk to the nearest newspaper stand. His obituary began on the front page in the Boston papers. It's news when a cop shoots himself. She didn't understand why he took his own life or why her family told a different account of his death. Finally, she had the rest of the story. She could thank her mother for that at least. But forgive? Not so fast.

"Thank God, there's only one more page." She read on.

By now you're asking why I didn't come clean with you before I died? Isn't that what most people do? Death bed confessions?

"Oh God, Mother, don't be so dramatic."

I'm sure you think I abandoned you. Just the opposite. All that I did, or didn't do, was meant to protect you. Mike's contempt for the truth and my fear of it bound us together with one common goal: to preserve your marriage.

You know our family history. We witnessed no strong, enduring male role models, with my father dying in the war, Matthew passing way too young, and you know the rest. I defended Mike because I believed your staying with him would get you to the happily-ever-after that my mother and I never achieved. I know now I was wrong.

So, I pray when you're able to reflect on all that lies herein, you'll be able to forgive, my darling KO.

Always,

Your loving Mother

P.S. Remember, divorce isn't the only way to cut the ties that bind.

"Unbelievable! What the hell does that mean?" Mumbling her mother's postscript, Kassie shivered and seethed as she lifted the long end of the chaise lounge, sliding it along the plush carpet to the bedroom doorway, scrawling a trail that looked like skid marks along the way. Flipping it on its side, she maneuvered it through the narrow doorway and dragged it down the hall. She reversed the process and managed to pull the chair into the bedroom she'd consider her sanctuary from then on when she stayed at the house.

Topher followed her, or was the chair the focus of his curious pursuit, pouncing on it as soon as Kassie had positioned it near the double window. He revved up his purring once she slung the afghan across the back of the chair, its rightful place as well as his.

Kassie grabbed her phone out of her pocket and sat on the edge of the chair so as not to disturb Topher who, with his head resting on his front white paws, had already drifted into la la land. Her first act was to prevent Mike from tracking her. She shook her head as she swiped through more than forty apps to locate Find Friends, stunned it had taken years for her to do this. Apparently he never cared enough to know where she was. Now was not the time to test that theory. There. Mike's blocked.

Crap. Four o'clock already. Both Mike and Chris would still be at the office. She texted Chris, "Make room. I'm coming."

Kassie grabbed a hair tie and pulled back her hair. She needed to get a move on and get out of there if only for a few days. She'd give Mike one of her often-used tall stories about a business trip. That should do it. Kassie figured she'd be back by Friday, if only to retrieve more of her belongings.

Or maybe by Friday she'll have calmed down and stay awhile at the house. It all depended on Mike's mood and whether she wanted to be around him day in and day out. For sure, she couldn't move in with Chris for the long term, on that they'd already agreed, and she'd rather not impose on Annie if she didn't have to. In her mind, the best scenario was still the original, well the second original, plan—live at home but separate from Mike and see Chris whenever she could.

To keep the illusion alive, after she'd packed a large suitcase, tote bag, and her briefcase, Kassie filled Topher's multi-day food and water containers. She rifled through the kitchen desk and found a folder labeled, Household Instructions. She found Topher's check-list on yellow paper stock. There were about a dozen copies paper clipped. She pulled one out and slapped a green Post-it note on it and wrote, "Mike, you know what to do. Be kind, he's just an innocent kitty." She placed the instructions and his pill bottle on the kitchen counter near the sink.

That reminded her. She took Mike's three pill bottles and placed them on the kitchen table. "Mike, please don't forget your meds."

It was five-thirty by the digital clock in her Mercedes. She couldn't remember how far ahead she'd set it when the government insisted the clocks move forward, but she felt sure Mike would hang around his beloved office for a while on his first day back. She put the car in reverse, pulled out, and pressed the remote, closing the door on the past.

Halfway down the driveway, she heard Mike's car before she saw him in her rearview mirror.

Mike got out and approached the driver's side window. Kassie clung to the steering wheel. He knocked on the glass. She stared ahead.

"Open the window." Mike knocked harder.

A voice echoed in her head, recognizing it was her mother quoting Emily Dickinson: *Saying nothing . . . sometimes says the Most.*

36

Office Space Aliens

As Mike pulled into his parking spot at Ricci and Associates early Monday morning, he noticed a stranger get out of an SUV across the lot. Must be the new guy. *What is his name?*

"Christopher Gaines." The new guy introduced himself and offered his hand to Mike.

"How do you do, son? Michael Ricci, but you can call me Mike." He pal-patted Chris on his back as they entered the building.

"I'm just fine. You can call me Chris."

"Well, good. You've been here for a few days, right? So I don't have to show you around."

"Yes, sir."

"Good. I was away last week, as you know. Need to catch up on a few things upstairs. I'll grab you later this morning. Looking forward to getting to know you."

"Sounds good."

An hour later, Mike called an impromptu meeting of the staff. They gathered in the large conference room on the first floor that seated sixteen comfortably. Every chair was filled. No absentees when the boss was in. One after another, he received warm welcomes. "Good to see you, Mike. Glad you're back. We missed you. The place isn't the same without you." *Bullshit. Bullshit.*

"Take a seat, though this won't be long. Thought I'd bring the family together. It's been awhile, right?" Mike started as he witnessed head nods and heard affirmative murmurs.

"Wanted you to hear from me about my sudden visit to Boston Clinic a week ago. Well, I guess it's just over a week ago now. Anyway, it all happened after I had a lovely dinner with Kassie on Holy Thursday. I must've eaten something bad because in the middle of the night I became quite ill. I won't get into the gory details."

"Thank you for that, boss," Bill said. The room chuckled.

"To make a long story short, the good doctors at the Clinic invited me to take a mini vacation over Easter weekend at their fine institution, where they poked and prodded to their heart's content. The highlight of the weekend . . ." Mike paused recalling his visitors. "Well, one highlight, Bill brought me cannolis."

The team clapped and hoot-hooted. Bill gave Mike a thumbs-up. He wondered whether it was for the cannolis or Amelia. Didn't matter. Sweet memories both.

"But I cannot tell a lie. Sorry, Bill, I didn't eat them. I gifted them to the nurses who were desperately sad to be working on a holiday but grateful for my thoughtfulness."

Bill first pouted, then chortled. "Sounds like you were a big hit with the ladies, as usual."

Mike shook his head yes and grinned. "So, the result of all of that drama is that I have good news and bad news."

"The bad news is that tests confirmed I have CKD, which means chronic kidney disease." Mike paused to let that sink in.

Mike heard a voice at the far end of the room and all heads turned.

"Excuse me, Mike," said Chris. "From research I've done on assignments on this topic, haven't they made great strides in this area?"

"Ah, yes. That brings me to the good news. Chances are I'll either start dialysis at some point or replace my bad kidney with a healthy one. You all shouldn't worry though, Kassie and I . . ." Mike stopped, his thoughts wandered as he spun his wedding ring. "Kassie has been a rock through all of this. I am so lucky. She and I are exploring the options. Anyone interested in donating their kidney to a good cause?"

Mike watched as the members of his team shifted in their seats and looked sideways at one another.

"Just kidding. From what I recall, there's no requirement for organ donation in your employment contract. At least not yet." Mike tried to release the mood that had stiffened. It worked as he heard a distinct sigh from Bill and a few other colleagues.

"Now, for even better news. I'm assuming you've met the newest addition to our family, Christopher Gaines." Mike motioned for Chris to stand. He did as he was told. "Christopher just demonstrated he's not shy, not afraid to speak up. If his writing is half as compelling as his self-confidence, he'll have a future here at Ricci and Associates."

Everyone clapped, except Chris.

As the staff filed out of the conference room, Mike caught up with Chris and invited him to his office.

They settled in to chat on Mike's two facing couches. Mike launched into a vivid backgrounder on the firm, how it's grown over the years, and bragged about the Who's Who of local and national clients they'd been honored to serve.

"I appreciate the opportunity to freelance here. A lot of my work on the West Coast was with tech companies, with some health care scattered here and there. Certainly Boston's base is similar. I'm hoping to get exposure to other industries, financial services, education—"

"Speaking of, did you know we're both Illini?" Mike pointed

toward his University of Illinois diploma hanging on a wall near his desk.

"Yes, I think someone told me that. Small world."

"Do you ever get back there?"

"To the school? No. To Illinois, yes. My parents still live there near Chicago. I visit them a couple of times a year."

"As all good sons should."

"I try. It's the right thing to do."

"So tell me, Christopher—"

"Chris is good."

"Chris, if you were living on the West Coast, and your family's in Chicago, what's the attraction to Boston?"

"That's easy. Opportunity. Who wouldn't take advantage of living in Boston and working for as fine a company as yours? And if things don't work out here as I hope they will, I can always go back to San Francisco."

"Any family or friends here?"

"No family. I plan to look up some college buddies—"

"You must come over for dinner some time. My wife is quite the chef." Mike stood and headed for the door; Chris followed.

They stopped near Mike's desk.

"Is that your wife?" Chris walked behind the desk and picked up a picture.

"No, my sister in her younger days." Mike chuckled.

"This is Kassie." Mike handed the wedding picture to Chris. "Her younger days, too, but she's still a hottie."

Chris nodded. "What does she do?"

"She's a marketer, like you and me. Works at a firm downtown. And she's off today, the marathon goes right by her building. Too bad I couldn't have introduced you two sooner, she could've taken you around town, shown you a good time."

"Kids?"

Mike groaned. "Nope. It wasn't in the cards. What about you? Married? Some sexy lady in your life?"

"No wife, no kids, that I know of."

Mike slapped him on the arm as they both laughed.

"Who knows, the woman of my dreams might be right here. In Boston." Chris handed the picture back to Mike.

"Is this your cat?" Chris touched the photo frame.

"He's Kassie's. Name's Topher. She adopted him about five years ago. Pain in the ass. But she loves him."

"I can see why. He's a handsome dude."

"Listen, Chris, here's my first lesson." Mike shifted from side to side as if he was dancing. "When you own your own company, display at least one picture of an animal, dog, cat, bird, iguana, doesn't matter, even if it's not yours. Clients love to talk about their pets. They're great conversation starters."

"I'll take that under advisement. It worked on me."

"Speaking of work, it's time we both get to it." Mike gave Chris a final welcome and pointed him toward the door.

Mike hunkered down in his office the rest of the day, eating the nutritionist-approved lunch Kassie had packed for him, catching up on the company's financials, and kicking back for a nap that lasted until Bill knocked on the door, even though it was open.

"How you doing? Long day, your first day back—"

"I finally appreciate Kassie's mother and her interior design expertise," Mike said pressing on the cushions and plumping the pillows.

They sat a spell and reviewed the client list and staff assignments. Bill repeated his earlier sentiment that it was good to have Mike back in the office.

"Don't mean to pry, Mike, how are things going with Kassie and her divorce craziness?"

"It's okay, Bill, you're not prying. Things aren't great, but they could be worse. She claims the timing was off. She hadn't meant for papers to be served when they were. Nevertheless, she's going forward with it."

"You're kidding."

"Wish I were. Our marriage was in the toilet before I got sick . . . sicker. But a lot went down that weekend, and she's pretty pissed at me. But, not to worry, I have a plan."

"I knew you would."

"I'm not insisting that she move out of the house. We are cohabiting."

"How does that work?"

"We agreed to separate spaces and shared spaces. And one night last week she let me into her private space if you know what I mean," Mike whispered and winked.

"You dirty dog. I always say the way to a woman's heart is through her . . ." Bill grabbed his crotch.

"Hope so. But it's just a start. And she's gotten all involved with my diet. Shopping. Making my lunch as if I was back in school. She's taking care of me. In more ways than one. And I'm on my best behavior. I think over time she'll come around. If she fell in love with me once, she could fall in love with me again."

"Is that what you want? Or what you need?"

"What I need is a new kidney." They both laughed.

"What do you think of Christopher, the new guy?"

"Getting up to speed fast. A quick learner. Smart, inquisitive, writes compelling, provocative copy. He's friendly, outgoing, quite charming. Handsome. A ladies' man, I suspect. The girls have been hanging around his cube, offering to show him the ropes. Oh, and there's been a change in their attire in the last couple of days. Did you notice the skirts and heels this morning?"

"More cleavage showing, too. Even if it's for him, we get to enjoy the eye-candy as well."

"He reminds me of somebody I once knew," Bill kidded.

"Who? You?"

"No, you, asshole."

Leaving the office a bit earlier than he normally would, especially after being out a week, Mike dragged his body getting into his car that evening. His mind, though, was energized. Being back where he was boss was like an aphrodisiac. He connected his iPhone and pumped up the jazz station through Pandora so loud the cars on the highway surely felt the vibrations as he passed.

Mike smiled as the deep blue evening sky and crisp spring air aroused a scheme of how to replicate the night he and Kassie had sex. If she were already cooking dinner, he'd offer to help. Maybe set the table. He'd compliment her on how lovely she looked. Perhaps feign an interest in the cat. He'd be sure not to invade her space, but somehow make their shared space stress-free and engaging so much so she'd gravitate toward spending time with him. Mike wanted to show Kassie he could still be charming, like the new guy.

His daydream was short-lived. As he pulled into the driveway, Kassie backed down. He blocked her from leaving. Where the hell was she going?

He jumped out of the car and knocked on her window. She ignored him, she didn't even look at him.

"Open the window," Mike demanded.

Finally, she did as he asked. He couldn't help but notice suitcases in her back seat.

"You going somewhere?"

She didn't answer him.

"Come on, Kassie. Don't do this. Stay. I want you to stay. I need you." His earlier good mood evaporated into the evening air. "I will not move my car. So you have a choice."

She turned toward him and said, "I got a letter from my mother today."

Mike's jaw dropped, shell-shocked, as Kassie maneuvered her car around his, destroying the lawn and peeling away.

Did she say what I think she said?

A letter from Patricia? Dead mother talking was not in his plans.

37

Cut to the Chase

Kassie didn't pass go, and she certainly didn't collect two hundred dollars. She wasn't playing any more games with Mike. She was a woman on a mission, except she wasn't sure where she would land.

She knew Chris was expecting her, but she couldn't bear to have him defend Mike again, although she was interested in hearing how his day had gone.

She opted for a pit stop in a Starbucks parking lot.

"Hey babe, where are you?" Chris asked. "Thought you'd be here by now."

"I'm having second thoughts."

"About what? Me?"

Kassie thought she could hear his lungs collapse.

"No, about tonight. I think I need to see Annie. Girl talk."

"What's going on?"

"You first. How was your meet-and-greet with the boss?" Kassie snarled.

"He speaks highly of you. Not so much about Topher."

"Huh?"

"He showed me some pictures in his office."

"So you saw the college photo with Karen?"

"Uh, no."

"It was a group shot."

"There were no group pictures. I'm sure of it. In fact, we talked about Illinois. If it were there, I think he would've shown it to me."

"That's odd," she said more to herself than to Chris.

"I'm jealous," he said.

"Of Mike? Oh, please."

"No, Annie. I thought I was your best friend."

"Best *boy* friend. That sounds juvenile, doesn't it? Sorry. Thing is, my mother left a letter for me with her attorney. I picked it up on last week but didn't read it until today. Annie knew my mom for years. She'll help me decipher it."

"What did it say? Your message sounded like you were unraveling."

"What didn't it say? Seems she and Mike were in cahoots to keep me from leaving him. I was such a fool. I should've walked a long time ago."

"What kind of cahoots? That's a pretty generic accusation."

Kassie explained that it was too complicated to go into on the phone but promised to let him read the letter the next time she saw him.

"And when will that be?"

Annie welcomed Kassie with open arms into which Kassie collapsed as soon as she entered Annie's townhouse.

"I'm not sure how much more of this I can stand."

"Well, you don't have to stand." Annie took Kassie's hand and led her into the living room where she'd positioned four overstuffed throw pillows around the gas fireplace. A bottle of pinot grigio, two glasses, and a plate full of cheese and crackers awaited their arrival.

Over the next three hours and two bottles of wine, Kassie and her best friend forever rehashed her history with Mike and Chris and Patricia.

"I'm such a slut," Kassie confessed, recounting the events of the previous Tuesday.

"When you made love to Chris, you were unfaithful, but not a slut. But you're right, when you slept with your husband, that's when you became a slut." They clinked their glasses saluting promiscuous women everywhere.

"What was it like after all these years?"

"I don't remember much. I was trashed. He seems to think we did it twice. I hope not."

"Was he as good as you remember? Did you feel anything toward him?"

Kassie sipped her wine and reached for a cracker, reliving the night in her mind. "Let's say, he hasn't lost his touch. Why would he? Once a skilled and passionate lover, always—"

"Like Chris?"

"Not like Chris, in that department anyway. In my humble opinion there are two kinds of lovers. Givers and takers. I had sex with both last week. You figure it out." She rose, put her hand on her heart as she giggled and staggered to the bathroom.

"You know why you fell for Chris, don't you?" Annie asked when Kassie returned.

"Do tell." She paced the room with her hands clasped behind her back.

"You can't see it?"

"See what?"

"He's a younger Mike. I've known Mike forever. Tell me you've never looked into Chris's eyes and seen Mike looking back at you?"

"Stop, you're freaking me out."

"And he's got that curl in his upper lip that makes his eyes twinkle when he smiles like Ryan Gosling. Especially when he smiles at you."

"Rubbish."

"And the way he tilts left when he walks—"

"It's not genetic. Chris injured his back as a child which is why he swims all the time."

"You sure about that? What's Mike's excuse for tilting that way?"

"He's crooked!" They fell back on the pillows laughing.

"Maybe. Just maybe, Chris is Mike's long-lost son."

"You're imagining things."

"I've got an idea. Why don't you do one of those DNA tests on Chris? See what you find out."

"What am I supposed to do, pull out one of his hairs while he's sleeping or ask him to spit into a test tube?"

"Or collect his semen. That would work, right?"

"Gross. You've been watching too many movies. That's enough wine for you. Here, read this. It'll take your mind off conspiracy theories. Well, maybe, it will."

Kassie handed Annie her mother's letter while she refilled their glasses. She lowered herself to the floor and re-fluffed the pillows, making herself comfortable for what she expected would be a long night.

"When did she write this? Why did she write this?" Annie said fanning the letter in the air.

"Sometime before she died."

"Obviously." Annie peered at Kassie over the frames of her glasses.

"I think she didn't want me to divorce Mike while she was still alive. That would've been too painful for her. Now that she's gone, she doesn't care."

"But it's not just about Mike. All this about your father's death and your wicked stepfather. You knew all that. Right? No big news there."

"Right. But she didn't know what I knew. Now she wants me to forgive her."

"Will you?"

"In the scheme of things, forgiving my mother is not number one on my priority list."

"What is?"

"At this moment, figuring out what she's trying to tell me. Do me a favor, read the postscript out loud."

"*P.S. Remember, divorce isn't the only way to cut the ties that bind.*" Annie read it, lifting her hands toward the ceiling as if to ask, what the hell does that mean?

"You know, in marketing, we put the most important message at the end. It stands out. Gets attention."

"I don't get it. Is she telling you to leave Mike without divorcing him? What good would that do?"

"I'm betting it's some kind of perverted riddle. You remember how she loved Emily Dickinson and her other wacky transcendentalist friends."

"Careful, all of us born in Massachusetts are related to them in one way or another." Annie raised her glass in their honor.

"What about 'the ties that bind?' What does that mean?"

"Ties could mean marriage, family, our religious beliefs," Annie offered before Kassie cut her off.

"No, that's too obvious for my mother," Kassie said as she curled up into the fetal position, lowering her head on her knees. "Blank isn't the only way to cut the ties that bind. Divorce isn't the only way to blank the ties that bind. Divorce isn't the only way to cut the blank."

"Maybe if you sleep on it, it'll make more sense in the morning."

A few minutes past midnight, Kassie and Annie huddled together in the guest bedroom as if they were schoolgirls plotting how to ask the football star to the prom. Even the room looked the part. Kassie's luggage occupied most of the open space, a black bra hung on a doorknob, her jeans slung on the back of a Queen Anne chair. The soundtrack from *The Big Chill* played loud enough to enjoy, but soft enough to not bother the neighbors. Leaving their heavy conversation downstairs, they spread across the king-sized bed, reminiscing about the good times, the fun times, the devil-may-care times.

"Was that the doorbell?" Kassie said rolling off the bed.

"Christ, were we making that much noise? Hope it's not the cops." Grabbing robes to cover their nightgowns, Annie headed down the stairs with Kassie close behind for moral support.

"Thought I might find you here," Mike said. "You blocked me."

"You blocked me in the driveway. I think we're even." Kassie tugged her belt tighter.

"Why are you here? It's after midnight. Couldn't you wait until tomorrow?" Annie said.

"Kassie, I need to talk to you. I can't sleep." Mike ran both hands through his uncombed hair and pinched his nose as if he needed to stop it from running. His wrinkled striped oxford shirt was mis-buttoned and hanging out of his jeans. His fly only halfway zipped.

Ever the good hostess, Annie invited him in and offered to make coffee.

"That won't be necessary. He won't be staying long." Kassie led Mike to the living room, but didn't offer him a seat.

"It's late. Stay the night, but come home tomorrow." Mike reached out to her.

Kassie stepped back avoiding his touch. "You're kidding, Mike. You're done telling me what to do."

"Listen, I can explain."

"Explain? Explain why you had a moral duty to Karen but abandoned your moral compass with me, your wife? The man I see standing in front of me is an imposter, a con man. My mother confirmed as much today."

"I'm sorry, I was wrong to deceive you. But damn it, Kassie, she promised not to tell you about the vasectomy."

38

Curve Balls

Two days after the "incident," code name for the night she learned Mike had deliberately prevented her from getting pregnant and her mother was a co-conspirator, Kassie's pain was as raw as having a Band-Aid ripped off along with the scab. She'd gotten out of bed only to use the john and to ask the woman in the mirror what she had done to be so mistreated. Each time her reflection provided no answers, she returned to the protection of the crumpled bed covers and prayed for something to heal the pain.

While Kassie wallowed in self-pity, Annie contacted Kassie's assistant. She'd be out the rest of the week. Stomach flu. Probably caused by stress over her husband and his ordeal. Just give it time.

By that evening, having heard enough of Kassie's moaning and sniffling, Annie intervened.

"You have a visitor," she said.

"Whoever it is, tell them to go away."

"Tell him yourself."

Kassie peeked out from under the comforter as Topher leapt

from Annie's arms and buried his white button nose under her chin. She wrapped her arms around him and clutched him to her heart.

"Thank God, it's you. I thought it was Chris."

"You think I'd let Chris in here with you stinkin' like last week's garbage? He'd make tracks back to San Francisco in a New York minute, whatever that means."

Kassie stared at her. "I don't know how I'll deal with all of this."

Annie continued, "Have you looked at yourself? I have a new nickname for you. Zombie Kassie. I'm surprised Topher recognized you."

Kassie stroked her cat. "What day is it?"

"Wednesday." Annie felt her forehead. "Listen, you're not sick, and I don't allow zombies in my house. If you want to stay, you need to get your ass out of this bed. It's time for you to shower and join the living. You've got twenty minutes." Annie yanked the covers off her. Topher flew into the air, landing in Annie's open arms.

Kassie was in no mood to argue, even Bad Kassie was in seclusion. In fact, having Annie take charge was just what she needed. She found Annie in the kitchen where a plate of spaghetti and meatballs and a basket of garlic bread greeted her.

"Well, don't you look better?" Annie said with her hands on her hips. "You smell better, that's for sure. Now eat."

"I'm not sure I can." Kassie stared at the fists in her lap.

Annie dragged a chair next to her and held Kassie's cold, shaking hands in hers.

"Listen, Kassandra O'Callaghan. This is not your mother, or Mike, or even Chris speaking. This is your friend who has been with you through all the hell in your life. I can give you tough love, or sweet love. Your choice."

Kassie kept her head down as her eyes welled up. How could any tears be left?

"Look at me, young lady." Annie lifted her chin. "Ask yourself, what do you have left to mourn that you haven't already? Your mother's been dead for over a year. Check. Your marriage has been dead for decades. Check. You came to terms with not having children a long time ago. Check. From where I sit, you're brooding over some very dead horses that don't deserve an ounce of your precious energy."

Kassie reached for the glass of pinot grigio, her hand trembling. Annie lent hers, guiding the wine to her lips.

"I know you don't want to hear this, but you have your whole life ahead of you. You'll divorce the bastard. And you have a gorgeous hunk of a man waiting for you. So smarten up. All that is bad is in your rearview mirror. Only good times lie ahead. The direction you choose is up to you."

While Annie cleaned the kitchen, Kassie retreated to her bedroom with Topher close behind. As she finished changing the bed linens, Annie walked in carrying Kassie's treasured afghan.

"Oh my God, where did you get that?" Kassie squealed, wrapping it around her shoulders.

"Mike. As I was loading Topher and all his paraphernalia—God he's got a lot of shit just like his mama—Mike came out and asked me to wait. He returned with the blanket and a box. He said to give these to you and tell you he's sorry."

"What box?"

Kassie and Annie spent the rest of the evening on the floor of Annie's bedroom. They sorted through hundreds of photos, restaurant napkins, matchbook covers, and swizzle sticks. Memories—places Mike and she visited, from their early days in Missouri, their vacations on the Cape, and their honeymoon in Italy—scattered everywhere. Kassie set aside a photo of them standing in front of a row of black gondolas with royal blue rain covers but kept returning to it.

She showed the picture to Annie. "See? I went on a gondola ride once in my life." She grabbed her necklace as if checking to be sure it was still there. "Once. With Chris."

"I can see that, silly. You and Chris right there." Annie tapped the photo.

"Don't start that again. That's Mike." Kassie pushed Annie backward. They both fell back all giggles.

"I need to call him," Kassie said.

"You're gonna call Mike?"

"No, Chris. God only knows what he's thinking."

"Not to worry. I called him. Didn't give him the details, but told him you had a blow up with Mike, that you were staying with me, and needed privacy. He sounded worried, but I assured him you'd recover in a few days."

"Thanks, Annie. I couldn't get through this without you."

The next day Kassie regained her courage and ventured out into the daylight. *I'm not a vampire after all.* Still a little gun-shy, she skipped Stop & Shop and drove out of her way to Wegmans. The time had come to return Annie's hospitality.

"She's in the kitchen." Annie greeted Chris as he arrived for dinner.

"Smells good in here," Chris said.

"What? Me or dinner?" Kassie turned away from the stove and rolled into his right arm. A bouquet of spring flowers occupied his left.

"Both." They kissed as if they hadn't seen each other in more than a week, because they hadn't.

"You are a sight for extraordinarily sore eyes."

"I'm betting you're on the mend." Chris glanced down as Topher brushed against his pant leg.

"Thanks to Annie and Topher." Kassie leaned down to pet him.

Chris picked up Topher and stroked him from the scruff of his neck down his back. Topher craned his head as if he was in kitty heaven.

"Careful. You'll be covered in cat hair," Kassie warned and chuckled.

"Not a problem. I'm assuming you have one of those handy dandy lint rollers. If not, I've got one in the car."

Kassie waited until they'd finished their chicken fajitas before bringing Chris up to speed on the incident, what had precipitated it, and her nearly nervous breakdown.

"Nearly? I'd say what I witnessed was a complete, unadulterated collapse of a human being. Right before my eyes, Chris, she transformed into Zombie Kassie." Annie snickered.

"I wasn't that bad."

"You had a right to fall to pieces. All these years you'd been a rock, and out of nowhere came this shock. Wow, I'm a poet!" Glasses were raised and clinked.

While Kassie cleared the table and brewed a pot of coffee, Chris read the letter from her mother. Annie rummaged through her liquor cabinet, retrieving a new bottle of Kahlua and her good crystal snifters, not the cheap ones she'd bought at a dollar store long ago for a neighborhood block party.

"Some letter," Chris said as they re-gathered around the dining table.

"This is what I don't get. Since she confessed so much in her letter, why did she fail to tell me she knew Mike had a vasectomy?"

"She did, Kassie, at least I think she gave you a clue. Read the postscript. Here."

Kassie brushed away Chris's attempt at handing her the letter. "I know it by heart: *P.S. Remember, divorce isn't the only way to cut the ties that bind.* I think it's a riddle." She tugged on her earring.

"I do, too. Think about it. Your mother knew Mike's vasectomy sliced your marriage in two."

"Ew." The two ladies cringed and crinkled their noses.

"Symbolically," Chris clarified. "It was the ultimate betrayal of your marriage vows. I think she's telling you that you didn't have to divorce him yourself because he'd already done it for you."

Kassie soaked in his theory as she swirled the Kahlua around the snifter.

"And because he'd already cut the ties, she was giving you permission to divorce him. Now that she was dead, that is."

"Like I needed her permission."

"Well, apparently you did," Annie interjected.

"So, that's the theory of the Patricia O'Callaghan case. What about Michael Ricci? Why did he hide his past? And to make matters worse, why did he play me like a fool as I jumped through hoops to get pregnant?"

"Have you seen her jump through hoops?" Annie asked Chris.

"No, but I'd like to."

Kassie laughed along with their little joke. "Get serious, you two." She smacked Chris alongside his arm.

"Okay. Okay. Let's put ourselves in Mike's shoes. You were both young and married only a couple of years," Chris launched a possible scenario.

"And then you had the miscarriage," Annie added.

"He had just started his business. I was doing well, too. We had our whole lives ahead of us. He knew I wanted a baby."

"It's pretty simple. I think he got scared," Chris said, shrugging his shoulders.

"Scared of what?" Kassie and Annie said in unison.

"Maybe he was afraid he'd do to you what he did to Karen. That he'd walk out on you. Desert both you and a baby, another baby. He loved you and was committed to you. So he had to do something to maintain the status quo. I can understand a man doing that." Chris paused and squeezed Kassie's hand.

"That's a sad, sad story, Chris." Annie wiped away crocodile tears.

"You're doing it again." Kassie pounded her napkin on the table, this time with a smile and a twinkle in her eye.

"Doing what?" Annie asked.

"He defends Mike all the freakin' time. I just don't get it." With that, Kassie gave up trying.

Chris's story sounded more like fiction than non, so she filed it in her brain under "Chris defends Mike." In the days and weeks that followed, Kassie stopped psychoanalyzing her mother and Mike, and instead decided to get on with her life.

She refused, or at least minimized, any direct interaction with Mike. She blocked him on both her personal and business phones. She put the two dozen pink roses he sent to the office on her assistant's desk. Annie accompanied her to the house to pack her belongings, gather her important papers, collect her favorite books.

Kassie directed her attorney to move forward with the divorce. And she and Chris fell into a routine of seeing each other one night during the week at the Charlestown apartment. And on Saturdays they'd do something special, like stay overnight on the Cape or take in a ballgame if the Red Sox were in town. Sex became not-so-spontaneous, yet still maintained its ooolala distinction.

"It's like we're becoming an old married couple," Chris said one night when they'd made love with the lights out.

"I promise to change that," Kassie said.

In June, month two of their separation, Mike showed up at her office one afternoon with bad news. He'd had an appointment with Dr.

Singleton that morning. Dialysis or a transplant were now on the table.

"I need your help, Kassie. Please."

Whether it was because he showed up unexpectedly or because she and her team just landed a new account, Kassie let her guard down and agreed to go for a walk with him.

It was a perfect day for a stroll around Boston Common. The cloudless blue sky was like a transparent umbrella protecting them from the internal chaos they each must have felt in that moment, but for different reasons. They rested a spell on a bench on which Kassie staked her life savings was the same one Robin Williams and Matt Damon had shared in *Good Will Hunting*. Mike had his doubts.

"Just go with it," Kassie urged him with a friendly shoulder nudge. "It's a sign. Good karma."

And so it was. Short of getting on his knees, Mike tried to make amends as best as he could.

"It's not just because I'm scared. I've had a lot of time to think over the past couple of months. When your fate is staring you in the face, you realize the error of your ways."

Kassie let him talk. She figured his words were mutually cathartic. And maybe Chris was right about Mike's fears. She was afraid, too, for Mike. What did the prospects hold for him? Was it fair she could see a bright future with Chris, yet Mike's tomorrows were cloudy?

"What about a donor? There's a national list. You must get on it. Now."

"I'm glad you brought that up."

Kassie reassured Mike she'd at least think about getting tested. How could she not at least offer to consider it when he sounded both contrite and pitiful? Yet, before proceeding down the testing path, she sought guidance from her three closest advisors.

"What are you crazy? What if you match? Are you going to give one of your healthy kidneys to a man who wouldn't give you a baby? The injustice of it all," Annie argued with Kassie each morning at breakfast and each night before bed.

On the flip side when she suggested the possibility to Chris one night in bed at the apartment, he said he admired her for considering it. "I've been working with Mike for a couple of months now. He's not such a bad guy."

"You weren't married to him."

"True, but you took vows, for better or worse, in sickness—"

"Not sure you're in the best position to quote my vows to me." Kassie rolled on top of him.

"Point taken."

"But you think I should do the test?"

"What do you have to lose? Oops, scratch that."

"Would you donate a kidney to someone?"

"That depends. For you, my mother, my father? Almost certainly. For a not-so-immediate family member? Hypothetically, I probably would."

Kassie interlaced her fingers with his and squeezed. "You, Christopher Gaines, are a wonderful, caring man. Which is why I love you."

"I don't know if it's Annie's influence, or the absence of Mike's, but you've become more compassionate in the last couple of months. You've come a long way on the road to forgiveness. I'm very proud of you. If you do this for Mike, you'll be giving him the greatest gift you've ever given him. Which is why I love you."

With a split decision, Kassie visited her mother's grave searching for a tie-breaker. Sitting on the dry ground hardened by the June sun, she read aloud the infamous letter which occupied a permanent home in a zippered compartment in her bag. This time rather than focus on the postscript, the words, "set you free" nagged at her. She wondered if Mike would forgive her infidelity if she gave him one of her kidneys. A fair exchange, she figured, though a steep price to pay for her freedom.

The verdict was in. She called Dr. Singleton.

Wouldn't you know? After all her consternation, Kassie wasn't a match.

Annie didn't hide her relief. "Oh, thank God. I thought I would have to lock you in a closet or move you cross country or maybe drug you. Yeah, that's what I'd do."

"The problem still exists, Annie. I hoped if I could be Mike's donor, I'd never have to feel guilty about Chris or about divorcing him at a time when he's frantic and scared."

"Frankly, my dear, you have nothing to feel guilty about. There is one way. It's as plain as the ring on your finger. By the way, why are you still wearing that thing?"

"I'm still married to the man."

39

Here Comes the Son

Getting on a plane to meet Karen was Annie's big idea. To say Kassie struggled with it would be an understatement. She had barely recovered from the incident when Annie convinced her to put on her big-girl pants and do the right thing. Where had she heard that one before?

Just for jollies, Kassie checked the list of the fifty states she kept in her planner. She'd visited thirty-eight for business or pleasure. New Mexico was not one of them, nor would she be able to cross it off her bucket list, also in her planner. She offered to meet Karen in Elephant Butte, but no, Karen insisted Chicago the day after the fourth of July would be mutually beneficial. After all, it would mean just a two-hour flight for Kassie, and Karen would be there attending a sorority reunion.

"It'll be a win-win, Kassie, you'll see I'm right." Karen shut the door on the possibility of Kassie getting a first-hand view of what Mike's monthly stipend had supported for over eight years.

"I'll do anything to help Mike," Karen bubbled when Kassie explained Mike's situation over the phone.

"Does that include promising not to tell him about our meeting?"

"Yes. I know Mike. He'd step in and derail it." Though Karen chuckled, Kassie cringed and flipped her the bird. *How dare you say you know Mike? He's still my husband.*

"Remember, you catch more flies with honey," Annie warned her to leave Bad Kassie behind as she packed for the trip.

As the plane approached O'Hare, Kassie closed her eyes and meditated, breathing in the cabin's stale, polluted air, exhaling all the grief Mike had heaped upon her.

Maybe the plane's next flight will transport my inner hell to a place far, far away.

Her hands clutched the armrests as the plane touched down. If she were to save Mike, she knew at some point she'd have to let go.

Kassie gazed around the sprawling hotel lobby with its palest of yellow walls, white accents, gold fixtures, stone-cold marble everywhere. Clearly Mike's money subsidized Karen's trip, even if he didn't know it. He probably wouldn't care if he did. She'd shrugged when Karen chose the five-star hotel. *Why not? She picked the city.*

As agreed, Kassie left a message for Karen at the front desk letting her know she'd arrived. There was no reciprocal message waiting for her, though she confirmed Karen had checked in as well. Kassie could've just called her room or her cellphone, but that would've been against the rules. And right now, Karen held all the cards.

Later that evening, Karen played one of them. A little after ten, with the Cubs about to score in the bottom of the ninth, tie game, bases loaded, two outs, Kassie heard a soft swish sound coming from the direction of her hotel room door. She swiveled the television so she could watch the action as she walked backward to retrieve whatever had been delivered.

Oh great! The Cubs won. Nice.

She turned off the tube, grabbed a water, and curled up on the king-sized bed. The envelope was small, pale blue, and sealed. It was addressed to Kassandra O'Callaghan, not Kassandra Ricci or Kassie Ricci, or any combination that would include the name Mike claimed Karen once wanted but could not have. How strange life was when you think hard about it. Karen had what Kassie wanted but could not have. Maybe that made them even.

Nevertheless, if Karen intended to send Kassie more than one message, she'd succeeded. This was her ballgame.

Kassie stared at the note. Unlike the plain white paper Karen used in her letters to Mike, this stationery aligned more with the Karen Copperman she'd visualized since learning about her existence three months ago. Its texture felt rich and her name, embossed in deep royal-blue script, screamed "look at how important I am." Pretentious. Entitled. It was the kind of stationery Kassie imagined she would've had to buy had she stayed at Mizzou and in the sorority. A rite of passage, she presumed. *Don't they ever grow up?*

Kassie was far from impressed. Before she left Boston, she predicted to Annie that she wouldn't like this woman and, so far, Karen lived up to Kassie's expectations.

Yet, Karen's note was simple enough. Even friendly.

So thrilled, Kassie, you agreed to meet here in Chicago. You won't be disappointed. Why don't you come to my suite at eleven? I'll order brunch for us. How do mimosas sound?

She signed it, *For Mike's sake, Karen. Room 1422*

Suite? If Kassie weren't on a secret mission, she'd call Mike right then and tell him to stop funding Karen's lifestyle. Short of that, she was relieved she hadn't signed the note KR.

Truth be known, Kassie was nervous about meeting Karen. After a night of tossing and turning, she got up early and went to the gym to work off some adrenaline. She grabbed a grande English Breakfast tea at Starbucks in the lobby, read *USA Today*, and still had three hours to kill before making her way to room 1422. On her way back to her room on the sixth floor, she noticed there was no floor designated thirteen. That meant Karen's room was on the thirteenth floor. Kassie felt her right eye and upper lip twitch. An omen? *Tell me this isn't so.*

Kassie had to do something to get on a level playing field with Karen. She tried on three outfits before deciding on white pants and a red silk top. As a lifelong marketer, she knew the power of red, especially in negotiations. But this wasn't a negotiation. It was a fact-finding mission and success would be achieved if and only if she walked away with the goods. Who was Mike's son and where was he? She replaced the red top with a striking, emerald green blouse with a stand-up collar that accented her shapely silhouette.

She checked to be sure she had a small notebook and pen in her purse. Of course, she did. Like other important things, she never left home without them.

The latch propped open the door to Karen's suite. When Kassie knocked, Karen greeted her with a sing-song, "Come on in, the door's open." And right on cue, two servers arrived behind Kassie with carts, plural, overflowing with typical brunch fare. The sound of a cork popping accompanied the competing aroma of Eggs Benedict, bacon, waffles and maple syrup.

"You're right on time," Karen said. "Mike always said you were a detailmonger."

All Kassie could do at that point was shake her head and apply the requisite two-cheek kiss, hoping Karen would keep the Mike-always-saids to a minimum.

"What a spread. It looks wonderful. Thank you." Ahead of time, Kassie had warned her alter ego to be polite, be a lady. And to focus. Remember the end game, which had broadened to include finding a donor for Mike, not just divorcing him.

Kassie shouldn't have been surprised when she met Karen. Even after all those years, Karen still resembled the co-ed in the photo she'd seen on Mike's desk, with her bright eyes and cheerful smile. Kassie had to admit if they stood next to each other, they could be mistaken as sisters, or at least related in some way. Bad Kassie wondered if being screwed in more ways than one by the same guy also evened the score.

What surprised Kassie was how likable Karen was on first blush. How could this be? Wasn't she Kassie's arch enemy, her competition? The woman who captured her husband's heart, as well as his manhood.

Karen spent much of the time over brunch, which the servers had set up on a table for two overlooking the Chicago skyline, talking about her late husband. How much she adored him, how devastated she was when he'd died. She hadn't been skiing since.

"I know Mike has been sending you money since Barry died."

"Oh, yes. Mike . . ." Karen said gazing out the huge picture window. "How is he, really?"

"He could use your help. We could." Kassie twirled her wedding ring.

And with that, Kassie opened a door she could not close.

Karen walked them down memory lane, sharing her side of the "Mike and Karen Ricci" story. Though Kassie had heard most of it before, she didn't interrupt her. It was comforting for Kassie to know there were some things Mike did not fabricate.

"I was devastated when my parents pulled me out of school. Away from Mike. I loved him beyond belief and wanted his baby. We wanted to get married, but everyone said we were too young. We'd ruin our lives." Karen shook her head as tears trickled down her right cheek.

"Excuse me. I think I need a tissue."

"Get one for me, too." Kassie could feel a sudden crack in her heart as she shared an overwhelming sense of loss with a woman she begrudged less than an hour before.

"What happened to your son, do you know?"

And this is where Mike and Karen's story diverged.

"My parents insisted I give the baby up for adoption. And so I did. But not in the conventional way."

"What do you mean?"

"Let me be perfectly, absolutely clear. Mike knows nothing about this." Karen stood up and paced the room. Kassie squirmed in her high-back chair uncertain about where the conversation was heading.

"Please sit, Karen, you're making me nervous."

"You know I was in a sorority. That's why I'm here this weekend. Our annual reunion."

"Go on."

"One of my sisters, sorority sisters, was graduating and getting married just before I was to give birth. She offered to adopt my baby."

Kassie froze. She struggled to process the words she'd just heard.

"You know who raised your son?"

"Yes. But I swore never to contact him, to never reveal I was his birth mother or who his father was."

"He's an adult now. And Mike needs him. Doesn't he have the right to know the truth? Don't they both have rights?"

"They do. And that's why I wanted to meet you here in Chicago. I can't contact him, but you can. If his parents agree."

There was a knock on the door.

Karen ushered in a well-dressed couple. Kassie stood to greet them.

"Kassie, I'd like to introduce you to Sarah and Charlie Gaines."

40

Drop the Mike

"What does that make me?" Kassie screamed at Annie the next night back in Boston. "Chris's stepmother?"

"Only if you want to be." Annie chuckled while she unscrewed a second bottle of wine.

"What's that supposed to mean?"

"You could either play the victim, or the heroine. The choice is yours."

"But *I am* the victim. Of my stupid belief that I, and I alone, could fix this. Why couldn't I have left Mike and his problems alone? But no, I had to insert myself into a situation where I had no business being. And look where it got me. I should've taken a page from my mother's handbook and backed off."

"It is quite comical you have to admit."

"Glad you think so. Why am I not laughing?"

They prepared to stay up late with pen and paper mapping out different scenarios.

"This would be so much easier if we had a whiteboard." Kassie ran her fingers through her hair, pulling it back into a ponytail. She primed herself to tackle the most consequential problem of her lifetime. And it was a humdinger.

She clapped her hands. "Okay, Annie Oakley, let's get to it."

"Sounds like you're back to your old self. When was the last time you called me that?"

Kassie rubbed Annie's shoulders. "Don't know, but it warmed my heart to say it, dear friend."

After a third bottle of wine and wads of yellow lined paper strewn around Annie's living room, they had Kassie's alternatives mapped out. There were two obvious paths. Either she did nothing, or she revealed all to Mike and Chris.

Annie agreed with Kassie that doing nothing was the path of least resistance. No one would be hurt if she kept Chris's bloodline a secret. Except for Mike who'd never know if Chris could be a donor. He'd just continue on the waiting list. And then there was the elephant in the room. Could Kassie have a future with Chris knowing what she knew?

"Would it be too weird?" Annie asked.

"Even if I consciously could get past it, deep in the crevices of my mind, I'd always see him as Mike's son. Wouldn't I?"

Kassie admitted that revealing all had its upsides and downsides.

"Let's assume Chris accepted Mike as his father, there'd be a fifty-fifty chance they'd match. If they didn't, the least positive outcome would be that father and son would unite for the first time. That's got to be good for something, right?"

"True. But that alternative is lose-lose for you. It would mean telling Mike you were unfaithful with the morals of a cat in heat, which could impact a divorce settlement, as well as ending a perfectly delicious relationship with Chris."

"I think you've had too much to drink. You're making me sound like a hussy."

Annie got up, holding onto the arm of the couch preempting the possibility of tipping over. "Perhaps. But it's better than slapping you and telling you to snap out of it."

Kassie stood and faced Annie eye-to-eye. "You wouldn't do that."

"Maybe not literally. But your immorality is the reason you're in this predicament. You have the power to steer this ship to port, Kassandra, and the authority to do so. And on that note, I'll see you in the morning."

Annie left Kassie alone with her thoughts. She'd lost Mike a long time ago, now she'd lose Chris, too. Whatever she did would impact Mike and Chris more than her. She knew what she had to do. It mattered.

The annual Ricci and Associates picnic was the following weekend at a park in Arlington. She called Mike and asked if he wouldn't mind if she stopped by. He sounded thrilled to have her come. She knew Chris would be there as well.

After warm greetings by many on the staff, she pulled Mike aside to a bench under an enormous oak tree. Kassie could feel droplets of sweat trickle from her armpits to her waist. Nerves or the result of a typical scorcher of a July day in Boston? Whatever, the shade provided at least some temporary relief.

Kassie bit her lower lip and took a swig of water from her purple bottle. "I have some good news, and some not so great news."

"Don't be shy. Go for it." Mike patted her knee.

"Well, the good news is I've found your son. So it's possible he could be a donor." She blurted out the cause and effect in one breath, hoping Mike would focus on how Kassie's pending confession would be to his benefit.

"That's amazing. How? Who?"

"Before I tell you the rest of the story, this all may be a shock to you. Please know I never meant to hurt you."

Mike reached for Kassie's hand as she said, "The not so great news is, I've been having an affair for the past few years." Her saliva vanished like a tsunami when all the water is sucked out to the sea.

Mike swallowed so hard she could hear it. He got up, walked behind the bench and stood behind her. Despite the heat, goose-bumps traveled up and down her arms and legs. An image of her stepfather flashed through her mind. Was he going to choke her?

Much to her relief, Mike placed his hands on her shoulders, leaned down and whispered, "Well, lassie, that makes the two of us. Now tell me about my son."

Kassie and Mike moved farther away from the picnickers and walked for an hour around the park. She told him the rest of the story. All of it. Her visit with Karen. Meeting his son's adoptive parents. How gracious and cooperative they were. And the final piece of the puzzle, the man she'd fallen in love with in Venice was Christopher Gaines, his son.

"THE Christopher Gaines. The freelancer from San Francisco? Imagine that."

Kassie buried her head in her hands and apologized over and over again until the word sorry sounded like "shorry" through her tears. She told him how they hadn't discovered Chris would be working at Ricci and Associates until Easter Sunday. Remember what a cluster that weekend was? And she didn't know their familial connection until she'd met Karen the week before.

They found another bench under a bridge on the opposite side of the park. Mike wrapped his arms around Kassie and kissed her forehead.

"I knew things were different when you came back from Venice. I hoped whatever it was would pass. Chris, huh? What a coincidence! And they say things like this only happen in Hollywood." They shared a laugh.

"What about you?" Kassie probed. "Who's the lucky girl?"

"Just a passing flirtation. Nothing as scandalous as you and Chris." He winked. "What do we do now?"

Kassie called Annie, who offered to host the soon-to-be father-son reunion. Mike and Kassie returned to the picnic area where she spotted Chris chatting it up with one of the twenty-something junior account executives. She suppressed the pang of jealousy in her gut, knowing her right to feel that way was fleeting.

"I saw you with Mike. Looked pretty serious. Is everything all right?"

Kassie shook her head, yes, and reached out and touched his heart. She invited him to visit her at Annie's that evening. As she walked away, she turned back toward him. "Remember what Emily Dickinson said. 'Truth is so rare, it is delightful to tell it.'" She blew him a kiss in front of God and everybody.

That night Mike, Annie, and Kassie barely talked as they waited for Chris to arrive. Annie poured Mike a bourbon. Kassie declined, certain she would throw up no matter what she drank.

Chris made things easy for them. He must've suspected something. First, Kassie's long walk with Mike that afternoon, then being greeted by them together.

"What's up, guys?"

For once, Kassie was relieved when Mike took control of the situation. She doubted she'd be able to speak, let alone say the right words.

Mike offered Chris a seat on the couch and joined him there. Kassie sat on a side chair with Topher on her lap. Annie stood behind her holding her hand.

"Would you agree, Chris, that life is a long road? And that it is an even longer road that has no turning?"

Chris said he'd heard that proverb before.

"I have something to show you." Mike turned over the frame of the college photo he'd kept on his credenza for years, the one with Karen on his knee.

Chris pulled the frame close to his face. "Hey, my mother's in this photo." First, Chris smiled and then frowned, looking confused.

"You're right," Mike said. "Your *mothers are* in this photo. Sarah your adoptive mother. And Karen your biological mother." Mike pointed to each young woman.

Chris looked at Kassie, then Mike, coughed and said, "That makes you my . . . father?"

"Told you so." Annie cleared her throat.

Kassie clapped her hands to her chest as Topher jumped off her lap and onto Chris's.

Mike threw his arms in the air. "Topher and Christopher. Now I get it. I get it all."

A year had passed since Kassie's brain might as well have exploded when she discovered she'd been having an affair with her husband's son.

It was dusk and quieting down in Venice; the lanterns coming to life as the daytime tourist crowd dispersed. Kassie had agreed to meet Annie in St. Mark's Square at the same café she'd first met Chris. She'd kept a napkin as a souvenir, so it was easy to give Annie directions.

They also agreed it was time for Kassie to find closure beyond forgiving her mother since everyone else seemed to be moving on with their lives. Annie convinced her this trip would cure all the demons she and her therapist had spent countless hours exorcising for months on end.

Her divorce, which she'd delayed until Mike's kidney transplant was completed and successful, would be final in September. As life would have it, Chris was not a match, but Karen was. No one had seriously thought of that as a possibility, except for Karen. She was tickled pink to give back to Mike after all he'd done for her.

Kassie suspected Karen would end up with the KR monogram she always wanted since she'd packed up all her cares and woe and moved her butt from Elephant Butte before the transplant to be near Mike and her newfound son. Once she settled into a short-term rental near Chris in Charlestown, Mike hired her as a receptionist at the firm.

After the big reveal, Chris requested a month off to spend time in Chicago reconciling with his adoptive parents. They had as much to explain to him about his adoption, as he had to tell them about his complex relationship with Kassie. Not surprisingly, he and Kassie agreed to take a hiatus without even one last roll in the hay. He returned to Boston this time to get acquainted with his mother and become a partner in Ricci and Son.

Kassie leaned her head back enjoying the cool breeze from the canal and swayed in her chair to *Por uno Cabeza*. She gathered it was a timeless selection of the St. Mark's Square dueling dance bands.

A tall handsome waiter, named Gino, placed a glass of pinot grigio on her small table. She tried to remember. Gino? Couldn't be. Maybe all waiters in Venice were named Gino.

"*Grazie*, Gino, but I didn't order—"

"No, *signorina, signore.*" He gestured toward a tall man with dark hair and a slight, yet attractive, afternoon shadow sauntering toward her. He wore a smile reminiscent of someone she once knew. Someone she once loved. Someone she'd always love.

"*Buono sera*, are you expecting someone?"

Kassie wiped her damp palms on her black skirt. "Annie," she whispered, at a loss for more words.

"She won't be coming. *Non tutte le ciambelle riescono col buco.*"

Kassie tilted her head and raised her eyebrows. "Say what?"

"Things don't always turn out as planned." Chris took her hand, lifted her, and they danced.

The next morning, they flew to Paris to start a new chapter. It was Bastille Day. There would be fireworks. There just had to be.

What's Not Said Playlist

On Spotify.com
https://spoti.fi/2sRDvp6

Access songs depicting the story on the *What's Not Said* Playlist on Spotify.com, which is free*!

The Sound of Silence, *Simon & Garfunkel*

Where Did Our Love Go, *The Supremes*

Runaround Sue, *Dion DiMucci*

I Left My Heart in San Francisco, *Tony Bennett*

Sweet Caroline, *Neil Diamond*

O Sole Mio, *Andrea Bocelli*

Will You Love Me Tomorrow, *The Shirelles*

Great Balls of Fire, *Jerry Lee Lewis*

Breaking Up Is Hard To Do, *Neil Sedaka*

All In Love is Fair, *Stevie Wonder*

You've Got A Friend, *Carole King*

Mrs. Robinson, *Simon & Garfunkel*

Photograph, *Ringo Starr*

Need You Now, *Lady Antebellum*

Come Away With Me, *Norah Jones*

Celebration, *Kool & The Gang*

The Sound of Silence (redux), *Simon & Garfunkel*

*Best browsers for Spotify's Web Player are
Google Chrome, Firefox, Edge, and Opera.

Book Club Discussion Guide

1. The expiration date on the Ricci–O'Callaghan marriage passed long before the novel begins. If Kassie hadn't met Chris, or if her mother hadn't died, would she have stayed in the marriage indefinitely?

2. What do you think about Kassie's theory that marriage should be a five-year renewable contract? What are the pros and cons? Could it ever work?

3. Both Kassie and her mother, Patricia O'Callaghan, embrace an Emily Dickinson quote: "Saying nothing . . . sometimes says the Most." Did this motto serve them well? How would Kassie's marriage and relationship with her mother been different had they both actually said something?

4. Kassie's childhood was marred by the death of her father and the abuse of her wicked stepfather. Yet, her mother wielded a strong influence on her, as did Uncle Dan. How did these relationships shape Kassie's view of marriage, family, career?

5. At the beginning of the novel, Mike is an unsympathetic charac-
    ter. Is he any more likable at the end of the story? What could he
    have done to redeem himself?

6. Are you surprised Kassie agreed to be tested to see if she could be
    a donor for Mike? What do you think she would have done if she
    were a match? Would you donate an organ to a relative, friend,
    or stranger?

7. When Nancy informs Kassie that her husband, Bill, saw her at
    the hotel, is Nancy acting as a friend or busybody?

8. When did you make the connection between Mike and Chris?
    It's been said, "no coincidence, no story." Do you believe in coin-
    cidences? Have you witnessed any in your life?

9. Discuss the ethics of Kassie's decision to unlock the first box she
    found in Mike's bureau and her determination to find and open
    the second. What do you think about her taking the money, and
    then putting it back? Would she have returned it if Chris hadn't
    suggested she do so? What would you have done?

10. Why did Chris defend Mike? Should he have taken Kassie's posi-
    tion? Are you surprised he didn't agree to spy on Mike at the
    office?

11. What makes Kassie relatable? Did you connect more with Kassie
    or Bad Kassie?

12. The characters in this story lie and deceive as easily as they brush
    their teeth each day. Whose deceptions are the worst, most
    unforgivable? Mike's lies? Kassie's crimes? Patricia's fibs? Or
    even Karen's dishonesty?

13. Was Patricia O'Callaghan Mike's accomplice or did she behave the way most mothers would? If you were Kassie, would you forgive Patricia?

14. At the beginning of the story, we learn that Kassie is a control freak. Is being a control freak a flaw or a strength in her character?

15. What do you think the future holds for Kassie and Chris?

Notes

The following quote, "Saying nothing ... sometimes says the Most," was used with permission. *EMILY DICKINSON: SELECTED LETTERS*, edited by Thomas H. Johnson, Cambridge, Mass.: The Belknap Press of Harvard University Press, Copyright © 1958, 1971, 1986 by the President and Fellows of Harvard College. Copyright © 1914, 1924, 1932 by Martha Dickinson Bianchi.

Acknowledgments

It's only fitting I properly thank the many people who supported me through the process of writing and publishing this book. Now is not the time to wonder what's not said.

To the eagle-eyed women on the East and West coasts who read and critiqued this book—Lyn Englehartson, Vicki Crumpacker, Deb Travers, and Ayse McCarthy—I am filled with deep love and gratitude. Friends forever.

Thank you to the entire *She Writes Press* Team—Brooke Warner, Shannon Green, Krissa Lagos, Mimi Bark, Samantha Strom, and Elisabeth Kauffman—for your industry expertise, creative talent, patience, and guidance throughout this journey. It's cliché to say I couldn't have done it without you, but I'm going to say it anyway. Further, I'm especially fortunate to be part of the New York-area group, comprised of amazingly talented authors, expert resources, and now, new friends.

A major tip of my Red Sox hat to Jim Alkon, Editorial Director of BookTrib.com, a subsidiary of Meryl Moss Media. Also a Red Sox fan, Jim is a trusted mentor, providing sage advice and responding to my panic attacks, even on holidays. Who does that? Only the best.

The following organizations, resources, and individuals were instrumental in transforming me from a writer with a dream to an author with a debut novel. Thank you for the lift and motivation. For craft, the Westport Writers Workshop, Jerry Jenkins and The Writers' Guild, Sara Salecky's Writing School, and Samantha Bohrman at Manufixed. For tech support, Joseph Michael, a.k.a., The Scrivener Guy; Jeff Goins; and John Burke at PubSite. For the business of writing, Jane Friedman, Kathy Ver Eecke, and *Green-light Your Book* by Brooke Warner.

To my loving family, who feared I might divulge family secrets in this book (relax, I don't), I appreciate your willingness to listen to me drone on about the writing and publishing processes. Fair warning. If you think this is my one and only book, think again. I've only just begun.

I can never ever thank Ayse McCarthy enough. Through health and sickness, career challenges, and sometimes even across three thousand miles, Ayse is my rock. Always encouraging, challenging, forcing me to raise the bar. Thank you from the bottom of my heart. You inspire me.

Grazie a tutti. Thank you all.

About the Author

© Lifetouch, Seattle, WA

Valerie Taylor was born and raised in Stamford, Connecticut. She earned a B.S. Marketing degree and an MBA from Sacred Heart University, as well as a graduate certificate in health care administration from Simmons University (formerly Simmons College). She had a thirty-year career in the financial services industry as a marketer and writer. After her divorce, she spread her wings and relocated her career to Boston and then to Seattle. When she retired, she resettled in her home state to be near her two grown children and granddaughter. She's a published book reviewer with BookTrib.com and a member of the Westport Writers' Workshop. She enjoys practicing tai chi and being an expert sports spectator. *What's Not Said* is her debut novel. A sequel is in the works.

WWW.VALERIETAYLORAUTHOR.COM

 valerietaylorauthor @valerieemtaylor ValerieETaylor

SELECTED TITLES FROM SHE WRITES PRESS

She Writes Press is an independent publishing company founded to serve women writers everywhere. Visit us at www.shewritespress.com.

Play for Me by Céline Keating $16.95, 978-1-63152-972-6
Middle-aged Lily impulsively joins a touring folk-rock band, leaving her job and marriage behind in an attempt to find a second chance at life, passion, and art.

Again and Again by Ellen Bravo $16.95, 978-1-63152-939-9
When the man who raped her roommate in college becomes a Senate candidate, women's rights leader Deborah Borenstein must make a choice—one that could determine control of the Senate, the course of a friendship, and the fate of a marriage.

Shelter Us by Laura Diamond $16.95, 978-1-63152-970-2
Lawyer-turned-stay-at-home-mom Sarah Shaw is still struggling to find a steady happiness after the death of her infant daughter when she meets a young homeless mother and toddler she can't get out of her mind—and becomes determined to rescue them.

Center Ring by Nicole Waggoner $17.95, 978-1-63152-034-1
When a startling confession rattles a group of tightly knit women to its core, the friends are left analyzing their own roads not taken and the vastly different choices they've made in life and love.

Clear Lake by Nan Fink Gefen $16.95, 978-1-93831-440-7
When psychotherapist Rebecca Lev's father dies under suspicious circumstances, she becomes obsessed with discovering what happened to him.

Profound and Perfect Things by Maribel Garcia $16.95, 978-1631525414
When Isa, a closeted lesbian with conservative Mexican parents, has a one-night stand that results in an unwanted pregnancy, her sister, Cristina adopts the baby—but twelve years later, Isa, who regrets giving up her child, threatens to spill the secret of her daughter's true parentage.